Als

MW01075497

A Lauren Beck Crime Novel:

WHAT DOESN'T KILL YOU, The Mystery
Honorable Mention, The 23rd Annual Writer's Digest Self-Published
Book Awards

The Ginger Barnes Main Line Mysteries:

THE MAIN LINE IS MURDER

FINAL ARRANGEMENTS

SCHOOL OF HARD KNOCKS

NO BONES ABOUT IT

A SCORE TO SETTLE

FAREWELL PERFORMANCE

LIE LIKE A RUG

And:
DYING FOR A VACATION

GUILT TRIP
The Mystery

By Donna Huston Murray

Please feel free to contact the author via her website:
donnahustonmurray.com

Dedicated to my marvelous role models:
Ruth M. Ballard and Florence K. Moore

Chapter 1

The bottom right drawer of the barn-office desk is the only one locked, so that has to be where my brother hides his stash. I already spent ten minutes scavenging for the key.

Dammit, Lauren, I scold myself. *Concentrate!*

Pulling an old cardboard box full of harnesses onto my lap, I dig through tangled leather smelling of cow sweat and buckles black with age. My reward? Dirt and bits of hay.

I drop the box and kick it back against the wall, wheel around and survey the room. Ron probably doesn't carry the key on him—too easy to lose out there working the fields. No, it has to be here, for convenience if nothing else.

"So where, Ron? *Where?*"

Back in high school a kid dared him to do a shot of tequila. True to his nature, Ron downed seven and nearly died of alcohol poisoning. The resulting reputation for risky behavior dogged him up until his wedding day, when he promised Karen once and for all not to "take stupid risks." If he's drinking in secret now, he's in trouble, the sort of trouble a man keeps from his wife. Considering his mortgage and the rent on the new acres, my best guess is financial. He's a farmer, after all.

And whatdaya know? Farming happens to be the most dangerous occupation in the world. A second of inattention and your jeans get snared in moving machinery. There goes your leg. You're driving your elderly tractor along a slope. It slips and rolls overon you. You're chopping the crust at the top of your grain bin. Fall in. Suffocate. These accidents happen to sober men. Attempting the work drunk, or even hungover, is pure insanity.

The tractor grunts have grown distant, but my brother will soon reach the edge of the field and turn back.

I hustle over to the shelf of seed catalogs and equipment manuals. Shaking the big binders with two hands yields nothing but clouds of dust and a pair of paperclips.

The tractor completes its turn and heads back.

My two little nieces got the giggles at breakfast the other day, a sound so heartwarming it inspired a fantasy about Ron and me actually getting along. I imagined us toasting marshmallows in the barbeque coals while Karen put the girls to bed, burning our fingers on the goo, marveling as fireflies floated up off the lawn, joking about the weather.

Ain't gonna happen. In his six-year-old brain I ended Ron's golden reign as an only child. Then while I was still a sweet little blonde with hazel eyes and messy pigtails, gawky, insecure Ronald Beck persuaded himself that I was our father's favorite. Nothing has been said—we are adults now, after all—but it probably didn't help that Dad sold the family homestead to pay my medical bills. My brother loved that old piece of ground the way lungs love oxygen.

Will he thank me for trying to save his life? More likely he'll kick me to the curb for butting in, and I can't say I'd blame him.

The desk deserves a second look. Centered in the room as it is, I can keep one eye on the door.

Nothing under the computer monitor or tower. The middle drawer holds only a stale cigar, a pen advertising a seed and feed company, three pencil stubs, and a comb. As I crouch down to check the kneehole, the office windows begin to rattle. I freeze, waiting, waiting, until finally—*finally*—the tractor grumbles through its gear change and commences its noisy drone back toward the far turn.

Another glance around and I spy a pair of muddy, army-green boots side by side under a bench. Reaching into the left one yields only worn felt and grit; but when I turn over the other, a silver key on a thin wire ring hits the floor with a clink.

A clink. The tractor noise stopped.

I lunge for the locked drawer and work the key with trembling fingers.

Inside is almost exactly what I expect. A black folder-style checkbook for doing payrolls and paying bills. A nudie magazine dated June, 2004. A twenty-two caliber pistol for shooting whatever or whoever dares to threaten the Beck family and its livelihood, ammunition elsewhere for safety's sake.

Plus three 1.75 liter bottles of vodka, one half empty, the others with unbroken seals—the same cheap swill I pour for the Pelican's Perch customers if they don't specify a pricier brand.

I want to grab Ron's sweatshirt in my fist and pull his face so close we're breathing the same air. I want to hit him upside the head and scream and stomp until he gets it, really gets it. Right now. Right this second. Life is precious. I learned that the hard way. Why hasn't he?

Unfortunately, finding a few bottles of booze doesn't prove a thing. The whiff I caught at breakfast might have been after-shave or mouthwash. Last night's stumbling/mumbling slipup could have been just that, a once and done.

My five years on the Landis, PA, police force taught me that accurate information is the best weapon of all. Without it, you have nothing. I need to summon the patience to monitor Ron's stash for awhile. If it turns out he is playing

Russian roulette with a bottle, I'll share my findings with Karen. She's the one he promised; he might listen to her.

I take a big, steadying breath, nick the level of the opened vodka bottle on its blue off-brand label, and return it to the drawer. I've just tossed the key back into the right boot before Ron bursts through the door.

"Lauren! Can you come back to the house?" His skin is drained of color. His eyes blink as if he can scarcely see. "The kids...Karen..."

"What?" I ask. "What's wrong?" I've taken a step toward him, but no more. He and I never touch.

"Toby. You know Toby...?"

"Sure. Karen's older brother."

"He's dead," Ron tells me. "Suicide."

Chapter 2

As he hurries across the driveway, my brother speaks into the cell phone he keeps on him for emergencies. "Yeah, yeah," he tells his wife. "She was in my office. Almost there."

Shadowing his long strides, questions buzz inside my head like trapped bees. How will Karen cope? What will they tell the children? How did Toby kill himself? Where? When? But most insistently, "Why?"

The man I met nine years ago at Ron and Karen's wedding would have been about forty now. Relatively young. Healthy. Employed. I can't help wondering what was so unbearable that he'd chosen to end his life.

One thing I did know. If no explanation for Toby's drastic choice ever comes to light, his death will be that much harder for his family to accept.

Two steps into the kitchen Ron halts so abruptly I nearly bump into his back. Sitting statue-still at their rustic round table, Karen is a portrait of Nordic-blonde despair. Charlene, the seven-year-old, grasps her mother's arm and stares up at her face with fear. Terry, the youngest, has nestled her head in mother's lap.

Karen rises. Runs into Ron's arms. Hammers his chest crying, "No, no, no, no, no." Then suddenly she pulls loose. Features distorted with rage, she informs the universe that, "Toby wouldn't. Not Toby. He had no reason. Not Toby," again and again with all the conviction of denial. "I know he didn't. Not Toby."

"Karen, honey," Ron tries to soothe her, and I fear Karen might scream.

Instead she draws in two deep, rugged gasps, doubles over, and moans into her hands.

Her terrified girls are crying, too—of course they are—and rather than say the wrong thing Ron has gone rigid and mute as a tree.

Pretending that adult meltdowns are as normal as rain, I drape my arms across my nieces' shoulders and suggest that we make dinner together. "Your mommy and daddy can wait in the living room."

Ron shoots me a glance that almost looks grateful, and an oblivious Karen allows herself to be led away.

I dump canned whole tomatoes into bowls and help the girls doctor them with Worcestershire sauce and sugar the way my grandmother used to. Stoic Charlene keeps her frightened thoughts to herself as she sprinkles the sugar. While I grate cheese onto the macaroni I cooked, her younger sister peppers me with questions. "Will Mommy be okay?" "What happens when you die?"

Without really saying too much, I reassure them both the best I can.

A little salad, a little bread, and we all gather around the table. Tear-weary and weak, Karen has no appetite. Ron makes an effort with his daughters but is clearly off his game. When Karen pushes away from her plate, he does, too.

"Please stay," Karen urges her husband. "I'm just going to lie down."

We complete the meal in silence, but even at midnight I still hear Karen's voice. *He wouldn't ...Not Toby."*

And yet he did.

Ron tapped on my bedroom door at sunrise. "Hey, Lauren. You awake? I could use some help."

Karen had already left for the airport. My brother would join her in Cleveland in a couple of days for the funeral. Considering the disturbing nature of the death, they decided that the girls should stay with me. The way Ron put it, "Think your boss can manage without you for a couple shifts?"

I said, "Yes," of course, but I had my doubts. Most of the Pelican Perch's wait-staff were so young they didn't belong on either side of a bar; and if Anthony Piccolo, the restaurant owner, brought in a temp, I was afraid I'd lose the few shifts he'd been throwing my way. That may not sound like the end of the world, but the reason I'd landed on my brother's doorstep was because a criminal had pulled every rug I owned out from under me, and in this predominantly rural area bartending part-time was the only job I could get.

Regardless, I threw on some clothes and headed for the kitchen. I fried bacon and scrambled eggs for Ron, his farmhands, and his daughters. I packed peanut butter and jelly sandwiches and juice boxes into purple and pink backpacks and walked two sleepy-eyed girls to the end of the lane in the dewy morning air.

You might think that an emotionally damaged cancer survivor who pretty much hid out in an attic apartment for four years would prefer an empty house, but you would be wrong. That wasn't me. Not anymore. Seeing the school bus's taillights disappear made me feel hollowed out.

Yet it wasn't until my brother returned home that I discovered how achingly lonely the farmhouse could be. Silly me, I'd been hoping Ron would ask about my experience with suicide, perhaps to help allay Karen's doubts. But no. The first evening he kissed his daughters good-night and slipped off to his barn office.

To avoid talking to me? Maybe.

To drink? Probably.

Did I dare challenge him without Karen there to back me up?

No.

His somber silence continued. By the fourth day I'd have settled for a remark about the weather or a gripe about the farmhands slacking off. Even the score of last night's Orioles game would have been welcome. Something. Anything. Ron volunteered nothing, and the one time I tried to learn more about Toby's suicide I was firmly told, "Not now."

My isolation reached critical mass on Friday. Walking back from the bus stop, I felt like a mouse trapped under a sky-blue teacup. I couldn't face another day of dishes, laundry, et cetera, ad infinitum with nothing but daytime TV for company. The very thought made me want to run screaming into one of my brother's newly planted fields.

Much to my relief, Anthony had scheduled me for that night's shift, but that meant my only chance to confront Ron was *right now.*

His truck sat just outside the barn. Swarthy farmhand Jerome, in his usual overalls and a worn plaid shirt, dozed in the passenger seat. Leather-faced Edmundo sat on the tailgate swinging his legs like a kid. Neither had much of a grasp of English, and in the week plus that I fed them breakfast neither made much of an effort. I learned to be content with their bashful nods.

My brother finally emerged from the nearby shed. Oblivious to my presence, he swung his heavy silver toolbox up and onto the truck bed then headed for the driver's door.

"Hey," I shouted. "Hold still a minute, will you?"

Ron turned toward me and blinked. "A minute, sure," he agreed, but his body language said that was all I'd get.

"Are you ever going to tell me about Toby?"

Our matching hazel eyes finally met, and I realized *That must be what my stare looks like, the one that used to stop thieves in their tracks.* That plus the gun in my hand.

"Tell you what?"

"Oh, maybe like how it happened?"

"You're not going to make a big deal out of this, are you?" he pressed.

"Not if Karen doesn't want me to."

That must have reassured my brother, because he lowered his chin and confessed. "Toby shot himself."

"With…?"

"A shotgun."

"Not the easiest thing to do."

Ron studied the ground. "No."

"Where?"

"What do you mean where?"

"In his bathroom, his office, what? I'm not asking for an autopsy report. It's just a question."

That piercing stare again.

Just when my frustration threatened to become anger, Ron capitulated. "The gun room of the Stoddard's hunting lodge. Toby and Chantal were there for her father's birthday party." A grimace and a glance toward the truck.

"The lodge is in Maryland, right? Not that far from here." Nothing in Maryland was that far from anything else in Maryland, at least not as the crow flies.

No answer. My brother's attention was on his employees, occupied as they are twiddling away his money.

I voiced the usual parting cliché. "Let me know if there's anything I can do."

Ron's head snapped around as if I'd cursed our mother, and that more than the days of silence delivered the message. If my family wanted my professional expertise, they would ask for it. Until then interference of any sort was strictly forbidden.

I lowered my eyes and waited for Ron to leave.

Wow, I thought as the truck finally rattled onto the road. Suicide by shotgun. *I hope somebody's looking into that.*

Me? I had a ton of housework to do.

Chapter 3

The following Thursday morning I was having a muffin and coffee at the breakfast bar facing the eastern field when I heard sneakers squeaking on the floor behind me. I swiveled around to find my sister-in-law carrying a basket of dirty clothes toward the laundry room.

Genuinely glad to see her, I said, "Hey, welcome home," with all the enthusiasm I felt.

My smile was not returned.

Here's the thing. As my stay lengthened, by the week, by the day, by the minute, I'd become increasingly hyper-alert for any hint that I'd overstayed my welcome. I feared that moment had come.

When Karen lowered her brows and said, "Would you mind taking your stuff out of the dryer?" I heard it as, "You're in the way. Get the hell out of my house!"

My palms dampened with sweat, I mumbled, "Okay," as I hastened to do my sister-in-law's bidding. Arms loaded with the offending clothes, I escaped to the bedroom I'd been assigned, Charlene's. She was across the hall with Terry for the duration.

In my borrowed space were the white iron bedstead from my childhood and the red and white shining-star quilt hand stitched by my father's great-grandmother. The clothing I considered essential fit easily into a child's closet and a small, pink dresser. On top of that were four framed photographs: my young mother in July of her final year posing in front of a massive white climbing rose; my father behind his new home in Albuquerque, New Mexico; and an aerial shot of the Pennsylvania farm he'd been forced to sell on my behalf. Across my photo of Corinne, my dear friend and almost step-mother, I'd draped the turquoise necklace she'd given me on the first birthday my oncologist had not expected me to achieve. A basket of toiletries resided on the closet floor along with three pairs of shoes and my winter boots. My rusting red Miata was parked out by the barn, and that was about it. People were what mattered to me now, and not much else.

Swallowing to ease the lump in my throat, I extracted three of my white bartender shirts from the pile on the quilt, shook them out, and hung them on hangers. I won't deny it; I was stalling. There's a karma to confrontation, and this didn't feel like my day.

Although maybe I was wrong. When I first arrived, hadn't Karen thrown her arms around me and insisted that I stay? "A slam-dunk no-brainer?" she called it. And hadn't she whispered, "Ron will come around," with a conspirator's grin?

Except for the suicide silence, my brother had been pretty good, too, what I'd call "accepting" about my extended stay. Two months was probably pushing it though.

I expected to find out where I stood from Karen, but the kitchen was empty.

Instead I heard crying. Forgetting about breakfast, I padded quietly toward Karen and Ron's end of the house.

My sister-in-law had braced her back against a dresser as if she meant to push it through the wall.

When our eyes met, her lips began to tremble.

"Toby?" I guessed. She was just back from his funeral, after all.

A wave of her head as she erased tears with the back of her hand. "No," she said, then, "Yes," then, "No."

Then she abruptly lifted her chin. "Never mind. I'm okay."

Before I could think of a response, Karen shook her head hard. "Sorry. I am not okay," she said. "Something's wrong with Ron."

Oh that.

"Yes." I drew out the word and nodded. "The drinking, right?"

Karen's head jerked, and her back straightened. "You know about that?"

I mustered a smile. "Bartender," I said. "See it all the time." Not to mention that I probably knew Ron as well as she did. "Any idea why?"

Karen pressed her lips together and shrugged, which figured. When my brother's privacy was threatened, he became part clam, part snapping turtle. If you valued your limbs, you circled wide.

Back still resting against the dresser, my sister-in-law sank to the floor. I slid my butt down the door jamb to join her.

"I think it's me," she remarked.

"Impossible," I argued, faking it this time because how would I know? I just knew that if those two had marital problems, the entire institution was doomed.

More tear-swiping and a sniff. "Then why won't he let me near him?"

Whoo-boy. My financial guess was way off. It had just been speculation anyhow. I sighed and blew out my cheeks.

Karen was watching me think, expectation in her eyes. She looked so miserable, so hopeful, that I would have invented reasons for Ron's negligence all afternoon if I thought it would make her feel better.

But hold on. Maybe I actually knew the answer.

"It's spring," I reminded his wife. "Ron's working his ass off."

Karen's eyes narrowed and her lips pressed tight. Her head waved as she hoisted herself off the floor.

"Not buying it, Lauren," she said as she eased toward the bed. "He always had time for me before." She selected a pink t-shirt out of her pile of clean clothes. Snapped it smooth. Began folding it.

The out-of-hand dismissal of my reasoning prickled like static electricity, but it also made my situation clear. I was kindling awaiting a match.

Karen placed the t-shirt down with a pat, then lifted her eyes to meet mine.

I couldn't hold her gaze, looked down at the folded shirt instead.

It was nestled inside an open suitcase half hidden by Karen's laundry.

Chapter 4

"Oh, look at the time," I told Karen, tearing my eyes from the opened suitcase. "Gotta get ready for work."

Even dragging my heels through what little I had to do—tidy the kitchen, put away my own clothes, shower and dress—I arrived at the Pelican Perch half an hour before my shift started. I couldn't escape the turmoil in my head, but at least Karen could deal with hers without me around.

The Pelican's Perch looked like what it was, a family friendly pub offering large drinks at modest prices, fried fish and potatoes, a couple of unpopular salad choices, two beef entrees favored by the biker crowd, and vanilla ice cream squirted heavily with Hersey's syrup for the kid in us all. Luckily, the former boat-storage barn retained its forlorn, but serviceable, dock for the summer sailors and a broad gravel parking lot for everybody else. If the food was merely fair, the locals didn't seem to mind; and who wants heart-smart mini-portions when they're on vacation anyway?

"You're early," my boss observed. A short man, Anthony was also stocky—probably from eating his establishment's food. His most arresting features were a pair of dark, close-set eyes and the gold Pelican earring dangling from in his left earlobe. Considering his nose, it wasn't a flattering comparison to invite; but if anybody cared, that person certainly wasn't Anthony. As a businessman, I'd say he was sharp with a soupcon of gullible. As a boss, he was casual enough to be ideal. That he noticed I was early surprised me more than if he'd noticed I was late.

He showed me half a smile. "To whut do we owe sucha pleasure?" He drew out the word "pleasure" as if it were a tasty food. Goes without saying, Anthony's New Jersey accent was thick.

Since my trifecta of bad luck had come up during my job interview—no money, no home, no job—I expected he would intuit the truth no matter what I said. I performed a What're-you-gonna-do head roll/shrug that made my curly blonde, work-appropriate ponytail wave like a red flag. Then I admitted I thought it was time to put a deposit on a place of my own.

Anthony's left eyebrow squeezed into an interesting S shape. He and Ron were friendly, so he knew where I lived.

"If you can work it out," I told him, "I could use some extra shifts." Part-time really wasn't cutting it.

Good man that he was, Anthony didn't blink. He consulted the resources in his head then made a clicking noise with his cheek.

"Yeah. Yeah, I can prob'ly swing a little more your way. Summer's comin'. Yeah. I'll think of sumtin'."

He rested his small hands on the top edge of his belt. "You wanna loan?" short for "How bad is it?"

I gave the reassuring no-thanks reply, and he waddled off to greet a batch of newcomers.

My shift proceeded in the usual spurts for a week night—pre-dinner tapering to an off-and-on flow before the hard-core drinkers settled in about ten-thirty. The night's tips were average, so my ability to move out on my own was pretty much the same as yesterday.

My mood slid from low to lower when I got home. Covered by a rainbow-colored afghan, my brother was sacked out on the living room sofa. Mouth agape, his head was pillowed by the shirt he wore earlier, and his right hand dangled near the boots and jeans he had carelessly dropped to the floor.

Leaning over his stubbled cheek to check his breath, I was transported back to a night when I was twelve. Feeling his way in the dark, Ron had stumbled into my room by mistake, tripped over my desk chair, and crashed face-first into my bedframe. My scream brought Dad running. A flip of the light switch revealed Ron's bloody split lip and chipped tooth.

Strictly speaking, we knew my brother's drinking to excess was not due to alcoholism. Lousy impulse control, the tendency to overachieve, latent immaturity, an I'm-going-to-do-what-I-damn-well-please attitude provoked by a large dose of self-pity? Throw in a reckless disregard for personal safety while under the influence, and it was yes on all counts. Ordinarily I'd have been strongly tempted to douse him with ice water, but not tonight.

Not after I'd seen his wife packing a suitcase.

The double toot of a car horn woke me around nine, and I hurried to look out the bathroom window, the nearest one facing the gravel lane. My peek through the curtain revealed a low-slung Ford Mustang in an orange that would make a pumpkin green. Dust from its skidding stop still billowed across the front lawn while its owner casually leaned against the opened passenger door. My instant impression was of a smug bridegroom waiting to whisk his bride off to a secluded island, but it was just a trick of memory. When Karen emerged from the house and ran to hug the man, I realized he was her younger brother Mike, whom I'd also met at Ron and Karen's wedding. Instead of a lover stealing her off to an island, it was Version Two of the old story: Disillusioned wife welcomed into the open arms of her family.

I clambered into a V-neck sweater and my denim skirt and ran.

"Hold on," I shouted as I stumbled out the door. The aforementioned suitcase was loaded and zipped and waiting on its rollers. Ron was nowhere in sight, and the girls were already at school. After a late shift, I usually slept until around eleven, so Karen's opportunity for slipping away undetected had been ripe.

Reacting to my shout, she released her rescuer and spun around to face me. A strand of corn-silk hair blew across her mouth, and she removed it before asking, "What are you doing up?"

"You can't go," I blurted.

Karen glanced at Mike as if he might know what I was talking about.

"Go where?"

"Go anywhere. You belong here. With Ron. Please don't go."

Another glance at Mike, whose lips twitched.

Karen doubled over and laughed. "You thought…?"

Thoroughly confused, I responded like an idiot. "Of course, I thought. What was I supposed to think when I found my brother sleeping on the sofa as if…as if…"

"As if we had a fight?"

"Yes."

"We did. He lied about having something to drink and, well, we made up this morning." Karen's expression allowed no room for doubt—the rest was none of my damn business.

"Oh, yeah? Then what's with the suitcase?"

Karen took three steps toward me, rested her palms on her thighs, and said, "The Roitmans, Chantal's parents, have invited Mike and me to fly to the Dominican Republic. They're going to scatter Toby's ashes in the Caribbean."

When I didn't respond, couldn't respond really, she added, "Chantal and Toby met at a resort down there, and it was her idea to, to…"

Karen shot her brother a needy glance then closed her eyes.

Mike drew her to his chest and stroked her back with his free hand. "Nobody from our family wants to go," he explained over Karen's head, "but Toby's wife—Chantal—she felt strongly that…anyway, we all thought she should get what she wants. Mom and Dad can't go because of Dad's health, but Karen and I, we couldn't think of an excuse."

"Karen?"

Her eyes met mine, and for a moment Mike wasn't there.

"You really don't want to go?" I asked.

She waved her head. "One funeral was one too many for me."

I relieved her of the suitcase and turned back toward the house.

Karen ran after me. "Lauren! What are you doing?"

"You shouldn't go if you don't want to."

"That's crazy! What will the Roitmans think?"

"Let them think whatever they want. You're never going to see them again. Why should you care?"

"I care about Chantal. She's, she's a mess right now. It would be awful to hurt her feelings. And Mike," she gestured back at her brother. "Mike shouldn't have to go alone."

"Okay," I said. "I'll go for you." I said it without thinking, but I liked what I said. Going in Karen's place would give her and Ron some desperately needed private time.

Best of all, I could see that the idea appealed to Karen.

"What will you tell the Roitmans?" she wondered.

"Don't know yet. I'll think of something on the way to the airport."

Mike and Karen exchanged a quick brother/sister glance, then Karen asked me how fast I could pack.

Chapter 5

"Remember you've got a plane to catch," Karen called after me as I tugged her suitcase over the doorstep and into the house. "A *private* one, but you shouldn't keep the Roitmans waiting."

"No problem," I shouted back out the door. "I'm taking your clothes."

The stuff Karen packed for herself would be short and tight on me, but I wouldn't be seeing Toby's in-laws ever again either, so I didn't care a flying fig how I looked. That said, I opened her heavy bag on my bedroom floor and set about making a few quick adjustments. Certain things you just plain don't borrow.

A bathing suit, for instance. I tossed aside her red one-piece and replaced it with the pink bikini with yellow polka dots I'd rescued from a bargain basket. I switched out all the underwear, and traded Karen's strappy summer footwear for my white Keds and the only pair of girly, high-heeled sandals I owned. A couple of toiletries, and I was ready for multiple days in the tropics inside of eight minutes.

Or was I?

Sitting on the edge of my great-great-grandma's quilt, I ran through the relevant facts, first and foremost Toby Stoddard's questionable suicide. Highly questionable according to Karen's emotional outburst.

Hope for the best. Plan for the worst. I didn't know whether passengers on privately owned jets got subjected to the usual security checks, but I suspected the odds favored no.

I took my Glock out of its lockbox, wrapped it in a clean rag, and tucked it in the bottom of the suitcase. I added a few bullets to the earrings in Karen's padded jewelry pouch, sighed to seal my decision, zipped the bag, and rolled. If the gun got flagged, I would simply stay home.

Waiting by the car, Mike and Karen were engaged in what seemed to be an affectionate private good-bye, so I stood aside and phoned Anthony to explain that I needed to go to an out-of-town funeral.

"Sure. Sure," my boss replied. "Do whatcha gotta do."

I promised to call him the minute I got back. Two absences in a month. Anthony couldn't be happy with me.

"Right. Right," he remarked. Then he covered the phone to greet a deliveryman, and just that quick I became old news. Exactly how old I would learn soon enough.

"So, Lauren Beck," Mike addressed me as we churned more dust speeding out the lane. "You've won yourself a fun-filled week with the Roitmans and me. I guess the question is, 'Why?'"

I gave that a careless shrug. "Never been to the Caribbean, have you?"

Mike steered with his right hand up high, which revealed the cuff button missing from his tan sport coat. Just visible underneath were the wide lapels and loud print of a Hawaiian shirt, and it occurred to me that a free trip to the tropics might be as much of a luxury for him as it was for me.

"Don't look a gift horse…?" he joked.

I returned his smile. "Nothing ventured…"

Out of the blue, a serious look. Maybe the years had added complexity to Michael Stoddard, or maybe the dancing doofus I remembered with the sweaty ginger-brown curls, florid face, and god-awful necktie had merely been stupid-drunk at his sister's wedding. Helluva first impression he'd made, not that he'd been trying. It would probably be a kindness to grant him a do-over.

I held out my hand. "Lauren Beck," I said. "Pleased to meet you."

"Likewise."

A minute later Karen's younger brother glanced away from the field-lined road and caught me staring at his gaudy shirt.

Brushing the collar twice with his fingers, he said, "Like it?" as if the answer were a given.

I told him it looked very tropical.

"Always good to blend."

"The way your car blends, right?"

Mike's impish smile stretched wider. "Exactly."

A cow pasture lay to our left, and he inhaled deeply through the slightly opened window. "Gotta love the smell of manure in the morning. Makes you feel connected to the earth, doesn't it?"

His eyes dared me to laugh, so of course, I did.

"Again like your car?" I teased. "Didn't they have shock absorbers back when they built this thing?"

"Careful, she'll hear you," Mike scolded. "Dolly's very sensitive about her parts."

I watched him drive for a minute but got nothing from his face.

"What else do you know about this trip?" I finally asked.

Mike spared me another glance. "We'll land in Punta Cana, although you won't be on land very long. Father Frank has secured a four-cabin yacht for the final farewell to his daughter's poor, disgraced husband."

"Disgraced?"

"You don't know?"

"Ex-cop. Nobody tells me anything."

"I see."

"So. You going to be like everybody else, or are you going to tell me what's going on?"

"Answer my question first."

"What question?"

"Why are you really here?"

I glanced out at our surroundings while I debated which of my motivations to share. The farm scenery had briefly given way to a cluster of buildings. A gas station. An International House of Pancakes. A bank.

I admitted that I felt like a stowaway on my brother's farm, "like I'm one meal short of being tossed overboard."

Mike's brow lowered as he waved his head. "Nope. Doesn't sound like Karen. Try again."

He had a point. He grew up with her, after all. Of course, I grew up with Ron.

I mulled that over until we stopped at a red light, when Mike challenged me with an expectant stare.

I met Mike's gaze. Then I told him I wasn't completely satisfied that his brother committed suicide.

He inhaled deeply then sighed out the word, "Why?" again.

"The method, you know? The houseful of people."

Mike's focus began to hop around, so I diverted my attention, too. To give him some time to process—if he needed it.

He didn't. He hit the steering wheel with the flat of his hand and exclaimed, "Sonovabitch." Then he deflated inside his clothes. Just plain deflated.

I gave him another moment. Didn't speak until we were cruising again.

"I take it you're not sure about the suicide either," I said. "May I ask why not?"

One quick head shake and a lengthy stare at the road. "Toby played baseball in high school, third base, but mostly he was a pretty good hitter."

He glanced my way, and I nodded for him to go on.

"Championship game senior year," he continued. "Score's five to four, bottom of the ninth, they're losing. Runners on first and third, two outs. Toby pops up. Game over."

"Toby lost his chance to be a hero."

"Correct."

"So?"

"So Toby went home, grabbed his wallet and Mom's car keys and ran out the door. I just made it into the Chevy before he squealed out of the driveway. He drove straight to the batting machines in the park near our house. Hot Friday night. Only a few other guys using the cages."

"Yeah?"

"Toby stepped into the first empty one and refused to leave. Must have paid for about a hundred and twenty pitches and hit most of them. Beat up his hands so bad they swelled up like catcher's mitts."

"That's it? That's your reason?"

"Not quite."

"When he got tired, he started missing pitches. When he whiffed four in a row, he smashed the aluminum bat into a metal post so hard he broke his wrist."

I thought I understood, but I wanted to be sure. "And this means…?"

"Toby was not a quitter. Suicide would never occur to him."

Was I convinced? Not really. Didn't I know first-hand that ambitious overachievers are perfectly capable of hurting themselves?

Mike caught my expression and smacked the steering wheel again.

"Dammit. Do you need more examples?"

"No. No, I get it. Type A personality, tenacious as all get out."

"Right. Right!" he said, calming down somewhat. "When I explained that to Mary, she practically packed my bag and kicked me out the door. 'Go,' she said. 'Find out what really happened. You'll never get another chance.'"

"Wow," I remarked. "Special woman."

"You don't know the half of it. I told her I didn't want to risk missing our baby being born—she's due next month."

"Yikes!"

"Guess what Mary said to that."

"What?"

"She said, 'You have to go because in six months or six years or six decades when Toby's suicide is still haunting you like a missing limb, I don't want you telling me I was right, that you should've gone on this trip.'"

"Wow! Hard arguing with that."

"You got that right. Plus it's Toby, you know? I loved my brother more than I love myself," a short laugh, "and my friends will tell you that's pretty much."

I took in his mischievous eyes and long curly lashes and dismissed my first impression altogether. "You're alright, Mike Stoddard. Aren't you?" I decided.

"Are you kidding? I'm awesome!" he quipped, and this time we laughed together.

A mile later I asked him how he'd planned to proceed.

His brow knit and his lips tightened. "Just keep my eyes open and my mouth shut. Why? What would you do?"

"Oh, keep my eyes open and my mouth shut…"

He chuckled. "So much more professional. Glad you're here."

According to all the signs, we were approaching the Chesapeake Bay Bridge, or officially the William Preston Lane Jr. Memorial Bridge. As we funneled into an EZ Pass lane along with about twenty other vehicles, Mike inquired, "You up for this?"

"Sure. Why do you ask?"

"Oh, no reason."

The span we entered consisted of three westbound lanes supported by towers with square openings. To our left lay its eastbound partner suspended on picturesque fans of wire. With no breakdown space the two oncoming lanes looked unnervingly narrow, and our three were plenty skinny enough. The guardrails seemed to be about chest high, and a steep incline lowered the choppy steel-gray bay water further and further away. To sample the briny air, I opened the window another notch, but the wind blew my hair against my cheek with enough force to sting. Even the seagulls had more sense than to venture this high.

"Swell place to be in a storm," I remarked.

"No," Mike asserted. "Oh, no."

"Exactly how high is it?"

"Hundred and eighty-six feet," he replied as if wasting energy on one more syllable might pitch us into the drink.

As a cop, I'd learned how to compartmentalize my fear, but combine the flimsy sensation of a Ferris wheel with being propelled at more than forty miles an hour and, caught unaware, I realized an ordinary civilian might suffer a panic attack or worse. The bridge should have warning signs like the ones for Space Mountain at Disney World.

Which made me worry just a tad about Mike's bravery. Right now his red-head pallor shone with sweat and his hands gripped the wheel as if they were the ropes of a descending parachute.

My next thought was that Mike loved his brother so much that he was willing to infiltrate the family that might have had something to do with his brother's death. Not the smartest move for an amateur, but emotions often overrule the brain. Wasn't I more than a little guilty of that myself?

After the tollbooth and a wide dogleg turn, Mike jockeyed us up into the center lane. Traffic aiming for Washington, DC, was thick, and naturally some impatient yahoo began to dog our rear end. Mike endured the dangerous aerial tailgating as long as he could but eventually signaled us into the right lane. Without thinking, I glanced down at the water and the sudden vertigo made my stomach roil.

"And how long is this thing?" I inquired, clearly meaning, *"How soon will we be off?"* Land appeared to be very, very far away.

"Four point three miles."

When we finally made it to the shoreline, Mike exhaled with a lengthy "Pshewww." If we hadn't been on the way to catch a plane, I think he'd have pulled over for a breather.

Glancing my way, he said, "Now you can say you've been on the scariest bridge in the world."

"Seriously?"

"That's its reputation. For twenty-five bucks you can get somebody else to drive your car across for you."

"You're kidding."

"Nope. It's an actual business."

"Wow. I guess I owe you twenty-five bucks."

Based on our surroundings and the traffic, Washington congestion was imminent. Rather than deal with the Beltway, Mike chose to stay on Route 50 and thread the interior streets of the city. Somewhere in the middle we joined Route 66 West toward our destination.

He and I spent the time getting acquainted in the typical impersonal way. It was much too early to explain how I'd come to be down on my luck; that much candor could wait. Instead I sketched out my background, how I'd studied criminology at Temple University then became a Landis, PA, cop. "If you don't count bartending," I told him, "my most recent job was investigating insurance fraud for AIA," Amalgamated Insurance Association of North America.

"Oh, yeah?" Mike seemed pleased. "I sell insurance."

I'd never have guessed. "Then we have something in common," I replied, unless he actually enjoyed the insurance industry.

"Beside Karen."

"Beside Karen," I agreed.

We chatted a while about her and Ron and the kids, then I got up the nerve to ask more about him. I was caught up on his Catholic upbringing and just beginning to hear about his University of Virginia education—the reason he'd settled in Charlottesville—when his cell phone rang.

"Mary!" he exclaimed after lifting the instrument to his ear. "Everything okay?" Never mind the lanes of traffic, or the speed, or the need to watch for his turn-off; Mike Stoddard was home with his wife.

I watched his eyes long enough to assure myself he could handle it all. Then I allowed the passing scene to blur and focused on the problem that had been weaving in and out of my head since we left the farm. With Mike totally enclosed in his personal love-bubble, maybe I'd be able to devise a solution before we got to the airport. I hoped so, because the more I thought about it the more worried I became.

Passing myself off as Karen's substitute might literally get me off the ground with the Roitmans, but it probably would not hold up over a week-long, undercover investigation. If one—or more—of Toby's in-laws happened to be involved in a staged suicide, the slightest slipup, such as accidentally asking the right question, could put both Mike and me in mortal danger.

"Pull into the next gas station," I urged the oblivious father-to-be as soon as he ended his call. "We need to talk."

Chapter 6

The city's congested asterisk pattern finally gave way to commercialized suburbs that, judging by the hectic traffic, still reflected the fervor of our federal government. No doubt the boutique airport would be farther out in the countryside where convenience stores would be scarce. I would have to find what I needed soon after we exited Route 66.

"There," I pointed. The establishment offered a dozen gas pumps on six sheltered islands and nose-in parking facing a bustling mini-mart.

As soon as Mike pulled in, I said, "Buy gas or something. I'll be right out."

He stopped under the island overhang; but when he opened his mouth to speak, I shushed him with a finger to his lips. "Right out. Park anywhere. I'll find you. First, please pop the trunk."

I took some things out of my suitcase concealed them in my big straw purse.

"Hurry up, okay?" Mike called after me as I trotted toward the building.

The doors were burping people left and right. I jostled myself through the nearest, narrowly missing a blue snow cone held by a very little boy.

Inside, I quickly chose three packs of sugar-free gum and popped the first piece into my mouth before my change had a chance to rattle down that little metal chute.

In the rest room I rolled my short denim skirt even higher and covered the lumpy waistline with my V-neck sweater. Change my footwear, fluff up my hair, rub on some peachy lip gloss, and I became someone else altogether.

Mike had parked the Mustang just around the corner and was anxiously watching for me through the windshield. Shame on me, but seeing that aging, high-school-jock face stare at me through the Mustang's window made me want to toy with him. In those high-heeled sandals it was easy, inevitable almost. I put a little extra sway in my hips and tossed a bit of blonde hair over my shoulder.

Mike's eyes widened as if he couldn't quite wrap his head around my new persona, so of course I sidled in beside him and planted a wet one on his cheek.

"Hey, hey, hey," he scolded, cringing away as if I were a Labrador retriever. "Stop that, will you?" He even slapped my hands.

Smirking, I'm pretty sure my amusement came off as a smirk, I settled back in my seat.

"Geesh, Lauren. Are you out of your mind? I'm…"

"Married. Yes, I know. And I'm trying to find out what happened to your brother."

"Yeah, I guess, but what's this," he wiped his cheek again, "got to do with…?"

"It's to keep us safe. If there's a murderer anywhere in the picture, neither of us can afford to let on that we suspect that. It would be like poking a rattlesnake with a short stick."

"But…"

"Please let me finish. You can't change being you," I conceded, "but I'm an ex-cop, *and* I have a connection to Toby's family. All I'll get from the Roitman's is the fit-for-publication version of everything, probably right down to whatever they ate for lunch. However, they don't know what Lauren Beck looks like, and, if I'm lucky, they may not even know I exist." I spread my hands. "That means I can go undercover as your girlfriend. Do you think you can deal with that for a week?"

Mike's cheeks scrunched up toward his eyes until he was peering at me through slits. "Do you have to be a bimbo?"

"Probably not," I admitted, "but being underestimated adds another layer of protection. I won't mean a thing to them."

"But Toby's in-laws? You can't possibly suspect...?"

"They're just our starting point, Mike. But if they find out we're not sure about the suicide, do you think they'll keep quiet about it?"

His eyes widened.

"Right," I confirmed. "They could accidentally share our doubts with the killer. Trust me, we can't be too careful.

"You're a lucky man," I reminded him. "You have a woman who wants you to be happy today, tomorrow, and the rest of your life. Let's just make sure that life isn't any shorter than it's supposed to be."

He finally nodded. Then a rueful smile. "I'll look like scum to Toby's in-laws."

"And I won't?"

Mike rolled his eyes. "They'll *really* hate you."

"I know. You up for this, or what?"

Another moment of thought, then his salesman swagger finally kicked in. He dropped his right hand onto my leg.

"Hey!" I said. "Save it for the Roitmans."

"Gotcha," he replied with a laugh.

Oh. Payback for the wet kiss.

"By the way," I cracked my gum as we rolled onto the road. "My name is Lori. Lori..."

"Ruggles," he finished. "My high-school crush was on Denise Ruggles. She was, uh," a furtive glance, "blonde, too."

Chapter 7

The Van Pelt Airport tucked into the Virginia countryside as anonymously as runways for private jets possibly could. Probably worried that we were late, Mike roared into the parking lot and snagged the last spot in the first row. As the dust wisped away in the breeze, I saw that we were surrounded by the same cars you'd find adjacent to a golf club's clubhouse, just fewer of them. Blazing brighter than the early afternoon sun, the Mustang labeled us just as surely as Mike's missing sleeve button and my shortened denim skirt. I figured I didn't need the chewing gum, so I threw it out.

Off to the right three long, low hangars sheltered the planes while front and center a trendy stone building protected waiting passengers from the elements. Dangling from the high ceiling inside was a small, yellow single-propeller plane, which coordinated nicely with the comfortable leather chairs grouped on the floor below. I estimated that the cost of the buttery furniture would cover the apartment deposit I needed and then some.

Mike had mentioned that the Roitmans had a fairly young daughter who wouldn't be with us because of school, but all four adults were present and accounted for. Judging by the debris on the short round table in front of them, they'd finished lunch from the adjacent café some time ago. Father Frank held a watery bloody Mary with a tassel of celery while the missus—Marsha was her given name—sipped at her remaining iced tea through a straw. Whether that was out of consideration for the dishwasher— her true-red lipstick could have greased a bicycle—or whether she was simply disinclined to reapply, too early to tell.

Looking rather awestruck, Mike mumbled, "Hope we didn't hold you up."

The Roitmans rustled, except for the son, who gazed out the wall of spotless windows with disinterest. I guessed him to be approaching thirty, my own age, although his body appeared to have been shaped on a squash court rather than an ordinary gym. His clothes—tailored to perfection. His nearly black hair had been brushed back, except one loose strand curled strategically over his left eye. The glance he spared me considered his chances then dismissed my indifference practiced ease. Could he be a murderer? Sure. Why not?

"No problem," the father addressed Mike. "Traffic through the city a bitch, was it?"

"Yes," Mike replied with relief.

To suggest that I wasn't exactly Mike's sister I had grasped his elbow as soon as he released the suitcase handles. Then I realized the Roitmans must have met Mary at the Cleveland funeral. Also, they knew perfectly well I wasn't Karen.

The moment was ripe for Mike to introduce me, but he seemed to be fascinated by his shoes.

"Hi!" I breathed into the silence. "I'm Lori, Lori Ruggles. Mike's, uh friend. Karen couldn't make it, so Mikey hoped you wouldn't mind if he brought me along. Please say it's okay. I promise I won't eat much."

The Roitman patriarch closed his eyes and drew in air. His buxom wife, with her stiff upswept honey-blonde hair and heavy gold chains, pressed those red lips into a line and dropped her shoulders. Forget that she was vain and a couple powder puffs past polished; the intensity in her eyes warned me to beware. Marsha Roitman was a woman and therefore complex.

An airport staffer sidled up and asked if he might clear the table.

When Frank indicated his permission with the toss of his hand, the authority he exhibited reminded me of a thug I'd arrested back on the job. Just bringing him in had required extra backup, and it took a District Attorney with the ego of Donald Trump to make the case stick. My spine stiffened just remembering the guy.

"They have internet there, right?" Mike asked out of the blue, and Toby's widow, Chantal, twisted around in her chair to check if he was serious.

I patted Mike's arm and whispered, "Yes, of course," into his ear.

Then Chantal addressed him with a question of her own. "Why couldn't Karen come?"

No response.

"Mike?" I prompted, but judging by the roll of his jaw muscles and the tightened flesh around his eyes, this was more than a momentary distraction.

From the outset I knew I was a varsity coach with a JV team, but it never occurred to me that my team might not show up. It appeared that my one and only ally had already left the building.

Time for an emergency adjustment.

Lori, the expendable, tell-her-anything, store-clerk/bimbo had to go. Like it or not, somebody from the Stoddard camp needed to exhibit enough intelligence and tact to elicit useful information from our hosts. Since Mike seemed incapable of forming a sentence right now, that left me.

Say hello to the much more suspicious, certain to be closely scrutinized Lori Ruggles. If she were to break concentration even once and allow the Roitmans to guess her intentions, Lauren Beck just might get stranded in a strange country—or worse. I didn't know if I was up to this new challenge, but it probably wouldn't take long to find out.

"Okay," I told the waiting audience as if with resignation. "This is what's going on. Karen opted out. Something about the Cleveland funeral being hard enough for her. Also, I think one of the kids has a cold or something.

"And Mike," I gestured toward him as if he were on display, "is obviously a mess over losing his brother, especially *how* he lost his brother, and since I care about *him...*" I sighed to give myself an extra second to think. "To tell you the truth, this funk he's in scares the hell out of me, and a week in a strange place with a bunch of people who don't really know him, no offense, didn't seem like a real good idea, if you know what I mean. So I talked him into bringing me along, and here I am. I hope you don't mind."

Marsha's mouth had dropped open, and she abruptly shut it. Gavin's eyes twinkled with amusement. Chantal merely stared.

The one to watch was Frank. With a granite expression I'm sure served him well in the boardroom, he fixed his dark, narrowed eyes onto mine. They did not waver. I found it difficult not to flinch.

After an uncomfortable five beats, Roitman stuffed his hands casually into his trouser pockets and strolled close enough to create a semblance of privacy. Chin lifted to a calculating height, he resumed peering into my eyes as if he hadn't quite finished downloading my life history. Sweat had broken out all over me before the left corner of his mouth lifted into a wry smile.

"Welcome aboard," he said with a curt nod.

Then he turned away.

Chapter 8

Frank Roitman acknowledged the obviousness of my being Mike Stoddard's mistress with a knowing nod. Then he grasped my pretend lover's elbow, swiveled him toward the door and called back over his shoulder, "Let's go, everyone."

As he spoke, he watched me without any visible judgment, so I allowed myself to breathe.

The group, including Mike, obediently queued up behind Daddy Frank, leaving me to bring up the rear pulling our two suitcases by their extended handles. Mine was a bit heavier than it should have been, and remembering why clenched my stomach as if I'd swallowed a pound of buckshot.

The March afternoon had heated up to the pleasant neighborhood of sixty degrees, and the sky had collected some cumulus clouds shadowed with a soft blue. For a small private jet, flying through them might be bumpy, although what did I really know about small, private jets except what I could see waiting for us on the tarmac.

"Welcome," said the pilot as he relieved me of the suitcases. His handsome Hispanic face grinned at my expense then lowered as he lifted my bag into the belly of the sleek, white plane. "Shoes?" he guessed with a raised eyebrow.

"Books," I fibbed before I realized he was teasing.

"Ought to get one of those e-readers," he suggested. "Easier when you travel."

"Good thought," I agreed as I escaped up the short stairs into the plane.

New experience. Stepping into the cabin was like slipping into a kid glove. The predominant color was cream trimmed with the dark brown of freshly brewed coffee. Eight ergonomic seats faced forward with an aisle down the middle. Every other seat could be turned backwards in order to share a small table. The fragrances of new leather and actual coffee perfumed the air.

The pilot had silently followed me in. "Something to eat or drink?" he inquired, gesturing toward the discreet kitchenette across the way. "It's just me today."

Surprised, I blurted, "No co-pilot?"

"Your host has his license," the gentleman assured me with a wink in Frank's direction.

"Oh! Oh, good." Then, figuring I couldn't be much more of a rube if I tried, I admitted I was starved. "No lunch." Or breakfast. Why I hadn't bought a sandwich at the gas station instead of chewing gum I couldn't guess, except that Mike had urged me to hurry.

"Un momento." The pilot hurried back down the short stairs and disappeared.

Frank and Marsha had claimed seats across from each other in front, their son and daughter just behind. Mike, blinking as if he might be ready to cry, settled into the fourth and final row in the back.

The pilot swiftly returned with long ham and provolone sandwiches garnished with avocado, lettuce and tomato.

"I think I'm in love," I told him, and he smiled so tolerantly I dared hope he forgave me for the extra weight in my suitcase.

"Drinks right there." He pointed to an almost invisible refrigerator then reminded us to, "Buckle up," as he entered the cockpit. I only got a quick glimpse, but it resembled a compact home theater for two, except with enough electronics to launch a rocket.

Take off was fast and smooth, the way I imagined a large bird might feel launching himself into the wind. Watching the late-winter patchwork slide by below reminded me of the aerial shot on my dresser of our family's lost farm. And naturally, that brought forth the deep, silent ache of causing my brother's disappointment, compounded now by the guilt of imposing myself on him and Karen. I hoped one day they would realize I was trying to thank them the only way I knew how.

With sun-tinted clouds drifting by us, Mike and I devoured the sandwiches with appreciative umms and nods and sodas from the plane's refrigerator.

At one point I asked if he ever expected to talk again, but he just eyed me as if I were nuts. By the time I stowed our trash, he was sound asleep.

Although I wanted to enjoy the flight, I'd closed the Pelican's Perch the night before then hustled out of bed because I thought Karen was leaving Ron. I slept until the jet's touchdown woke me.

The pilot turning our luggage over to the two waiting porters caused me a small panic, but the trolleys remained in our distant sight. Instead I forced myself to observe the crowds entering the single-story thatched buildings that made up the Punta Cana airport.

A few hundred tourists disembarking from large commercial planes got shunted together with us, every one of them carrying something—a large colorful tote bag, a straw hat, one of those ubiquitous black carry-ons. I saw Chantal cringe away from a teenager's purple backpack as if it contained anthrax. Crowds tended to bring out prejudices and phobias, and clearly Chantal had a couple of both. Germs? The proximity of strangers? I couldn't be sure.

I ended up walking alongside Marsha, who chose to talk to me as if no one else within earshot spoke English. "The first time we came here," she said, "the airport didn't even have rest rooms."

"Wow," I replied.

"They had all this," a sweep of her arm to indicate the zigzagged line we had just joined. "Just no rest rooms."

"The airport wasn't done?"

"No, it wasn't. But we're at sea level, don't forget. Plumbing was a costly problem they hadn't yet solved."

"I guess that means you've been coming here for a long time."

"No, not really."

Oh. Welcome to the third world.

"Your young man," Marsha cocked a chin in Mike's direction. "You can keep him from doing anything drastic?"

Mike was acting like a ticking bomb. If I'd been his host, I'd have asked the question, too.

I answered, "That's the plan."

"I certainly hope so," she declared as she eased out of my conversational range.

I dropped back to thread my hand through the crook of Mike's arm.

"You alright?" I inquired.

"I'm fine." He had been reading a text on his phone, which he deftly slipped into a belt holder underneath his jacket. Wise in such a tight crowd.

"Try not to be so weird," I suggested as I squeezed his sleeve.

He showed me his confusion. "I thought that's how you wanted me to act."

"Distraught is good. Suicidal is bad." Mike did need to return to earth if we were to bring off our deception, but I probably should have used another word to deliver the message.

He waved his head as the line inched forward. "I shouldn't have let you come," he decided. "I could have handled this myself."

"Too late now."

"I'll say."

Somewhere beyond the booths that addressed the business of entering the Dominican Republic were three men playing island music. The beat of a bongo drum carried over the noisy hum and bustle of impatient tourists. Overhead wide fans twirled under the roof thatching, but they did little to dispel the body heat of the crowds. Behind us more arriving passengers had closed us in. Claustrophobia was a possibility, but I fought it off just as I'd had to during the cat scans I endured back when I was sick. A wave of gratitude that I was now considered to be "cured" washed over me. Not the first time today, and certainly not the last.

In contrast to his finicky daughter, Frank Roitman appeared to tolerate the cattle chutes of humanity with a patient, businesslike, expression. When he arrived at the first desk to pay the small fee required of each of us, he made good eye contact with the hardworking clerk. Then he did it again when his and Marsha's passports were stamped. I admired him for that.

Gavin and Chantal approached each desk together, but separately, if you know what I mean. Chantal never entirely shed her cloak of mourning. It pressed down on her head and caused her shoulders to slope. Even her stance seemed to have widened to accommodate the weight of her loss.

In contrast, Gavin Roitman absorbed his surroundings without sharing anything of himself. I wanted to know why he was so different from his father. I wanted to point out that *aloof* was no way to go through life. Too bad I had to keep it all to myself. He was missing out on some good advice.

Mike tipped the musicians a dollar as we passed by, so at least part of him was in the here and now.

Then came the awkward moment when we were required to stand still to be photographed with two Dominican women in costume, a procedure that assumed everyone came here for fun, certainly not to scatter a loved-one's ashes into the sea.

We were told our photos could be purchased off a certain airport wall before we left the country.

If there were one or two fewer people in our party on the way out, I wondered whether the photographer would notice.

Chapter 9

At the last minute Frank Roitman bypassed the door being held open for him and hefted his firmly packed two hundred pounds into the limousine's shotgun seat. He loved his daughter, but being confined in close quarters with Chantal's grief made his knee bounce and his palms sweat. *Toby adored the beach. Beef stroganoff reminds me of Toby. Toby Toby Toby. What'll I do without Toby?* The sooner they sprinkled the misguided young man's ashes offshore from that damn resort where they met the happier he, Frank Roitman, would be. A week of mourning and contemplation? A week away from the dying days of a rotten winter was more accurate—at no small expense, by the way.

His wife prevailed. Of course she prevailed. *Chantal needs this*, Marsha claimed. *You can afford the time just this once*, she argued. *It'll be good for you—for all of us—just wait and see.*

Well, he would wait, and he would see.

On one of his visual sweeps of the passing landscape, Frank happened to meet the limo driver's eye. The man had a lived-in face dotted with skin tags. He wore a sweat-stained straw fedora with a faded purple band. Even when he whipped around one of the motorbikes or miniature cars so prevalent in the Dominican Republic, his weathered brown fingers tapped along with the soft plink plink of the radio music. All that contentment sparked an unfamiliar pang of envy, which Frank disguised by swiveling his head the other way.

Lately nothing loosened the steel bands of tension constraining his ribs like the rings of a barrel. Marsha knew some things but not even close to everything. When he'd been mugged by the brother of the unfortunate young woman from that damned lawsuit, there had been no hope of hiding the resultant broken wrist from his wife. Unfortunately, her overreaction made sheltering her from everything he possibly could imperative. Luckily, one of the benefits derived from his early environment was the ability to replace whatever he needed to conceal with whatever he chose.

With Marsha you never had to guess if she was faking. She was. Although maybe not faking so much as amplifying. Thirty-six years into their marriage and you'd think she was still a newlywed. The kids joked that the gaudy baubles he presented to her on every possible occasion were the only reason she still doted on him. He traveled too much, they pointed out. He was a workaholic, married to his job. All true. He also knew that his youthful good looks had gone the way of his hairline.

He would never admit it, but he found his wife's honesty about her jewelry fetish endearing. After long years of building a billion-dollar conglomerate, her transparency was a welcome antidote.

Behind him the strained conversations between his family and his guests had devolved into staring out at the same billboards and unkempt jungle that Frank saw, only he saw all of it and he saw it first. If a sniper happened to be waiting on the flat roof of the upcoming motorcycle showroom, he liked to think he would be quick enough to duck, one of the silly, but maybe not-so-silly, thoughts that flashed in and out of his brain these days, and one that he made sure to hide.

The road was much more complete than he remembered, the Dominican government finally having replaced the barely competent contractors they'd entrusted with the chore for far too long. Except for the gated and guarded resort complexes that had sprung up like so many sand castles, the countryside looked much the same. Lush green and bleak all at once, with single cows munching on vegetation behind fencing so recently live the posts had taken root and sprouted leaves.

Traffic stalled for no discernible reason, and Frank found himself staring at a three-sided shack. In the shade of its corrugated roof, three dark-skinned men in slacks and loose, short-sleeved shirts malingered on two chrome stools and a red wooden chair sipping whatever the locals drank during the day. When one glanced toward the shiny black van and their eyes met, Frank felt as if he'd been caught with his zipper down. He was grateful when they began moving again.

Next came a mostly yellow, patched-together house with a flea-bitten mongrel foraging for food. Across the way lay an abandoned construction project, stacks of cement blocks with no apparent purpose.

Nothing and no one even remotely suggested a threat to the Chairman of the Board and CEO of Roitman Industries, which made perfect sense. Why bother following him all the way to the Caribbean when he could be ambushed entering a building that bore his name or in a house firmly attached to four hundred acres of real estate? Why indeed? Yet, once established, the habit of vigilance was hard to shake.

Hoping it wouldn't be noticed, Frank allowed himself the luxury of a deep, deep sigh. As he sipped from the plastic bottle of cold water provided by the limo company, he allowed his eyes to drift shut. It was the most unguarded moment he had permitted himself in days, if not weeks.

Naturally, the van bounced over a pothole and shocked him back to reality. If a threat existed within the Dominican Republic, it would come from one of two strangers holding hands in the back of this vehicle. Mike Stoddard, the overgrown boy, so insecure that he resorted to ridiculous clothing to inspire affection. His brother's suicide had hollowed him out, no question; but even though the case could be made, so far nothing indicated that he blamed Frank for that.

The tall woman was another matter altogether. A beauty with hardships concealed behind those unusual, pale gray eyes. Muscular and voluptuous, she seemed to be indifferent to her own appearance, confident yet vulnerable. A contradiction, and therefore an enigma. He couldn't fathom what she saw in Mike, and that alone bore watching. If they were a couple, the reason would emerge. If not, well, Frank would deal with her the way he dealt with any obstacle.

In the meantime he indulged in a satisfied smile, a personal pat on the back for allowing this *Lori Ruggles* person to join them. More neighborhood wisdom—put potential enemies at ease in order to lure them close.

"We are here, Mr. Roitman," the driver announced.

And they were. The van had just rounded a block of pastel buildings to reveal the placid blue water of a marina and a spectacular hundred-foot yacht. As the limo drew to a smooth stop, the sun shone across the borrowed vessel's name, "The Constitution," painted in gold. Far larger than an ordinary yacht, it had been moored at the water's edge alongside a long walkway leading to a restaurant.

"Damn," Frank swore to himself as he admired the multi-million dollar trophy. He was going to owe a helluva lot of favors before this week was over.

Chapter 10

Mike and I followed the Roitmans onto the sleek yacht like orphans pretending to be royalty. I think I scanned its perfectly polished appointments discreetly, but inside I was gawping like a five-year-old at the circus. Blond wood and chrome, pristine white paint, taupe cushions—the vessel was floating modern art, sparse and appropriate without visual or spatial waste.

After wending our way down a set of open stairs, Frank briefly assessed the four staterooms then assigned them with a gracious wave of his hand. Later I would learn that another farther below   accommodated the crew, a husband and wife duo who took care of everything, especially us.

On either side of the platform bed Mike and I were about to share, smooth wooden cabinets conformed to the shape of the hull. Unpacking into mine took three minutes, but Mike dawdled through the chore as if he were reluctant to commit. When he finally finished, he flopped onto the bed like a snow-angel.

"Tired?" I surmised. To pick up Karen he'd gotten up even earlier than me, and his in-flight nap had probably been too short to make up the difference.

He glanced my way as if he'd forgotten I was there. Something was going on.

"Mary's been texting you, right?" Silent, easy to keep private. Checking messages in the middle of a live conversation wasn't exactly polite though, unless…

"Is she okay?" I asked with sudden concern.

Mike rolled away from me. "I shouldn't be here," he complained into the pillow.

"Whoa, there. You said Mary insisted. She even packed your bag."

He sat up and propped himself on arms as taut as barbed wire. "This is ridiculous. What difference does it make whether Toby killed himself or not? Nothing's going to change. He's gone. Gone! End of story." He raised his wrists to his eyes.

Something had brought on these second thoughts, but now wasn't the time to ask. If he got any more worked up, I was afraid he might do something really crazy, like expose us to the Roitmans. When he settled down enough to listen, I would remind him once again how dangerous that could be—for both of us.

I sucked in a huge breath and blew it out slowly. Then I patted Mike's knee and said, "I'm going to shower and get dressed for dinner. Get some rest. Then meet me on the deck when you're ready. Okay?" Like it or not, he was here now. If I left him alone, maybe he would figure that out for himself.

He dropped back onto his side and slept.

Forty minutes later, I tiptoed up onto the rear deck in my strappy sandals. I was wearing one of Karen's dresses, a floor-length, blue and white print sundress that, on me, exceeded the boundaries of cleavage decency. If the Roitmans had any doubts about my relationship with Mike, the dress, or lack thereof, would erase them.

Father Frank's eyes graciously swept past me to his wife, who pretended not to see me at all. The corner of their son's lip lifted and his eyes narrowed. *Blonde trash* seemed to be his verdict, although he had no problem enjoying the view.

"What would you like, Miss?" inquired a ropy middle-aged guy with leather skin. He wore white shorts, a faded blue cotton shirt rolled halfway up his forearms, and deck shoes. Had to be the captain manning the bar, another svelte table with storage just off-center of the social area. A breeze lifted his sun-bleached hair and ruffled my dress. Above us the softening sky displayed pastel shadows on swollen early evening clouds.

"It's Lori," I introduced myself. "How about a gin and tonic?" Easier to switch to plain tonic later, assuming I got the chance to ask.

"George, at your service. Lime?"

"Sure."

Mike bounded up the stairs just then, and everyone glanced his way. "Fell asleep. Hope I'm not late."

"I don't think they have that word down here," Frank offered with a generous smile. "Please tell George here what you'd like to drink."

"What're you having, uh, Lori?"

He could see the ice and clear bubbles through my tall plastic tumbler, never glass on a boat I would soon realize.

"Um. No, thanks. Got beer?"

"One Presidente, coming up. Local favorite."

Mike and I lounged side by side on the seating that followed the curve of the yacht's railing. Frank and Marsha were to our right, Chantal and her brother Gavin across from us facing the Caribbean.

Before we could get a conversation going, a willowy woman with a gray streak in her straight, dark ponytail, offered us little puff-pastries filled with lobster and a mango dipping sauce.

"I'm Anna" she told us all, reconfirming my perception that this was not the Roitman's yacht. Making eye contact with each of us individually, she added, "Please let me know if you need anything. Anything at all."

The last person to say that to me had been the nurse administering my chemo, and she obviously meant "within reason." There on the hundred-foot deck of The Constitution the options appeared to stretch as far as the horizon, a heady notion that literally froze my brain. I couldn't think of one thing to request, not even in jest.

Frank leaned his elbows on his thighs. "What do you do, my dear?" he inquired. The family had met Mike before. I was completely unknown, and that must be addressed.

I told them I was a bartender, "at the moment."

"Oh?" Marsha responded instantly. "I'd have thought a dancer or model or maybe even an actress."

"Mother was an actress," Chantal supplied.

Gavin reacted a drumbeat slower. "At the moment?" he repeated, then, "I'll have another." He drained his plastic cup and held it toward me. Not an endearing guy, Gavin. I looked forward to digging through his baggage.

While I offered Gavin my blankest smile, George, the captain, deftly intercepted the empty cup, freshened the ice, and covered it with an ample amount of top-shelf bourbon. I was familiar with the label.

"An actress. How interesting," I prompted Marsha like the good guest I was pretending to be. "Have you been in anything I might have seen?"

"Oh, no. You're what? Twenty-five?"

"Thirty," I confessed.

"Still too young. No. I left the theater behind when I met Frank." She adored him with her eyes. He beamed in return.

In my head I invented the scenario. B-minus actress attracts ambitious young admirer, wisely chooses that fork in the road and doesn't look back.

Anna waved to her husband, who announced that dinner was ready inside. A half dozen beautiful salads waited at yet another sleek table attached to the floor. I tried to imagine this high-end hotel being tossed by fifteen-foot waves and failed. Surely, the weather wouldn't dare.

Throughout dinner Mike's mental absence became even more apparent. Rather than getting the Roitmans to talk about themselves, he was answering Frank's questions with one and two word answers. "You're in the insurance business, aren't you?" prompted during the gazpacho. *Yes.* "Couldn't help noticing your Mustang. Fun drive, is it?" over the steak. *Yes.* "Where did you two meet?" as our desserts arrived.

"Charlottesville," I supplied when Mike hesitated too long. Then I deliberately addressed Marsha. When one's boobs are on display, one does not speak to anybody's husband until the missus signals her permission, a slight smile perhaps, or a softening around the eyes. Marsha and I were not there yet. "So," I asked, "how did you and Frank meet?"

Either I finally said something right, or whatever she was drinking was having an effect. She tilted her head and leaned in.

"*Come Blow Your Horn* at a small Philadelphia theater," she opened with the panache of a well-rehearsed story. "I played the love interest and Frank's date's brother had the lead." Several gold bracelets clattered down her arm as she indicated her husband with a perfect pink nail.

"They were seated in the third row," she continued, "and when I glanced at the audience all I saw was Frank's mouth opened wide enough to catch flies."

Both her children delivered the *catch-flies* line with her, igniting Marsha's face and pressing her lips into a flat line. Neither Chantal nor Gavin noticed their mother's displeasure, but Frank did.

"That was the last of the date," he said, "and the beginning of this." He took her hand and gave it a kiss.

Mouth still drawn, Marsha stared at the fork on her plate.

Gavin stood. "I'm going over to the club," he announced.

"Nowhere else?" Frank inquired, and my cop instincts applauded.

"No, Dad. I'm not that dumb."

Mike sensed an opportunity to escape and seized it. "Sorry, folk. If you don't mind, I'm going to turn in." Not a glance my way, and most revealing of all, no *Lori and I are going to turn in.*

"Be down soon," I told his back, but it didn't help. Marsha and Chantal had fixed their attention entirely on me. Had we been friends, they'd have quizzed me about my relationship with Mike as soon as he disappeared.

I smiled benignly, and it was Marsha who blinked. Pushing away from the table, she mumbled something about speaking to Anna about tomorrow. Frank left to confirm the morning's plans with George.

Meanwhile, Chantal stared at me the way cops watch a suspect through a one-way mirror, and if I hoped to remain "undercover," that would not do. Also, she was the only Roitman openly mourning the deceased, so I needed whatever she knew. Getting that required her trust.

"This must be so hard for you," I sympathized.

"Yes, thanks." But neither of us knew what to say after that.

Social decorum eventually forced her to look off at the water and the sky, which were rapidly becoming one.

I grabbed two straws from the table, quickly stuffed them up my nose, puckered my mouth like a fish, and crossed my eyes.

Chantal glanced back and barked out a loud laugh.

So loud that her parents peeked around the corner to see what the hell was going on.

Chapter 11

Still chuckling, Chantal's eyes glittered like the stars gradually dotting the twilight sky. Until then I might have passed her without notice on the sidewalk, in the mall, at the grocery store, but laughter revealed a subtle beauty that I suspect grew on you over time. For men, the appeal would be as a foil or an anchor rather than a trophy or, God-forbid, a competitor. It had been mourning that transformed her into a well-kept secret.

Turning away from the elder Roitmans, I snatched the straws from my nose and put on an innocent face. Swiveling back around, I caught them dancing around the moment as if it were broken glass. After mumbling their good-nights, they disappeared down the stairs.

Chantal slapped her cheek and laughed again. "Ohmigod," she said pounding her fists on her thighs. "That was the last thing I expected you to do."

I joked that the devil made me do it.

"The hell you say. Who are you anyway? I can't see you with Mike. I mean, he's a nice guy and all, but that's just it. He's too nice to screw around on his wife."

"Used to be childhood friends," I lied easily. "Then…we really do love each other, but…it's complicated, you know? Really complicated," I allowed my voice to trail off.

"If you say so."

"How about you? Who is Chantal Stoddard? What gets you up in the morning?"

She snorted. "Tomorrow? Scattering my late husband's ashes into the Caribbean. After that…?"

Fatigue had blurred her edges a bit. Considering the direction our conversation just took, it was a good thing I'd nursed my one drink until it was nothing but ice water.

"Tell me about Toby," I prompted. Behind her a distant outcrop of land sparkled with the shoreline lights of hotels and garden pathways. The backdrop made Chantal look like a bronze mermaid with fireflies in her hair.

"Toby was a good man," she began. "Funny. I loved his laugh. Honest. Handsome," a brief, girlish smile. "Smart. Very smart, a genius at crunching numbers. He was one of the few people Dad really listened to."

"What do you mean, listened to?"

"He was Dad's CFO. You didn't know that?"

Chief Financial Officer. No, I did not know that, and my pulse regarded that little detail as rather huge. With Toby responsible for significant amounts of money, a business motive for his murder sounded even more likely than a personal one.

"Sorry," I apologized to his widow. "Mike never mentioned that." And I hadn't asked. We'd been too focused on setting up our deception.

Chantal's sniff alerted me that she was silently crying.

"Did you have any idea…?"

"…that he was suicidal?" She huffed sarcastically then lifted her chin to consult the sky. "Nope. Not a clue, and that's what's driving me crazy." She swiped her nose with a crumpled tissue.

"He didn't leave a note?"

A barely perceptible wave of her head.

Since the silence between us began to grow, I decided that asking more tonight would resemble prying more than sympathy. I looked out at the sea to indicate a change of subject. Then I suggested we should probably get some sleep.

"Yes," Chantal seemed to agree gratefully. "Yes. Sunrise comes early."

We both rose and headed toward the stairs.

"Sunrise?" I asked.

"We're scattering Toby's ashes at sunrise. Something else you didn't know?"

Since missing the entire purpose of the trip would be worse than inexcusable, I asked if Chantal would mind knocking on our door to wake us in the morning.

The stairwell light revealed her confusion. "Just leave Anna a message," she replied.

"Oh! Oh, sure." A mental palm to the forehead. Wake-up calls were included in the *anything* the captain's wife offered. So fast we forget.

Mike was sprawled on the bed in his clothes, his cell phone lying next to his hand.

I let him sleep while I dug his charger out of his dop kit and plugged it in. The last text message was still visible, imagine that, and I'm afraid the professional snoop in me couldn't resist.

"Cramps turned out to be nothing. Not to worry. Love, Mary."

No wonder the guy turned into a zombie. He was afraid he was going to miss the birth of his first child, or worse, that something might be going horribly, horribly wrong.

He woke up when I took off his shoes. "Whaaa…?"

"Lori, your lover," I provided. "Punta Cana. You're on a small ship. Yacht. Whatever…"

A glimmer of recognition, then alarm. "My phone. Where's my phone?" He felt around with his right hand.

"Charging in the bathroom," I answered. "Pardon me: *head*. I'm going to change into a t-shirt or something."

Anything but the short lacy thing Karen had packed for sleeping. "You may want to do the same?"

"Uh, okay."

The fact that Toby Stoddard had controlled the Roitman conglomerate's finances still made the hairs on my arms stand on end, so now that Mike was mostly coherent, I told him to listen up. "First chance we get I need more information about your brother. First chance! It's important, okay?"

Urgent would have been a better word, but the guy was already stressed to the max. He didn't need to know that what began as an unfounded theory, most likely an invention of grief, showed signs of becoming a bona fide murder investigation. I would tell him, of course, just not today.

"Sure. If we get the chance," was the lukewarm response.

Meanwhile, Mike was shedding clothes as if I wasn't there. Modesty, the least of our problems: solved.

Chapter 12

I woke up because my world was rocking and I knew I wasn't having sex. Confusing because someone a third larger than me was also under the covers.

Clutching the sheet with my fists, I attempted to look around.

A loud rap on the door shocked me into lunging for my gun.

No gun. In place of my old maple night table with the wobbly drawer was a puny rounded shelf that wouldn't hold anything larger than a paperback.

Details began to fill in. Engine noise and splashing sounds confirmed that I was inside a boat that was moving. My Glock was in my suitcase where it wouldn't slide around and attract attention. And Mike. The man's name was Mike. His reaction to the hammering on our door was to cuss and roll over.

"That's our wake-up call. Get out of bed, you big lug," I said, thumping his back and nearly pushing him to the floor.

"Okay, okay," he whined, laughing as he stumbled into the bathroom.

Only the tiny nightlight next to the sink saved him from broken toes. He flipped on a better light and the close quarters were revealed to be a beige and white, lived-in mess. The pitch black outside our two portholes seemed to be brightening toward charcoal gray.

Mike had said so little last night that to get him talking, I inquired, "Everything okay at home?"

"Uh, sure. Why do you ask?"

"Because you started this trip taking the possibility of Toby being murdered seriously, but now you're pretty cavalier about it. Have you forgotten that one slip-up might put us both in danger?"

Mike stopped lathering his face to glare at me. "What is all this to you anyway?" he sniped. "You never even met my brother."

Getting through to him was so crucial that I knew my answer had to be perfect. I could say I loved Karen and loathed murderers, but would that be convincing enough?

I told him I believed he and his family deserved to know whether Toby took his own life or if someone else was to blame.

Mike moved in so close to the bed that he loomed over me. "And...?"

What else did he need?

"And I also swore an oath to uphold the law."

That earned me a disgusted look. "If I'm not mistaken, you're not a cop anymore."

"I swore an oath," I snapped back with a vehemence that surprised me, "and I owe Karen big time. If you don't want to help me learn the truth about Toby's death, just look me in the eye and say it."

The air went out of him. He retreated to the sink, eyed himself in the mirror, then dropped his head and waved it. "Exactly what am I supposed to do?"

Finally.

"Maintain the fiction," I said. "Put your arm around me. Look into my eyes. Make like we're a real couple. You said you could do that, but you haven't even tried."

"Why not just tell the truth?"

"Because a killer who feel threatened will kill again in a heartbeat. Kill us in a heartbeat, Mike. We can't let anybody know we suspect Toby might have been murdered."

Mike rolled his eyes. "Okay. I'll put my arm around you and look into your eyes. Is that all?"

"No. Quit grunting one-word answers—yesterday you sounded like Frankenstein. And please please please leave your cell phone in your pocket. Checking it every other minute is rude."

"So now you're my mother, too?"

"I know this isn't easy for you. Just do the best you can, okay?"

He widened his hands and exhaled. "You can't seriously believe that one of the Roitmans killed Toby."

"Correct *me* if I'm wrong, but wasn't he in an isolated location, and, as far as we know, his wife's relatives were the only other people there. Bottom line, I don't know what happened yet, and neither do you. That's pretty much the point."

"The Roitmans are as normal as you and me, Lauren. Now that you met them, surely you can see that."

The statement was so ridiculous I had to laugh. "Oh, do tell. What does a murderer look like? I've always wanted to know."

Mike circled his head toward the ceiling then flicked a blob of shaving cream at me.

I assumed we were a team again. What else could that possibly mean?

The next pressing problem was what to wear for a final farewell at sea. Karen's cropped pants, bare feet and a long white shirt seemed to be the best of my choices. Mike opted for jeans and a cotton sweater over an undershirt. He had deck shoes his wife must have packed, so he wore them.

When we emerged from the stairwell, we found ourselves to be anchored offshore about half a mile. The remaining overnight lights of a sprawling beach resort seemed to hop up and down with the rolling of the yacht, while the surrounding ocean churned like a Maytag washing ink out of a giant load of jeans. A briny breeze coming in from the sea dampened our clothes and chilled our skin.

The amazing, anything-you-want Anna stood by the bar minding a plastic pitcher of Bloody Marys, which both Mike and I declined. I assumed he wanted to stay sober in Toby's honor. I wanted my hands free in case I needed to grab something stationary.

The Roitmans obviously possessed better sea-legs than us outsiders. They each held a tumbler of spicy red hair-of-the-dog except for Chantal, who hugged a dark rectangular box to her chest.

"Well, shall we?" Frank prompted, as if our arrival was a signal. One by one the three drinkers relinquished their plastic cups, although Gavin chugged his dry first.

With the yacht floating perpendicular to the beach, we lined up on the northernmost side with an indirect view of the slash of yellow slicing through the clouds to the east. I felt the first cold plop of rain on my arm when I stepped out from under and reached for the rail. The rain gathered momentum as the others took their places, but no one dared acknowledge the downpour or attempt to avoid it.

Our position was perhaps ten feet above the water with the staterooms just below our feet and the deck for fishing—or whatever—and the captain's equipment and canopied seat above. Chantal stood at the notch in the hull used for climbing on and off when the boat was docked. Presently, it was closed off by a removable rail. Frank and

Gavin stood to the widow's left. Her mother clung to her right side. Then came me and Mike.

"Say something, darling," Marsha shouted at her daughter due to the splashing waves and the chilly breeze hissing in our ears.

Already tears cut a path down Chantal's cheeks, which may be why she extended the box out over the water instead. Unfortunately, a wind gust flipped up the loose lid and sent it twirling into the Caribbean. A seagull gliding by in the hope of scoring something edible complained with a squawk and angled sharply toward shore.

Evidently no one had thought to check inside the crematorium's container, because it seemed to come as a surprise that Toby's ashes were secured inside a thick plastic bag. Chantal was forced to remove it, turn it over, and dislodge a strip of tape before she could begin to scatter anything. Considering the trouble, not to mention expense, her parents had gone to, dumping the contents all at once would have been unseemly and anticlimactic, so she closed off perhaps a third with her hands and tilted it down slowly.

"Good-bye, Toby," she said with a sob. "I miss you."

Some of the particles dropped soundlessly into the sea, but some ashes got taken up by the breeze and got swept back toward Chantal's father and brother.

Frank managed to tuck his face beneath his arm, but Gavin didn't have his father's foresight or good luck. He uttered a disgusted "yuk" and ran for the stairs. Frozen in place, nobody dared breathe, let alone look around, until the footsteps ended and a door slammed.

By now Chantal's sobbing was painful to hear, so painful that her mother drew her to her breast and murmured into her hair. The box quickly became an awkward problem, though, so the moment didn't last.

Free again, Marsha wiped the mascara running down her face with the napkin she'd kept in her hand. "Just do it," she advised her daughter, and the shivering widow complied.

While the rest of us wondered what to do next, Chantal grasped the railing with both hands and stared ahead like a pioneer woman trying to imagine the west.

So there we also stood thinking our respectful thoughts until a large rolling swell doused us all with cold, salty water.

"That's it," Frank announced, retrieving the bottom of the box from the deck and flinging it into the next oncoming wave. Turning, he lifted his head and shouted up to our waiting captain, "George! Get us out of here."

The anchor chain squealed its mechanical ascent even as we filed off toward the stairs. Frank chose to climb upward, presumably to speak with George, while his wife and daughter headed to their respective staterooms for warm showers and dry clothes.

Mike and I lagged behind, but Accommodating Anna and the pitcher of Bloody Marys were nowhere to be found.

Chapter 13

Somehow the morning slipped by. Chantal hid in her stateroom, perhaps with her mother. Gavin probably finished sleeping off his night out.

Meanwhile, Frank settled in at the end of the dining table and took turns tapping his laptop and speaking on his phone. He seemed to be acquiring a company that imported coffee. I knew this because I'd curled up in the adjacent lounge with a wrinkled paperback of Lee Child's first thriller that I'd found on a bookshelf.

When the rain blew away around a quarter to eleven, a brilliant sun cut sharp edges on the elegant buildings alongside our mooring. Since our yacht was so big, it was the only one stretching along the reinforced water's edge next to a macadam walkway. Just beyond lay a strip of flowered lawn adorning a widely windowed restaurant attached to a resort.

As I wandered down to check on Mike, Chantal and I nearly collided as she emerged into the small hallway we shared.

"Oops, sorry." "Excuse me," we said in unison, then Chantal predictably burst into tears.

I waited to hear what she would say and wasn't surprised when she blurted, "It was a disaster, wasn't it?"

I folded my arms as if to think.

"Oh, I don't know," I waffled. "You said Toby had a good sense of humor. Maybe it was his way of getting everybody to lighten up."

Something bubbled up from Chantal's throat, a snort that may have been a chuckle that took her by surprise. Her hand covered the O of her mouth, and she blinked so hard the waiting tears ran down her face in a rush.

"You think?" she said, and this time she really laughed. "Oh my lord. You really are something. What's your name again?"

"Lori." For now, anyway.

"Lori. You really are something." She proceeded up the stairs as she'd originally intended, but her shoulders had lost some of their slump and her steps rang on the wood like little hammers.

When I entered our stateroom, Mike finished a text message before looking up.

"The sun is out," I said. "You ever going to leave this foxhole?"

"Yeah, sure." He stood arms down, almost at attention.

"You promised to act more like a couple, remember? Got a bathing suit?"

"This is it." He pinched the leg of a baggy blue and white garment that looked like ordinary shorts to me.

"Fine. Let's go to the beach. Give me five minutes, okay?"

"Sure. I'll be up on the deck." The phone went into his pocket, a towel over his shoulder. Pulling the cabin door shut behind him, he left me alone.

To make sure Mike didn't renege, I hurried into my pink bikini with the yellow polka dots. Karen had thoughtfully provided an opaque white cover-up that closed in the front and nearly reached the middle of my thighs.

To my shock and delight, in the few minutes it took me to change, Mike had buddied up with Gavin for a windsurfing date.

"Darling, do you mind?" His brow wrinkled, and he actually wrung his hands.

"Sure, honey," I said. "I forgot what a windsurfing fiend you are."

"Since college," he supplied. Maybe he was finally playing his part. Or maybe he really was a windsurfing fiend.

Gavin spied Anna eavesdropping from the galley. "We'll pick something up for lunch," he told her, and, simultaneously, me.

The body language at the airport, the club outing last night, and now the windsurfing escape with Mike began to build a profile of Gavin Roitman hint by hint. Perhaps he wasn't completely anti-social, just adverse to his family.

Which made me wonder. Were he and Chantal like Ron and me or just ordinary siblings? Were he and Frank two lions vying for the same pride, or were their differences merely a generational gap? Had Marsha been too controlling, too motherly, or maybe too self-involved for Gavin The Youth to tolerate? So many reasons why a family member might disconnect, most of them sad.

And some of them toxic.

I decided the beach could wait. To kill the hour until lunch, I took the Lee Child novel and some coconut-scented suntan lotion topside. With the only shadows hidden under the furniture, I had to tiptoe over to one of the cushioned lounge chairs facing the cove. From inside the adjacent resort came the slow, pock...pock music of a tennis game and the rattle of an awning flapping in the breeze. Across the marina an engine roared to life and grumbled its way out to sea.

My skin began to glow with tiny dots of sweat, and soon my whole body felt limp. I exhaled a deep, luxurious sigh.

"Nice up here, isn't it?"

Marsha's stage voice sat me upright, and Lee Child dropped to the deck with a slap.

"Sorry. Didn't mean to scare you." She had a tilted smile when she said that. "Do you mind?" She gestured toward the lounge chair to my left.

"Of course not. Please." I waved her into the seat that was rightfully hers to begin with.

"You puzzle me," she said as she smoothed the pink terrycloth robe beneath her legs.

Suddenly worried, I replied, "Oh?"

She looked me in the eye. "You can eat twice as much as me, and look at you."

My body unclenched by a very small increment.

"How do you do it?"

"Five miles every other day." Weight lifting, target practice, jumping rope, farm chores for Ron, house chores for Karen, standing on my feet bartending for several hours whenever I got a shift.

"You run?" She seemed to equate that with eating grasshoppers.

I shrugged and said I liked food.

Then I mentioned that I'd never met Toby. "What was he like?"

Marsha's face hardened as if the subject was distasteful.

"For the most part a pleasant man," she allowed. "Very good with money. Lucky, because he certainly liked having it." She tilted her head briefly in thought. "A good husband, I guess. At least Chantal seemed to think so."

We sat there metaphorically chewing our cud for a moment or two. Marsha relieved her neck by facing forward. She crossed her ankles comfortably and grasped the armrests like a sphinx.

Then she asked, "Why are you really here?"

Yikes! Guts and pitch-perfect instincts. She hadn't bought my minding-Mike's-mental-health story, and now she was calling me out on it. I would have to watch myself around this one.

"Time together," I answered simply.

"Yes. Any chance you can get, I'll bet. It won't work out, you know. You do know that, don't you?"

I gave her a tiny nod of acknowledgement.

"Yes. Of course you do. I should ship you back home in a cardboard box, but…"

The silence that fell required me to say something. "But you won't. Why?"

Marsha huffed irritably. "Because Chantal could use a friend right now, and for some reason, she likes you."

I treated myself to a nice, normal breath.

"Chantal is not a strong person," her mother remarked. "Sometimes I wonder how that happened with parents like Frank and me, but she simply is not and never will be. Toby. It's too bad…Toby seemed to appreciate her." Marsha tidied the pink terrycloth covering her knees. "Now he's gone, and she must learn to adjust."

Love, horror, and disappointment briefly comingled on the former actress's face. Then just as quickly her inner thoughts passed. When she faced me once again, I swear I felt a chill.

"Help distract my daughter, Ms. Lori Whatever-your-name-is, and I will tolerate your presence among us. Otherwise, it's the cardboard box. Do I make myself clear?"

"Crystal."

With that, Marsha Roitman swung her slippered feet onto the deck and stood. Her parting words were spoken into the stairwell.

"I'm going to help Anna. Tell Frank lunch will be ready in ten minutes, will you?"

Chapter 14

So much for sunbathing about as far away from care as a person can get. How had I ever convinced myself that pretending to love a guy I just met and getting inside the heads of our four hosts would be easy? It was a dangerous delusion, and the fact that I'd sold it to myself bruised my very recently mended confidence. I truly felt lucky not to be flying home in a cardboard box.

Most of the criminals I encountered as a small city cop were not brainiacs. They drank too much and hit their wives, or killed a rival drug dealer. Some let their parking meters expire or jaywalked. Others tried to hire prostitutes who looked like me or hid "free" groceries under their jackets. Rarely were they CEOs of billion dollar enterprises or their deceivingly perceptive wives.

In high school I once dated a guy who attended a famous Philadelphia prep school. It took me longer than it should have to pinpoint what was different about him and his friends. And no, it wasn't money. My boyfriend was a scholarship student, and so were some of his friends. Their common denominator turned out to be the entrance exam. They had all passed.

CEOs of billion-dollar enterprises get to be CEOs because they have brains. It follows that to be interesting to a smart man, a woman probably should be intelligent, too. Their children? Genetically, the odds favored better than average IQs. Maybe the exposure to luxury was giving me a sugar high, or maybe Mike's conviction that the Roitmans' were innocent had eroded my common sense, but whatever it was, I needed to snap out of it or it was entirely possible that I might not be up to this challenge.

The ribbon along the bottom of the flatscreen in the lounge read, "Breaking News."

Children gunned down at school? A government building bombed? An assassination attempt? Whatever it was, Frank Roitman appeared ready to tackle it personally. His feet met the floor like a sprinter's braced against the starting block. The fists at his sides pressed into the sofa cushions as if they were crushing rocks. Had I smashed a lightbulb on the coffee table in front of him, I doubt that he'd have flinched.

I eased onto the arm of a chair facing the television.

"So far six confirmed dead and forty-two injured in the derailment of a Washington, DC, Metro train," the CNN reporter announced. "Emergency crews quickly responded, but access was made difficult due to a damaged stairway…"

The devastation resembled a war scene. Four long train cars lying in a twisted pile. Clouds of smoke and dust hanging in the underground air. Uniformed rescuers carrying heavy stretchers across the screen. Other medics crouched alongside passengers whose hold on life remained unclear.

"No word regarding what caused the crash, but because the accident occurred so close to government offices, terrorism has not been ruled out. As yet, no one has come forward to claim credit…"

The announcer was a news veteran. I'm not good with names, but everything about him conveyed professionalism—his suit, his calming voice, the honesty that easily closed the distance between us. I appreciated the stability he managed to convey, but Frank required something more. Bourbon on the rocks, perhaps. His thick hands now shielded his entire face. He released a heavy sigh then rubbed this temples with stiffened fingers.

Mentioning lunch would have been an obscenity. When his wounded eyes returned to the video coverage, I slipped behind him and into the galley.

Anna was balancing an enormous shrimp on the edge of a dish lined with lettuce, her lips pressed together so tightly that I thought she might have seen the news.

"This way, dear," Marsha physically corrected her placement. Then she raised her eyes and asked, "Did you tell Frank?"

"Uh, no," I admitted. "He was watching CNN, and I..."

"Not again." She slapped a dishtowel onto the counter and huffed off around the corner.

I had just caught on that Anna's personal bad news was Marsha when the "anything" woman shot me a look that dared me to take over where her meddling guest had left off.

"I'll just be..." I pointed my thumb toward the rear deck, and Anna mouthed what appeared to be a heartfelt, "Thank you."

Chantal and I ate at the shady table that doubled as a bar.

We talked about nail polish.

Chapter 15

Frank Roitman shut off the satellite TV and reached for his drink. The air-conditioning in the yacht's lounge area cooled his knees below the madras-plaid walking shorts Marsha had purchased for him in goddamn Bermuda, for chrissake, years before, and the ice from his bourbon on the rocks chilled his thick fingertips. His eyes felt dry and gritty from staring at images of mangled metal, the same damn images he'd already seen who knows how many times before.

It seemed to him that the Metro accident was taking the course of no course at all. Compelled to speak, reporters repeated the obvious facts, dressing up their accounts with speculation that ranged from likely to very unlikely, from responsible to extremely irresponsible, all safely phrased as questions. Could this tragedy have been caused by human error? Or was it the work of a terrorist organization? Will we know in a few hours, a few months, or never?

Tired of the repetition, Frank's mind chose to dredge up another, more familiar, disaster life had provided to make him miserable at a moment's notice.

Darryl Sykes, father of twenty-two-year-old Luanne Sykes. Darryl had lost the civil lawsuit he brought against Roitman Industries for selling a very small part of an anti-lock brake system to the domestic automobile manufacturer that produced the first car Luanne ever purchased. After failing to secure a job in a law office doing anything, she'd become an x-ray technician in a Chicago hospital—Frank forgot which one. Happy and eager to show off her new engagement ring—her fiancé was an intern, Frank remembered that because of the cliché—Luanne had skipped dinner to make the two-hour trip to her parents' house somewhere in rural Illinois. The weather was vile— driving rain and gusting wind—but Darryl's attorney claimed the flashing lights of the broken-down truck that blocked the right-hand lane had offered plenty of warning time for Luanne to apply her brakes. Yes he argued, it was likely, just as the truck driver claimed, that cars going the same direction in the adjacent lane prevented her from going around the truck. However, the real blame for the fatality belonged to the manufacturer of the anti-lock brake system that failed, not to Luanne herself, or God, as some might suggest, for making it rain.

Did Frank dwell on the fact that the young woman's car slid into the truck at enough of an angle to thrust her into the passing lane, taking her life and seriously injuring the driver of an SUV? Not really. The mind protects its owner against intolerable information.

Instead Frank identified with how Darryl Sykes must feel about losing his civil suit against the Roitman Industries subsidiary that produced the part. He supposed it was the proportionate opposite of the relief and outright joy experienced by him, his family, and anybody else whose livelihood depended on Roitman Industries. Frank wouldn't rank the victory higher than Marsha saying yes or the birth of his children, but neither would he admit to anyone but himself how close the judge's verdict came. Factoring in the ramifications? Uncomfortably close.

Or maybe not. Maybe the girl had been too distracted, or hungry, or her nose itched at the wrong moment. Nobody could be sure, hence the judge's decision. Deep down inside himself, in the place that ordinary honest people visited but a multi-millionaire with well-stretched bootstraps visited only during the occasional dark moment, Frank recognized that he would harbor Luanne's tragic accident almost as long as that guy Darryl. In his own context, granted, but still…

Frank drank a slug of bourbon. Then he rattled the ice and threw back another.

As long as he was contemplating disasters, what about Gavin falling in love with Darryl's remaining daughter? What the hell had Frank done to make himself a target for that much bad luck? Fate certainly had a twisted sense of humor. His horndog son spotting an attractive babe in the courthouse hallway. Really? The two of them getting serious was like the investigation that would never end, the jury staying out forever. With so much at stake it simply could not be allowed. Let Gavin think his dad was an asshole. Frank hadn't made big bucks spilling his guts every time he made an unpopular decision. Sometimes "because I said so," was all you got.

Which brought him to Toby Stoddard, and there Frank's mind balked.

He switched the TV back on. Another reporter was taking another lame stab at analyzing a senseless disaster.

Welcome to the club, Frank thought. Welcome to the club.

Chapter 16

I had a lovely run on the beach during low tide. Wide swaths of differently colored lounges defined the territories of the resorts. Sunbathers cooling off chatted as they bobbed in the waves. Others walked or jogged back and forth along the water with me. Island music and multi-lingual announcements blaring from the beach bars' sound systems urged lazy tourists off their butts into the surf for aerobics, onto the sand for volleyball. Parasails lifted one and two daring souls into the sky at a time. Lengthy empty lots lay in between resorts as well, populated with short palm bushes, trash, and the occasional vendor hoping to sell bright native crafts.

I regret to say that not even paradise was perfect. Guards wearing brown slacks, tan short-sleeved shirts, and pith helmets stood at various intervals, each looking both bored and vigilant. In a way, I'd been there, done that. I wished them cool drinks and shrimp cocktails and many boring days to come.

When Mike burst into our room at a quarter to four, I was showering in that miniscule glass-enclosed triangle. I heard Mike sit down hard on the bed.

When I was half dry and completely decent, I sat down beside him. He smelled like salt water and beer. His ginger hair was tightly curled and sandy, his skin pinkish brown in spite of the extra-strength suntan lotion he'd smeared all over before he went out.

He also looked a bit shell-shocked.

"You've seen the news?" I asked.

"Uh, no," he admitted, so I filled him in.

"Tragic," he murmured, looking scarcely more stricken than before.

"They still don't know the cause," I added. Seven dead, though, and fifty-eight injured as of twenty minutes ago.

Already Mike had collected his cell phone from the charger and had begun to tap the screen.

"Wait." I interrupted. "Before you get all involved, tell me what you learned from Gavin."

Mike glanced at me with narrowed eyes. "Not much. We went windsurfing, remember?"

"Not for five hours you didn't. Out with it. What did he say?" I crossed my terrycloth arms as if to stand my ground.

An impatient sigh. "Toby gave Gavin financial advice. Sometimes it was good. Sometimes it wasn't."

"Okeedookee, Batman. What else you got?"

Mike managed a smile. "He has a girlfriend, but his parents don't like her. That's one reason he lives forty minutes from them and thirty from work."

"What's work?"

"He's president of some small company, I think. Maybe one that belongs to Roitman Industries."

"What kind of company?"

"No idea. We mostly talked about sports." The default language of men.

"Do you mind? There's a text from Mary."

"Yeah, yeah. Go ahead."

The message must have been short, because he immediately dropped the phone on the bed, fisted his hand in his hair, and closed his eyes. If possible, his neck and face glowed even redder than before.

"What?" I asked.

It took Mike a second to recognize me. Finally he said, "Mary's had more cramps."

"More cramps?" I wasn't supposed to know about the first batch. "When did that start?"

"Yesterday. Her doctor called it false labor, 'No big deal.' Now it's happening again."

"She's eight months, right?" I checked.

Mike just looked at me.

"...so even if the baby's early, she should be okay, right?"

The stare took on intensity.

Okay, so I don't know much about babies, but I do know when to get lost. I dressed in record time, then just before I excused myself, I informed Mike that dinner would be at seven in the resort restaurant right beside the boat. Yacht. Small ship. Whatever.

Blank stare. Or should I say glare.

"Dress nice," I added, "and don't forget—we're in love." I meant that as a joke, and Mike definitely took it that way. His snort could have been mistaken for a laugh anywhere.

The restaurant's hostess smiled her greeting and counted out menus from a rack while clinking dishes, subtle music, and the patrons' animated conversations drew us in. To the left wine bottles covered the wall floor-to-ceiling. The three dining rooms surrounded a lighted fountain, and waiters balancing trays on their fingertips wove between tightly clustered tables like graceful matadors.

Mike and I strolled behind the Roitmans with linked arms; and when we arrived at our long table for six, he graciously helped me into my chair. Although he had assured me that Mary and the baby were okay, another frightening message was always a possibility.

Also fearing that opportunities to watch the Roitmans interact might abruptly come to an end, while drinks were being ordered I began to catalog my impressions.

Whatever Chantal requested it was without enthusiasm, and her dress reflected her somber mood. It was a floaty thing in a hue so funereal that her body almost disappeared into the shadows. The bright note—her fingertips had been freshly painted pink.

Marsha consulted Frank and together they chose a bottle of red. Based on the effervescence in Marsha's voice, it probably should have been champagne.

Check that. Champagne would have suggested that tonight was an occasion, so red was the right choice. Points for Marsha. The forehead swoop of her immoveable French twist remained perfect, her linen sheath as unwrinkled as linen allows. Her lips, always a focal point, were still that unflattering true red, and I wondered whether the color might be calculated to draw attention to her every word.

Frank struck me as tired and hungry, or perhaps dispirited by the disturbing news he watched off and on all day. Fortunately, the restaurant had no televisions, so his eyes flicked from table to person to menu and back. Being out with his family seemed to relax him somewhat, but being relaxed was not his usual state.

Gavin was as animated as I'd seen him so far. He had begun narrating windsurfing stories as we collectively left the yacht and continued across the macadam path, up the walk and into the beautiful dining room. "...and then the wave slapped him on the ass again and flipped the board up over his head. It was a wonder he didn't get decapitated, right Mike?"

"Right," Mike grumbled, and I finally realized the stories were all at his expense.

"Oh, come on, boy. Cheer up. You had fun today. Admit it."

"Yes, I had fun." It pained Mike to say it, but only I knew why. Guilt, of course, for revisiting his college-age passion while his wife revisited the emergency room.

"Yes, I had fun," were also the last words he cared to say.

The drinks arrived, the wine poured, and with a hand on his father's shoulder Gavin proposed a toast. "To Calvin Graffam, Esquire," he said in a hearty voice.

Frank's eyes widened, but he met his son's gaze and lifted his glass. We all did, but Chantal leaned toward me and whispered, "Company attorney. Just won a big case."

After we all sealed that with a sip, she lifted her whatever-it-was and said, "To Toby," which brought us down to earth again.

Dinner progressed slowly from beverages to the salad bar, which included sushi and an array of delectable choices I couldn't begin to name. Mike opted out, preferring to brood into a second Presidente beer.

"Darling," I said when his silence had been noted by everyone but him. "Here. Try a bite. It's amazing." I didn't care whether the stuff on my fork tasted like marinated sole of shoe. Compared to him, even Chantal seemed downright giddy.

When he waved me off again with the rest of our party watching, the time seemed right. I threw down my napkin.

"You're thinking about her, aren't you?" I accused loudly enough to turn heads two tables away.

I stood up to emphasize my make-believe anger.

"Admit it, Mike. Go ahead. Be honest for once in your life. All you can think about is your wife."

Mike's shock was genuine, the ripple effect alarming. Conversations halted. Eyes swiveled my way. The closest waiter beamed with a cynical smile.

"I can't believe you're treating me like this," I ranted with clenched fists. "After all these years…I'm done, Mike. Done." Across from me a sixty-something woman smirked in triumph while her husband just plain stared.

I put my limp hand to my nose as if to staunch the sniffles then rushed for the door and out into the night.

It took Mike longer than it should have to follow me, a nerve-racking eternity, to tell the truth. I paced back and forth on the macadam at least three times—under a streetlight so he wouldn't miss me.

When he finally caught up, I bapped him in the chest with my knuckles. If anyone were watching, a Roitman for example, I would still look angry, which I was a little.

"What took you so long?"

"I…uh…what the hell was that back there?" He looked stricken, scared, pissed.

"That was your out, you idiot. Now you can go home."

"Wha…I thought you wanted me to buddy up with the Roitmans. You said you couldn't do this without me. 'We're a team.' That's what you said."

"Yes, and a great job you've done so far. You found out Gavin is president of a company, not which company, just a company. I could have found that out on the Internet."

"Excuse me for trying. I suppose you're doing better?"

"Better than you." I found Marsha's revelation that she thought Toby was excessively fond of money informative, especially coming from her.

"Wait. You said I can go home?"

"Yes, Mike. Go home. Please go home."

He hugged me.

"Hey! We're supposed to be fighting."

"I don't care." He kissed me on the lips.

I slapped him.

He stepped back and rubbed his cheek. I couldn't have scripted it better if I'd tried.

Mike waved his head and laughed. "And how do you suggest I get out of here?"

I folded my arms and probably looked a little smug. "You walk around there," I indicated the entrance to the lobby of the resort. "You tell somebody you need a taxi, and you give them a tip. Then you take the first commercial flight back to DC. Go straight home. Do not pass Go; do not collect $200."

"What are you going to do?"

"Act angry. Say horrible things about you. Same stuff any scorned woman would say."

"You're going back in there?"

"I sure am. Frank ordered me my first Lobster Thermador." Also my purse was under my chair, and my Glock was still on the yacht hidden in my suitcase.

"You'll keep in touch?"

"Oh, yeah. And you better, too. I want to know if Mary and your daughter are alright."

"Not me?"

"You are alright, Mike Stoddard. That's already been established."

Chapter 17

So what if Mike Stoddard hadn't really been here while he was here, our room felt hollow without him. Trying in vain to fall asleep, I reminded myself I should be relieved to have him gone. Sure, he was a thoroughly nice husband and almost father, an insurance salesman who danced like a fool at weddings. Nothing on his resume qualified him to probe the Roitmans' private lives for murder motives. I should be glad he wasn't here to accidentally give us away, super glad I was no longer responsible for his safety. We would keep in touch, at least during the rest of my stay—the "Guilt Trip," I'd dubbed it in honor of our mutual objective—but when we were both satisfied that Toby's demise was his own choice, our tenuous connection would expire. I convinced myself I was okay with that. I really was.

I fell asleep fingering the empty side of the bed anyhow.

In the morning, Father Frank left the three of us women to dawdle over our scrambled eggs and optional mimosas while he paced the rear deck and spoke into his phone. I heard the words "bicycle manufacturer" a couple of times. The man didn't know the definition of the word "vacation."

The rest of us didn't talk much, probably because the air was ripe with my supposed embarrassment.

Then Gavin showed up, raised his eyebrows, and asked, "Where's Mike?"

Chantal shot her brother a glare of warning. His mother wriggled in her chair and affected disinterest.

"Gone," I answered over my toast.

"Sonovabitch," Gavin observed with a bark of laughter. Then he aimed an expression at his mother so fraught with private meaning that I made a mental note to quiz Chantal about Gavin's love-life first chance I got. Discreetly, of course. It might not have a thing to do with Toby's death, but then again it might.

I knew the socially correct thing for me to do would be to follow Mike's example and go home, but what would I do about my Glock? Simply leaving it behind would be irresponsible, and anyway I couldn't afford the airfare. All things considered, I thought it best to leave my fate in the Roitmans' hands. If they wanted me gone, I felt certain they would arrange it. Bottom line, we wouldn't be here that much longer anyway.

Apparently, I should have been paying attention because Marsha had departed and Chantal and Gavin were faced off like a pair of mountain goats about to smack heads.

"You're such a bastard," Chantal told her brother through clenched teeth. "You apologize, or, or..."

"Or what?" Gavin pressed. "All I did was ask a simple question—land breeze, or sea breeze? Maybe I'm planning to windsurf again, you ever think of that?"

"No you were not, Gavin Roitman. You just wanted to rub my nose in, in what happened yesterday. Admit it." She rapped his shoulder with her knuckles.

Gavin grabbed her hand and lowered it to her side.

"You're wrong. If I'd wanted to do that I'd have asked whether the scrambled eggs were clean enough to eat."

Chantal lashed out again, faster and harder.

Gavin caught her fist before it did any damage.

Talk about awkward. Chantal flounced into her seat and tapped her clawed fingers on the table. Gavin poked his scrambled eggs as if they were radioactive, then made a point of saying "ummm" after every bite.

Finally, he shoveled the rest of the eggs onto a triangle of toast, topped it with another triangle, snagged his coffee mug and headed up to the top deck.

"Maybe we should do lunch someplace different," I suggested to Chantal. "Know any restaurants on the beach?"

She looked at me as if I'd sprouted a second head. Then she said, "Uh, sure," as I set my empty mimosa glass aside. It was a tall plastic thing with the waistline of a woman and a purple paper umbrella resting on the lip. I've never understood the point of those frou frou things, and I'm glad to say my boss at the Pelican's Perch didn't either. Heck, Anthony didn't even approve of crushed ice.

Travel half a mile in any direction and it's a different world.

Chantal and I wore bathing suits, the pink with yellow polka dots for me plus Karen's white cover-up, a one-piece job with flattering gathers for Chantal and a flimsy tie-dyed wrap, which she'd crossed up high in front and knotted behind her neck. Probably purchased down here on a previous trip.

We'd walked half a mile along the beach, carrying flip-flops and sneakers respectively, and pointing out interesting sights to each other—a big breasted woman sporting neon stripes, a swarthy man wearing a thong of strained black elastic, newbies who hadn't applied strong enough sunburn protection. A pretty child with a red bucket.

"Ooh. Look at that hat. I want that hat," Chantal gushed. It was widely brimmed and black with some sheer strips that cast pretty shadows on the wearer's skin.

"Very Hollywood," I observed. "It would look great on you."

"Puh," she responded modestly.

We finally found a bar open to the public on the edge of the beach. Across the way children splashed in a kiddy pool fifteen feet across. In the center a cement frog about two feet tall spouted water from its mouth. Two naked little boys with flawless mocha complexions laughed and shrieked as they ran through the questionable water. I was kinda glad I wasn't a kid anymore.

For lunch I had a cold salad of little tiny scallops that had been pickled. And a beer. It was hot even under the awning due to the noon hour and the complete lack of breeze. If Chantal's brother really had planned to windsurf, he was out of luck.

"So what's going on with Gavin?" I finally asked.

"What do you mean?" Chantal cleared a strand of hair from her face.

"He had sort of a strange reaction when I said Mike was gone. I just wondered why."

Chantal's eyes widened, and her mouth dropped open. "You're not interested in him, are you? Please tell me you're not interested in him."

"Oh, no no no," I demurred.

"You sure?"

"Totally sure. Oh, no. I just thought there might be a story there."

Chantal monitored my face for a moment. Then her shoulders relaxed and she swayed into a more comfortable position. "You know about the lawsuit against one of Dad's companies? We toasted the attorney who won it last night."

I shrugged. "Over my head."

"Lucky you. We've been living through that thing for months."

Briefly, she explained about a man who filed a civil suit against a Roitman's subsidiary blaming the company for the wrongful death of his daughter. The company produced anti-lock brakes, the failure of which Darryl Sykes, the father, claimed caused twenty-two-year-old Luanne to crash into the back of a disabled truck.

"Okay," I said tentatively.

"Gavin's been seeing Darryl Sykes's other daughter."

"Oh," I said. "Oh, dear."

"Oh dear, indeed," Chantal agreed. "Dad threatened to cut Gavin off if he didn't drop her."

To me, that sounded surprisingly harsh, but all I said was, "I wonder why."

"Spite?" Chantal guessed with a shrug.

Another facet of Frank Roitman to explore.

"More iced tea?" I asked after we pushed our plates away.

Toby's widow patted her stomach and shook her head, so I blurted out the other thought that had been flitting in and out of my mind.

"You're pregnant, aren't you?"

Chapter 18

Chantal gasped. "Wow! How did you guess? I haven't even told my mother."

"Bartender," I reminded her. "You haven't been drinking alcohol."

Confirmation of my suspicion had jacked up my pulse with excitement. And relief. To me, Chantal's mourning always appeared to be genuine, so I never really saw her as a murderer. Now that she admitted she was pregnant, I felt I could safely place her in the Highly Unlikely to Kill Her Husband category.

Also, I couldn't believe the Toby Mike described would leave Chantal to raise their child alone, unless…

"Did your husband know?" I inquired carefully.

"We were a little superstitious," Chantal admitted shyly, "so I didn't test right away. But I'd say yes. He smiled at me as if we shared a secret. He'd hold doors for me, pull out my chair. Little things he only did once in a while he did more often." She glanced off toward the Caribbean then back at her lap. "Yes, I'd say we both knew."

Unfortunately, her answer sounded more like an informed guess than a certainty, so suicide still couldn't be ruled out.

"I'm sure you're right," I said. "But I wonder, was there any one particular thing he said or did that made you sure he knew? Something for the baby book perhaps?"

"Why?"

"Because…if he knew, I can't imagine why he…?"

I let my voice trail off because Chantal had instantly become angry, whether at me or her deceased husband, I couldn't tell. Either way, the damage was done.

"He knew, dammit. We both did." Tears pooled in her eyes.

"Okay, okay." I made those keep-it-down, patting gestures you do when people around you are staring. "Then why do you think he…?"

"Business." She almost spit the word. "Something at work."

Now she seemed angry about Toby's job. With her father. I was finally getting somewhere.

Suddenly, Chantal stood up from the table and marched away from me. She showed no sign of stopping until she arrived back at the yacht.

A surprise, but it was fine with me. I'd planned on picking up the check anyway.

I'd also had enough walking on sand, and I didn't want Chantal to look back and find me stalking after her. I'd disturbed her delicate peace, if indeed she'd attained anything resembling peace; and she would not benefit from seeing the person who disturbed her again anytime soon.

Maybe I should hand out a card:

Lauren Beck

aka Lori Ruggles

Persona non Grata

After washing off my feet at a faucet beside the kiddy pool, I put on my sneakers and squeaked my way over to a paved path that led toward a road that more-or-less led to a town center. Not many people were about since it was still hot as blazes, but enough were around to suggest that some commerce was being conducted. A pale green bank, which looked more like a solidly built storefront, stood on the near corner. Windows of thick barred glass allowed me to observe two tellers standing in wait and a man at a desk dealing with a woman in a colorful dress.

A motorcycle business seemed to be a popular hangout for the local men, and even covered up I drew at bit more attention than I liked. Keeping traffic between me and the men, I hustled along the road and soon came upon an enclave of shops geared toward tourists like me. The shade was welcome and the prices extremely reasonable, much better than anywhere near the yacht—go figure—and I almost allowed myself to succumb to a pink hat with a yellow flower. It was large and floppy and Lori Ruggles would grab it up in a minute. Me, not so much.

When I wandered back outside, opportunity knocked. Thirty yards away Frank Roitman was coming toward me with a purposeful gait. Since almost all I'd learned about the head of the family was that he preferred to buy companies connected to something he liked, I thought it might be interesting to follow him.

So, keeping one eye on Frank's progress, I ducked back into the shop, snatched up the hat and its matching tote bag, muttered "Changed my mind," and hastily paid in US dollars.

"No problem," I was assured.

Waiting behind a display for Frank to chug on by, I donned the hat and my sunglasses, stuffed the store bag in my tote and held my breath.

Frank happened to be wearing a white, short-sleeved shirt and brown slacks, not the most distinguishable clothes around, so I hustled a bit to keep him in sight. He turned right along a stone path then left to a long aisle of small stores lining the edge of yet another resort. They appeared to be high-end shops, confirmed by the tony tourists meandering along in the shade of the shrubbery. When Frank ducked into a small pink building labeled Lady Luck, I was able to saunter along until I could see into its window. Jewelry. Along with the usual beautiful gems were pieces featuring a pale aqua stone I'd never seen before. As always, I admired the bling and the craftsmanship but personally had no use for it. Marsha Roitman, however, wore the stuff every day. And I mean *every* day.

Standing at an angle near a tall, bushy hedge I observed Frank conducting a transaction. A good-looking gentleman with confident posture had emerged from behind a one-way mirror, the same sort used in police lineups. He opened the hinged, rectangular box he brought with him, extracted a necklace and handed it to Frank. Frank admired the piece, nodded, and the local gentleman secured the necklace back in the box. Frank then dug some cash out of his wallet and dealt out several bills into the man's waiting hand. So far, so good.

Except what happened next was not so good. The bills disappeared into the gentleman's pocket, freeing his right hand to hold a pen and his left to steady his receipt tablet and fold the previous store copies out of the way. When he finished writing, he ripped off the customer's copy and made like he was handing it over, except before Frank got his thick fingers on it, the guy lifted it out of reach like a fifth grader taunting a classmate with a candy bar.

A short conversation ensued. Frank slipped another bill from his wallet. The man made a "more" gesture. Frank argued, lost, and grudgingly delivered another bill into the greedy shopkeeper's hand.

The cop in me assumed the receipt had been written for an inflated amount, useful to Frank to impress his wife or as proof of value if the necklace ever got "lost" or stolen. Premeditated insurance fraud, in other words. If something other than that was going on, I couldn't guess what it was.

I ducked behind the opposite hedge just in time for Roitman to emerge with his slim package and his anger. He paused long enough to wipe his brow with a handkerchief then set off at a purposeful pace toward the road. Which way he might turn was a tossup, so I cut through a small garden, around another business the size of my niece's bedroom, trotted past a family with three wilted children and just managed to see Frank turn toward the motorcycle men.

"Damn," I muttered, certain that Harleys were yet another Roitman passion.

No. Banks were. After Frank mopped his brow once more, tucked his handkerchief away, and entered the establishment, I hurried across the street to stand out of sight at the edge of the bank's dusty plate glass window. Peeking through its bars, I watched as Frank's stepped over to the one and only desk. Whereupon the guy manning the desk popped up and offered his hand to be shaken. Clearly, the banker's gesture wasn't just a surfeit of cordiality, because he covered Frank's large mitt with his dusky brown fingers and finished the greeting with a warm pat. These guys had done business before.

Trying to look inconspicuous in spite of the huge pink hat, I dug into my tote and came up with a sale flier the clerk had stuffed in there along with my receipt and the plastic store bag I hadn't yet thrown away. The flier would have to do. I leaned against the green, cement-block wall and fanned myself with the thing. Now and then I hazarded a look around that included the inside of the bank and Frank's back.

While I'd been busy looking languid, the banker had disappeared.

About four minutes later, my flimsy excuse for being there had worn uncomfortably thin. Glancing at a non-existent watch was out of the question; this was the Dominican Republic. Nobody cared what time it was.

Ah. The banker returned carrying a white envelope. He sat down, removed the contents, and began motions that closely resembled the counting of currency. A not insignificant pile of currency.

Frank appeared to have made a large withdrawal, which meant he had an established account. An oddity to tuck away for further thought.

When the money was back in the envelope, another cordial handshake was performed with a happy nodding of heads. The envelope disappeared somewhere on Frank's person—a logical guess, because it wasn't in his hand when he exited the bank. Of course I'd turned my back on the door as soon as he stepped out of my sight behind the cement-block wall. A couple more paces put him outdoors again, but by then I was bent over tying my sneaker with my butt sticking up.

I waited at the curb and crossed over to the beachside of the road soon after Frank did. Then I followed him with my eyes at a greater distance until I was certain he intended to return to the yacht via the beach.

With all that money on me, I would have, too. Every resort along the way had armed guards watching every inch of sand.

Chapter 19

"Since Lori is a bartender," Marsha told Captain George that evening before dinner. "Why don't you let her take over for awhile?"

Well played, Marsha, I thought as the breath went out of me. *Way to demote me from an unwelcome guest to an employee.*

George shot me a glance to check how I felt about the switch, but what choice did I really have?

I ambled into position. Smiled cordially. Asked, "What will you have, George?"

Marsha's lips parted and her eyes stretched. It was the first unguarded response I'd seen her make; but if she expected George to react to my cheekiness, she was doomed to disappointment. He raised his gnarled hands and bowed back without a word.

"Who wants a tequila sunrise?" I offered the family as one. "Pina colada? Bourbon on the rocks?"

Frank accepted the latter, which provided Marsha with the perfect opening. She eagerly informed the unenlightened among us, sadly just George and me, that Frank had bought a distillery a few years back. "Didn't you, dear?"

Doing his part, he added, "It was on the rocks, too."

"Not now, though," Marsha boasted, stepping on his line.

"No, not now." Frank's smile replicated the private satisfaction my father got from a profitable real-estate deal, the sideline he'd adopted when farming failed to cover my medical bills.

"That seems to be a habit of yours," I remarked, and Frank flinched as if he thought I referred to the bourbon.

"Oh no," I amended. "I meant investing in your personal preferences—coffee, bourbon, cars..." More specifically car parts, such as anti-lock brakes. Which was probably a sore subject. Maybe I should just shut up.

"For fun," I hastened to add.

"Oh, yes," Frank replied without discernible pleasure, "for fun."

"But only if he thinks he can make a buck," Gavin contributed, which garnered an unreadable glance from Dad.

Chantal requested a cola with a benign smile. When we'd met on the stairs only minutes before, I'd apologized for upsetting her at lunch. To my surprise and relief, she tilted her head and lowered her brows as if I'd confused her. "I can't imagine what you're talking about," she said, and in a way I guess that was true.

I poured a vodka and tonic for myself then took a seat at the edge of the group.

"Go on, Daddy," Chantal prompted. "Show Mom what you found today."

"Well..."

"Go on."

Roitman extracted the serpentine necklace from his pants pocket and dangled it carelessly between his thick thumb and forefinger. Even in the dim surroundings the diamonds at the tip of each S-shaped link found light to reflect.

"Anybody here lose this?" Frank inquired casually. "I found it on the beach."

"Oh, Frank," Marsha scolded. "You're such a tease." She collected the necklace the way a pickpocket collects a wallet. "Thank you, dear. What are these light aqua stones? I've never seen them before."

Obviously pleased with himself, Frank explained how larimar is only found in a small area of a mountaintop in the Dominican Republic. "The color will fade with sun or heat, so don't wear it to the beach," he cautioned.

"As if I'd wear diamonds to the..." she rapped Franks arm, then grabbed him with her talons and reeled him in for a kiss.

"Dinner's served," Anna announced.

Her husband bent down toward me. "I'll take that," he said with eye contact as he relieved me of my empty tumbler.

"Thank you, *George*," I said.

Marsha did not notice my excess of manners, but Frank did.

To avoid the twilight breeze coming off the water, we dined inside by candlelight.

Later, as the rest of the family dispersed, Gavin crooked a finger my way and stepped out on the aft deck. From the sidewalk below the yacht's mooring came the light conversation of two couples exiting the restaurant, and deeper into the marina a few small parties seemed to be in full swing. Water lapping against the hull was a given, and I'd grown to love the sloshing sound and the briny fragrance that permeated the air. Above, thin wisps of cloud slid across an ebbing moon.

Standing in its shadow, Gavin told me, "You look cold. Here."

Without waiting for an answer, he swung his sweater from his shoulders to mine. It was warm from his body heat and smelled of spice. Giving in to a shiver, I finished wrapping it around my bare arms.

"Thanks," I said, slightly worried about where this was headed. For me, the only thing right about Gavin Roitman was his age.

He leaned against an angled support of the upper deck. "How are you holding up?" he asked.

I shrugged. "Oh, you know. You win some; you lose some. Mike's where he belongs—I guess. I'll be okay—I guess." Blah blah blah. I could have gone on like that all night, except I'd have had to listen to it, too.

"Come to the club with me. Have some fun. You'll feel better."

"Oh, I don't know…"

"Com'on. Dance a little. Get loaded. I promise I won't bite unless you want me to."

"When you put it that way, how can I resist?"

The shadowy contour of his dimple deepened, so sarcasm he got. Good to know. Best not to alienate the unsub (unsubstantiated suspect) until I got what I needed, such as any reason he might have had to kill Toby Stoddard.

I returned the sweater and ducked downstairs to grab the wrap Karen had thoughtfully packed. Then Gavin and I strolled companionably around the perimeter of the restaurant along softly lighted pathways leading throughout the resort. After the big finale of a tropical dance revue—we heard the beat all the way back at the yacht—a steady flow of older tourists shuffled past us on the way to their beds. The few parents carrying sleeping children over their shoulders kept well to the side.

Three bars close to the main lobby each conducted a brisk business in their own style. One seemed festive and bright and appeared to attract young marrieds. The dimmer, larger one located at the edge of the lobby catered to singles, especially the twenty-something crowd. The small, shadowy one lighted only with tiny candles seemed to be the last stop before the boudoir. This I based mainly on the cleavage of the woman on the lap of the man in the corner—and experience. Been there. Done that. Certainly not going there tonight.

Back under the palms where relative silence reigned, a cigar vendor bent to light a customer's purchase. The smoke smelled sweeter than my uncle's cigars back home. Either Cuban or Dominican. The good stuff, if you were into tobacco.

"We're a little early," Gavin remarked. "Want to try the casino for a few minutes?"

"I don't…" I didn't have much money with me.

"Oh, com'on," he said. "They have nickel slots."

"Okay."

A red-jacketed doorman-cum-guard ushered us into a room about the size of an eight-car garage, much smaller than I expected. It was crisply air conditioned, and much less frenetic than an American casino, perhaps only twenty-five or thirty patrons casually testing their luck.

"What do you want to try?" Gavin inquired.

"Nickel slots sound good."

"Seriously?"

"Seriously."

He handed me a five-dollar bill. "Live it up, kid. I'll just be…" he circled his finger to indicate that he'd be around.

Half an hour later, I sidled up behind him at a poker table. The dealer was a gorgeous Asian woman who used a no-nonsense attitude to keep the players from flirting. She dealt swiftly and with such concentration that I couldn't imagine calculating my hand fast enough to keep up. Slap, slap, slap, scoop. Repeat.

While he watched her perform, Gavin's graceful fingers toyed with a small stack of multi-colored chips. What they were worth I couldn't begin to guess.

He raised his eyebrow at me when the current hand ended and his bet was gone. "Ready?"

I returned his five dollar bill and an additional fifteen cents.

"Big winner," he observed with a chuckle. Then he tucked the five into a pocket and dropped the fifteen cents back in my hand.

"How'd you do?" I inquired.

"Not as well as you."

He cashed in, and we headed back out into the night.

"You always that frugal?" he asked.

"Yup. Have to be."

"What's it like, living like a church mouse?"

"Is that a real question?"

"Yes, I suppose it is."

"Why? You expecting a reversal of fortune?"

"That's pretty personal, wouldn't you say?"

"So was your question."

"Humm."

We hooked arms and strolled a few yards. Then he asked whether I was going to answer him.

"You go first."

"My father threatened to cut me out of his will."

"Because...?"

He thought for a moment. "Nope. You got your answer. Now you."

"Okay. I discovered that if I have enough for necessities and a beer at the end of the week, I'm content."

"Content. Not happy?"

"Material things don't make a person happy."

"You've met my mother, right?"

"Hmmm," I said as if considering. "Make that 'material things don't make *me* happy."

"Atta girl." Gavin congratulated me. "Keep those expectations low."

We stood at the stairs to the disco, or whatever they call a dance club these days. I'd never been to one. Frankly, I had no desire to step foot inside this one.

But step foot we did. It was dark, except for strobe lights on the dance floor and a row of bulbs behind the liquor bottles that silhouetted the bartenders and gave the couples and singles on the stools a halfway decent look at each other.

Gavin drank three drinks to my one, and we danced. His moves were practiced and fun to watch; but when he noticed my lack of enthusiasm, he began to drink faster and ogle other women.

One thing we did not do was talk. Yell at each other to be heard, yes. Talk, no.

After about an hour of that, Gavin leaned across the tabletop and shouted, "Let's go."

His pronunciation was overly careful, not a good sign, but he'd said exactly what I wanted to hear. I performed a mental fist pump and grabbed my wrap.

"Wanna walk back on the beach?"

"Absolutely." So there we were—barefoot, shoes dangling from our fingers, kicking cool sand and meandering through the shadows with nobody to watch us but the occasional guard.

Gavin steered me up against a coconut palm and moved in for a kiss.

"Whoa, fella," I said pushing his chest away with my own palm.

He tried to move in again.

I ducked under his arm.

"Whasup? You don't have a boyfriend anymore." He was huffing, getting angry.

"No," I admitted, because it happened to be true. "But you have a girlfriend."

"Shit," he said. "What's that to you?"

Strike two. I had been appalled when Gavin dredged up the scattering-of-the-ashes fiasco to Chantal this morning, and now he had disrespected his girlfriend. His *serious* girlfriend from the sounds of it. Frank wouldn't have bothered to threaten him over her otherwise.

I like to think that Lauren Beck would have used more restraint, but I was too deeply into the Lori Ruggles persona to hold back.

"You may be president of some damn company or other," I heard Lori say, "but you're also an asshole."

Gavin's head jerked. Lips twisted with anger, he took one drunken step. Then the sonovabitch lunged for my neck, so I used his forward momentum to flip him on his back. The sand made for an easy landing, but I heard his teeth click when his head bounced off the tree trunk.

When he opened his mouth again, nothing came out but curse words, so I kicked sand at him until he spit and yelled, "Stop."

Flashlight bobbing along the ground, a guard hustled over to us. Shouting to be heard over the crash of the incoming surf, he asked us what happened in English with a Spanish lilt.

"He tripped," I told the guy, holding out my hand to help Mr. President up. He was still wiping sand out of his eyes with his sleeve.

"Tell the officer what happened," I prompted as the cop's flashlight played across Gavin's face.

The glare he aimed at me would have melted metal. "I tripped," he said, then spit at my feet.

"We'll just go home now. Okay, officer?"

The guard stepped back, reluctantly, but he did step back. While he watched, I took Gavin's arm and playfully pushed him in the right direction.

"Oops," I remarked to the guard. "Forgot our shoes."

By the time I picked them up and turned back, Gavin was nowhere in sight.

Chapter 20

After breakfast the next morning, I drifted into the lounge area to watch CNN with Frank. Since no terrorist group had yet claimed credit, a diverse panel of people I didn't recognize was discussing the Metro crash in hypothetical terms.

We learned that the driver had been on the job for twenty-four years and had no history of drugs or alcohol, nor were any discovered during the autopsy. His finances were in good order. His wife still loved him. In short, no reason had emerged to explain why he had been driving excessively fast.

"It isn't a very difficult corner..." remarked the only female on the panel.

"No, but the proximity to strategic government buildings..." by the moderator, a man wearing pinstripes.

"Anything useful on the black box?" the recording device usually associated with airplanes.

"Unfortunately, no. The accident happened too fast for anyone to log a reaction."

Lacking any real news, the moderator began to describe some of the nut-case confessions that cost investigators dozens of precious hours.

Frank clicked off the set. "Déjà vu all over again," he remarked with a disgusted sigh.

Then he noticed me. "Something I can help you with?"

"No, oh no thanks," I said, realizing I'd intruded yet again. "Just wanted to thank you for, for everything. You've been extremely gracious."

Frank's nod struck me as a little curt, but perhaps he didn't take compliments well.

"Chantal likes you," he conveyed with a warmth that made me miss my father. Maybe instead of a deposit on an apartment I could visit Dad in Albuquerque, mention that I needed a place to live, settle in…completely destroy their honeymoon glow…

I told Frank I didn't think Marsha shared Chantal's impression of me.

Settling back against the sofa cushion, the CEO's face took on a forgiving sort of fondness. "Marsha enjoys having something to bitch about. She thinks it keeps us on our toes."

I began to say, "I guess it would," but just then Frank's cell phone buzzed. He scowled at the caller ID. "Excuse me," he said. "I have to take this."

To offer an illusion of privacy, I carried my empty coffee mug around the corner to the galley. I wasn't really out of earshot, but Frank didn't contribute more than a word or two to the conversation anyway.

When silence suggested the call was over, I peeked around the corner. If I gave my host a wide berth, I might be able to return to my stateroom without bothering him again.

No precautions were needed. Frank had forgotten I was born. Still on the sofa, elbows resting on his knees, he looked like a man who'd just been hit with a rock. His eyes were blank, his lips slack. The gray of his skin would have made a heart attack victim look healthy.

I debated whether to ask if he was okay, and my hesitation prompted him to glance up.

"The family will be leaving this afternoon," he announced. "If you'd like to stay longer, I can make arrangements…"

No sign of pain, other than emotional.

"Not a problem," I said, although my heart was beating a quick retreat of its own. Why on earth had I brought that Glock? "I don't mind going home early, but thanks for the offer."

Probably still digesting his new business emergency, Frank didn't seem to pick up the tremor in my voice or noticed my reddened face.

"Guess I go...pack," I said, but Frank had stopped listening.

So far as I knew, Gavin's first appearance of the day was at three PM when we gathered ourselves and our belongings on the sidewalk to board the van for the airport. He didn't speak to me, nor I to him. He also climbed in last, insuring that we wouldn't end up side by side during the ride.

The airport bustled with what I guessed to be a few hundred travelers—noisy kids, sleepy seniors, impatient youths, placid Europeans. We got the word that our private plane was delayed, so Frank, his wife, and his daughter wandered up to a members-only lounge.

Gavin pulled me aside at the bottom of the stairs. "They'll page us," he said cryptically, then led me through the duty-free stores and upstairs to another slightly less frenetic, marginally cooler waiting area.

We found two seats together facing the chaos. Gavin extended his long legs and slid his ass down to the edge of his, laced his fingers over his belt buckle, and said, "So. Where did you learn how to deck a man with one hand?"

While I chose what Lori Ruggles would say, I tucked a stray curl behind my ear.

"Self-defense class."

"And why would you need a self-defense class?" he pressed.

My face asked whether he really needed an answer.

Relaxing with a distant thought, he smiled. "Been different if I was sober."

"Sure would," I agreed. "You'd be in a Dominican jail."

His mouth opened, but he quickly closed it. We both slouched back in our seats as if we expected to be there a long time.

Hoping to finally get to my original agenda, I asked his girlfriend's name.

"Julianne," he confessed. "Not exactly my girlfriend anymore."

"Sister of the unfortunate Luanne Sykes?"

Gavin did a double-take. "How the hell do you know that?"

I admitted that Chantal told me. "What I can't understand is why your dad gives a flying fig who you're with now that Roitman Industries won the lawsuit."

Gavin's hands kneaded air as he sighed out a chestful of angst. "My father isn't the most forgiving person you'll ever meet."

"Inflexible?"

"Think re-bar." Those rods they use to reinforce concrete.

"Your mother seems to get what she wants out of him. Why can't you?"

He huffed out a laugh. "Because my father gets a perverse pleasure out of watching me fail."

That surprised me, and I guess it showed. "But you're president of one of his widget factories."

Gavin's expression looked like pity. "A custom car mat company," he corrected me, "and who gives a shit whether that succeeds or fails? Certainly not my dad."

"Then why own it?"

"To give me something to screw up so he can justify cutting me loose to my mother."

"Seriously?"

Gavin didn't bother to reply.

I folded my arms across my chest. "Huh. So how is business anyway?"

"Up fifteen percent last month." The president of the widget company spread his hands. "When people hold onto their cars, their floor mats wear out. Also, we ran a new ad."

"Good for you."

"Thanks." Gavin's modest smile revealed how pleased he was to thwart his father's plan—if Gavin was correct and that really was his father's plan. Maybe Frank had simply thrown his son into the deep end of the pool to teach him how to swim.

All of which was interesting, but not at all what I needed.

"Was Toby smart?" I wondered aloud.

"You get right to the point, don't you?"

Yeah, so?

"Toby," he mused. "The favored son." Gavin shook his head. "The replacement son's more like it."

"You resented him?"

"I wouldn't say that." Yet from the stiffening of Gavin's body, resentment was exactly what he felt. I'd finally unearthed a motive, the classic Eliminate Your Rival. Not that I was happy about it.

Chantal appeared at the entrance to our area and waved both hands above her head. I noticed because I was facing that way, but Gavin was busy twiddling his thumbs.

"So," I said, appearing to tick off the facts. "You're president of a widget factory, and you behave like an asshole in your free time. What's up with that?"

Gavin rested his forearms on his knees and showed me a slow smile. "You've seen the Queen Mother's nose turn up, haven't you? And Frank? He freezes up so tight it's a wonder he can take his morning shit."

He was tweaking his parents' noses? Was he that immature? Unlikely. Devious? Skillful? Calculating? Controlled? I suddenly realized none of my impressions of Gavin added up. Perhaps he had inherited Marsha's penchant for acting; he certainly knew how to keep his audience off balance.

"Ga-vinnnnn?" Chantal shouted across the crowd.

We both stood. I grabbed my purse, and Gavin slung his duffel over his shoulder. When I didn't immediately extend the handle of my suitcase, he gave me a curious look.

I told him, "I don't believe you."

"What!"

"I think you behave like a juvenile delinquent to keep expectations low. Then if you do screw up your widget factory, the fall from grace won't be very far."

He lifted my chin with his index finger, and his face took on a wistful softness.

Then just that quick his eyes were daggers. "You could get into a lot of trouble being that smart," he warned.

Chapter 21

For my second and probably final flight in a private jet, I vowed to stay awake and enjoy every moment. However, as the fifth person and a relative stranger to everyone else, I ended up having the last short row of seats to myself, and, consequently, no one to talk to. I slept until the wheels bounced ever so lightly on that obscure runway in the middle of Nowhere, Virginia.

The Roitmans held an all-too-obvious discussion about what to do with me in the terminal lobby with the little yellow airplane hanging overhead.

"Since it'll be too late for our driver to take you home tonight, we'd like you to stay with us another night," I was told. "Somebody will get you wherever you need to go in the morning." This from Marsha, who appeared not to have slept on the plane and clearly should have.

"Whatever works best for you is fine with me."

Outdoors again, night was rapidly falling along with a heavy dew. The swaths of dampened grass alongside the runways gave off a green, fertile fragrance. Low on the horizon a pale polka-dot in the sky was probably the planet I'd wished upon as a girl. Later I found out it wasn't a star, which probably explains why none of my wishes came true.

I scanned the parking lot but detected no orange glow; Mike's Mustang was gone. The last I'd heard from him, Mary was home again but confined to bed rest. With luck, the only reason Mike hadn't contacted me again was because he had nothing to say.

"I guess this is good-bye," Gavin remarked as he dug car keys out of his pocket. Even in the parking lot lamplight he wore his put-on playboy look as naturally as a slob wears ketchup.

I extended my hand. "A pleasure meeting you," I said.

A kiss to his mother and sister, a nod to his dad. The trunk of a nearby car popped open. Gavin was the president of a widget factory. He did not live with his parents.

Transportation for the rest of the Roitmans and me came in the form of a seven-passenger van with a driver. My suitcase and I kept each other warm in the back seat, mainly because the cargo compartment was full of Louis Vuitton.

As we bumped out of the lot onto the adjacent back road, I texted Mike with the subject line "Guess what" then told him we were back in Virginia "for business reasons." Also that I'd lucked out and would be spending another night with Toby's in-laws. Since nobody in the van could see what I was writing, I added, "Had an interesting talk with Gavin," before I pressed send.

Twenty minutes later we entered a curving uphill driveway to a front circle complete with an operating fountain. Crickets chirped in the dark. Tall pines rustled like the surf and flavored the night air with their sap. As one might expect, the massive Federal-style mini-mansion had been built with long-lasting Virginia brick.

A large brass fixture under the portico and lamps shining from within the house were all that illuminated your way inside; but when you got there, the first impression was a whopper. An urn of fresh flowers over two feet tall, walnut paneling to chair-rail height, paintings done by somebody with talent.

The driver assisted Frank in offloading the luggage and hauling it into the front hall. I did my own and got no objections.

"Daddy! Mommy!" shouted a girl of eleven as she ran to hug her parents. She was bouncy and round and had on an old-school uniform—white blouse, pleated plaid skirt in navy, burgundy and white, navy knee socks, laced leather shoes.

"Abby, sweetie, shouldn't you be getting ready for bed?" Frank seemed both pleased and concerned.

"Dad-dy. It's only eight o'clock. Lana told me I could stay up anyway."

The girl was shoulder height to Frank, ear height to Marsha. Tortoise shell glasses slipped down her small nose, and even with braces on her teeth she was beautiful. Perfect skin, brown hair that glowed with red and gold highlights, blue eyes the shade of sapphires—just a little more weight than necessary. While she was waiting to become a knockout, she would be self-conscious.

When we were introduced, young Abby Roitman assessed me as if I were a horse she wasn't sure she wanted to buy.

"What are you doing here?" she inquired as if she had the right to know, which maybe she did.

I glanced at her parents for a clue about how to answer.

Chantal jumped in. "She's a guest, Abby. Mind your manners." The expectant mother sank into a brocade chair. "You think Lana has anything for us to eat? I'm starved."

It occurred to me to wonder why Chantal hadn't gone her separate way like her brother. Maybe she was in no hurry to return to an empty house, a house without her husband.

With Abby skipping along behind we all wended our way through a formal dining room, an old-fashioned pantry, and into the kitchen.

I guesstimated that the house had been built sometime after Abraham Lincoln but before Rosie the Riveter, but the kitchen had been updated last week. The hood over the six-burner stainless-steel gas stove appeared capable of sucking the whole stove through the ceiling. White marble countertops, mullioned cherry cabinets, and a cook in a pale gray dress with a white bib apron. She looked disturbed by my presence, like a hostess who hadn't set out enough plates.

"Svetlana, this is Lori Ruggles. She'll be staying in the pool house tonight. Are the sheets fresh?"

"Yes, ma'am," the cook/housekeeper replied. As expected, her accent sounded Russian. I would later learn that "Lana" had come to the United States from Belarus, that she was university educated, and that she had a sarcastic sense of humor.

What I saw just then was a woman of perhaps fifty with a sad, sagging face, thin, straight brunette hair laced with white strands and held off her face with combs. Her suspicious eyes bored pinholes into my skin.

I told her, "Hello."

Chantal opened both sides of a French-door refrigerator. "What can we have, Lana? Help me out here."

The evil eye blinked, and animation resumed. Frank shooed Abby off to a bath and her pajamas. Lana handed platters covered with plastic to Chantal, who arranged them on the vast island in the middle of the room. Marsha dug into drawers for utensils and napkins, unceremoniously foisted them on me, then waved at the rectangular table jutting out from the back window.

Everyday earthenware plates were set beside cold chicken, string-bean salad, fresh rolls, mayonnaise, German potato salad, and cherry pie. Frank supplied ice-water, or beer, or wine; and we all helped ourselves as if we'd done it a hundred times before. Go figure. The Roitmans appeared to be regular people.

While we ate Lana escaped to a room off the kitchen, and we could hear the theme of a familiar cop show set a low volume. When we finished, Marsha tapped on the door, and Lana emerged once again to tidy up our casual dinner.

"I'm sure you've had quite enough of the Roitmans," Marsha hinted as the others said their good-nights and slipped away. "Chantal will settle you into the pool house. I'm sure you'll be comfortable there."

Chantal flipped a light switch beside the door at the back end of the house, and a rolling lawn came into view. Halfway down the hill lay a rectangular pool still wearing its taut green winter cover. To the left a small bungalow with a pitched roof snuggled in behind a clump of mature rhododendrons.

Both of us tired, my suitcase bumping along on brick pavers, Chantal and I took our time getting to the door.

"Just so you know. I'll drive you home tomorrow," she offered, reinforcing my suspicion that she was reluctant to return to her own home.

"Where do you live?" I inquired.

She said she and Toby had been living outside of the town where Roitman Industries was headquartered. It was indeed on the way to DC.

"We'd just bought another house though. More bedrooms. Nicer yard. I was able to get out of the agreement after Toby died, but I can't stand being in the old place without him so I left it on the market. Keeping it ready to be shown is a total pain in the butt, so I'm staying here for a while."

"Old bedroom?"

"Yep."

"White furniture. Pink walls?

"Canopy bed. Lavender walls."

I looked over her shoulder toward the mini-mansion. "Which one?"

"Back corner on the right."

"Gotta be a good view."

"Yes, it is."

We both fell silent, and I thought the moment was finally right to ask. "Have you ever wondered whether your husband really committed suicide?"

"You mean the hint you dropped that day on the beach?" She said it without shock or any emotion at all. "I thought of it, sure." She exhaled a puff of air as if she were laughing at herself. "But it was."

I thought of the odd method Toby chose to die, Karen's doubts, Mike's doubts, the house purchase, the baby she was carrying; but I was far from ready to implicate anyone in her family. Not until I ruled out the possibility of other suspects. A visit to the hunting lodge might help with that.

We exchanged sad smiles, and she handed me the key to the bungalow.

"Want me to show you around?"

"I'll manage."

She gave my arm a grateful pat and said she'd see me in the morning.

The setting was splendid, the night air pleasantly cool on my face. I lingered in the doorway while Chantal plodded uphill toward the mini-mansion on the bumpy brick walk. She was looking at her feet though. She would be okay.

Then a gunshot sliced through the space between us, and she ran for the door like a hen fleeing the butcher.

Chapter 22

Contrary to what his wife thought, Frank loved being home. True, he wasn't here much; but when he was, he loved it. Like now. Slippered feet extended on the bed, extra pillow behind his back, a short glass of bourbon neat within reach. And Marsha half undressed futzing around in the adjacent bathroom. Oh hell, yes, a news program was on the wall-mounted TV just across the room, but why not? He could keep an eye on that and Marsha, too.

"...the terrorist possibility now categorized as a 'movie-plot' threat, as opposed to what terrorists actually do..."

The comment caused Frank to swallow more bourbon, which failed to dissolve the knot in his belly. If not a terrorist, who or what were the investigators going to blame? His eyes drifted back to his wife.

Marsha pursed her lips in concentration as she removed the slender diamond tennis bracelet she'd worn on the flight home. He noticed she laid the bracelet on her dressing table with the reverence he reserved for cash.

"...speculating whether the engineer may have experienced something similar to road fatigue or highway hypnosis..." The man is dead, though, isn't he? So we'll never know.

Lifting both arms, Marsha busied herself undoing her hair. Each small motion caused her breasts, in profile from where Frank sat, to flex and jiggle in a way that slipped a smile across his lips. The woman certainly had good genes—good skin, good figure. Most days he would say he was a lucky man.

Of course there were times he considered strangling the breath out of his wife, but this was marriage, for god's sake, what else did he expect?

"...many reports over time of a peculiar fishy smell originating from the Metro train's brakes." Oh, please!

Marsha watched her eyes in the mirror as she fingered hairpins out of her French twist. She knew the style was as old as earth, but it accentuated her jawline and neck. When the throat wrinkles became ugly grooves, she would consider a change, but not yet. No, not just yet. At random moments Frank kissed the nape of her neck, and she was nowhere near ready to give that up.

Like always, she felt the pull of Frank's attention. She also knew she was sharing him with the news. Frank's fascination with all things transportation irked her on an ordinary day, but coverage of the Metro crash and all its ramifications nearly pushed her over the edge. If she wasn't already half asleep, she would run over there and swipe the remote right out of his hand.

Tonight she was too tired. After Frank confided his *situation* at work, she had packed in a helluva hurry, so of course their borrowed plane got delayed. She knew she shouldn't look a gift-horse in the mouth, but pushing and shoving through the sweaty hordes jamming Punta Cana airport then sitting in that tiny lounge with nothing to do for what felt like a week—who wouldn't have bags under her eyes?

She needed her nightgown. As she rose to go get it, the dressing table chair slid to the left and the foot supporting her weight rolled. Catching herself before she fell, her arm swept the tennis bracelet off the dressing table onto the floor. To steady her balance, she staggered right/left while reaching behind her for the back of the chair.

She missed. The chair wobbled, and rather than fall, she sat. Something crunched. The chair leg had landed on the bracelet. Marsha's manicured fingers flew to her mouth.

Afraid of what she might find, she bent down and scooped up last year's birthday present as gently as if it were a baby chick. Half an inch of the narrow row of diamonds set in gold had been twisted and crushed.

Two of the small stones had even cracked in two. Holding the bracelet aloft, she turned to confront her husband.

He sensed her stare.

"*What is this?*" she demanded, emphasizing each word like a threat.

Frank Roitman always knew he'd married a formidable woman, but until this moment she had yet to frighten him. As sudden as a dog's bite, the qualities he depended on his wife to possess were gone. In their place were all of the ones he never expected to see, the ones from other men's horror stories, tales full of damning adjectives and demeaning laments. Intellectually, he knew a woman's wrath could turn an honest man into a thief, cause him to hide inside alcohol, even prompt a primeval violence that would condemn him to prison for life. It had all seemed theoretical.

He saw now that it was not.

"I can explain," he said.

"Then start."

He stood. He stuffed his hands into his pockets. He walked a crooked path to where Marsha was seated. He raised his left palm as if to minimize what he'd done. Then he told her, "I needed some money off the books."

"What for?" They stood face to face now, like two marionettes dangling on fragile strings.

Frank's chin lifted. "If I wanted to tell you, I'd have told you before."

Instinctively, Marsha left that statement alone. Instead, she asked, "How much?"

He answered.

She swore. "So is all my jewelry fake now?"

He reached for her hands.

She yanked them away.

"Are we broke? Tell me the truth, Frank, or. Or…"

"Don't say it. Don't even think it. I was protecting you from an unpleasant situation, that's all. In business there are things that no one should know but me."

"You could have trusted me, Frank. Why didn't you?"

Because, my dear, baring my soul to you is not in my own best interest.

He deflected.

"It's the legal system, Marsha. It just wasn't—*isn't* prudent—to tell you all my problems."

"The legal system?" she scoffed.

Frank knew that Marsha would not be reassured by a more complete explanation. True, a wife could not be compelled to testify against her husband, but if she voluntarily told someone else, spousal privilege was broken and all bets were off.

Or, if they happened to divorce, nothing could protect him from her wrath—and these days divorce was a statistical coin toss. Yes, risk was certainly integral to most of his business accomplishments, but trial and error had educated him well. He had learned to recognize when accepting risk was prudent and when it was not.

He had just begun to offer his wife a reassuring hug when they both heard a shot.

Marsha startled and gasped.

Frank lurched toward the sound in time to see his daughter running, stumbling, and running toward the house, shrieking and flailing the air like the scarecrow in the *Wizard of Oz.*

"Hand me the phone, Marsha," he said. "I'm calling 9-1-1."

Chapter 23

The shot came from the dark side of a long row of thick evergreens to my right. Thanks to the light by the poolhouse door, I dumped my suitcase, grabbed bullets out of Karen's jewelry case, and loaded the Glock inside of ninety seconds.

The rhododendrons to the left of the bungalow were huge. Sneaking between them and the wall proved to be impossible and rounding them would have left me too exposed. Instead, I wriggled past some naked bushes on the bungalow's other end then on through a narrow gap in the evergreens. Sensing a barrier, I stopped to listen.

From the middle distance came the grumble of a car speeding away. There had to be a road or a lane out there, but no headlights showed in any direction, and soon the shooter was gone.

I'd come to a string of wire dotted with familiar white ceramic knobs—electric fencing surrounding a pasture. Not too excited about getting zapped, I turned right hoping to skirt the perimeter and eventually check into that road.

By now my night vision was fair, certainly not great. White-tipped fence posts helped me judge the terrain—up, down, even—but bushes and trees regularly blocked my path, and clumps of last-year's overgrown grass often tripped me up.

In roughly five minutes I reached a stand of tall, dense arborvitae that appeared to mark the corner of the field. Thin light from something high up shone toward me from the other side.

I did not get that far.

"Freeze," said a voice deep with authority.

Grasping the Glock with both hands, I pointed it toward the voice and inched the rest of the way around the evergreens.

Light spilled from a bulb attached to the underside of a barn's roof. Silhouetted a dozen feet in front of me was a man using the exact stance as mine.

"Drop it," he said.

"You first."

"Not going to happen."

I sighed. "Since you haven't shot me yet, I'm guessing you work here."

"I still could," he informed me, "so lower your weapon and slowly lay it on the ground. Then back up till I tell you to stop."

If I hadn't heard a car without headlights leave, and if the vibes from this guy had felt more offensive than defensive, my response would have been different. As it was, I trusted my gut and followed orders.

While I backed up, the silhouette moved forward. When he arrived at my Glock, he lifted it by the barrel and gave it a good sniff.

"Okay, sweetie. Who the hell are you?"

"Sweetie? Really? That's so...so yesterday."

"Okay, you fucking idiot. What were you doing running around in the dark right after a gun was fired?"

"It wasn't mine," I argued, "but you already know that."

"Huh," he snorted. "You going to tell me who you are, or do I have to beat it out of you?"

"Does Scorsese know you're using his material?"

"Who. Are. You?"

"An invited guest," I said, crossing my fingers behind my back. "I'm staying in the pool house."

"You better have a suitcase."

"Of course I have a suitcase."

"We'll see." He tucked my Glock in the front of his belt, grabbed my arm and propelled me over to some open lawn. From there the pool house and mini-mansion looked like toys sitting in pools of phosphorous.

My adrenaline high had crashed back at "Freeze," and my sneakers were soggy with dew. The silhouette's hand around my arm was the warmest thing in my universe, but I began to regret that I hadn't had a chance to give *his* gun the sniff test. How embarrassing would it be to die just because of one little miscalculation? I started to shiver and couldn't stop.

Whoever-he-was began to march me uphill. Rather than the strong stride I expected, his gait was the side-to-side wobble of a long-established limp. Still we made it to the bungalow in record time.

"There. You happy now?" I said gesturing toward my, correction—*Karen's*—suitcase. The surrounding clothes resembled an after-photo of a Christmas morning involving small children, if one of them happened to wear size 32B.

Below the shadow cast by his baseball cap, the silhouette smirked.

Then he returned my Glock handgrip first, doffed his cap, and gave me my first look at his eyes.

The door light wasn't kind, but the eyes were. They smiled from within deep creases that told of fifty-some years, many of them hard.

"Sleep tight," he said.

"You, too," I replied, but the Roitman's security man wouldn't be resting anytime soon.

Up at the main house, the revolving lights of at least two police cruisers were bathing the evergreens with a garish wash of red, white, and blue.

Chapter 24

The bungalow's soft furniture had been slipcovered with blue and white ticking, the light knotty pine floor softened with slip-proof blue shag rugs. Driftwood and sea shells here and there made for a beachy, family-friendly décor; but after the shot somebody fired toward the Roitman's home and my subsequent tramping around in the dark, all I cared about was a hot shower and a pillow.

I slept like a hibernating bear.

When I finally woke up, I dressed in the warmest clothing Karen's suitcase offered—cut-off white slacks and a thin cotton sweater—and headed for the kitchen.

"Good morning," I greeted Lana, the cook, who briefly looked up from rolling out pie dough.

She wiggled her hand over a couple of covered dishes sitting on a hot plate. "Ham, eggz, rolls over there. Hep yourselv." Warm food, if not a warm welcome. I poured coffee and loaded a plate.

"Thank you," I said softly since the rest of the household still seemed to be comatose.

Pushing into the pantry backwards through a swinging door, I learned that I was wrong. Female voices bleeding through the door to the dining room sounded shrill.

I carefully set my coffee mug and plate on the lower pantry cabinet and held still. The last thing I wanted to do was walk in on an argument.

"I bet you anything it was that Sykes guy whose daughter died. The man who lost the lawsuit."

"Calm down," Marsha told her daughter. "You're overreacting."

"Overreacting?" Chantal repeated a decibel louder. "If somebody shot at you, you'd be ready for a straight-jacket."

"Darling, you're too worked up over this. The police seem to think it was a prank or an accident. They're going to look around more this morning, but..."

"Never mind. You're not listening to me anyway."

A heavy sigh and a fraught moment. "Would you like me to get you one of my tranquillizers?"

"What! No, Mother. I'd rather not, not until...You really don't know?"

"Know what?"

"That I'm pregnant?"

Marsha emitted something between a roar and a moan. Then when her lungs were sufficiently re-inflated, she stammered, "No, I...I..."

"Seriously, Mom, if Lori figured it out...you really didn't have a clue?"

"I'm going to be a grandmother. I'm going to be a *grand*mother!" Next came a loud slap on the table and a heartfelt, "Dammit, Chantal! Why didn't you warn me?"

"Warn you? About something wonderful happening for Toby and me? Not everything is about you, Mother."

Not the best moment to burst in with a plate of ham and eggs. I gingerly lifted my breakfast off the cabinet and prayed that the door back into the kitchen wouldn't squeak or flap back and forth after I backed through.

Lana glanced up from her pie filling just as unfriendly as before. "Do you mind if I...?" I jerked my head toward the rectangular table where we all sat last night.

Distant footsteps thudded up the center-hall stairs as the first swinging door hit the pantry cabinet with a whack. Then a red-faced Marsha barged through the kitchen past

Lana and me with fire in her eyes. Outside, she plowed through the patio furniture and disappeared around the corner of the house before I had time to blink.

Getting a ride out of here this morning wasn't looking too good. Before any of the Roitmans might spare me a thought, they had their tempers to deal with, and also the police.

With Lana busily denying my existence I figured I might as well polish off my cold breakfast. Then I grabbed an apple for a snack and headed back downhill to my temporary lodging.

I'd finished the Lee Child book, and the only paperbacks in the pool house were three thick bodice-rippers and two Agatha Christies that appeared to have spent time in a bathtub. Not a fan of either, I watched a cooking contest on the flat-screen over the credenza, a first for me. The food the contestants prepared looked tempting, but it was the personality conflicts I enjoyed, exaggerated though they were. Anything to spice up the show.

Someone tapped on the door. Maybe the police?

Nope. Abby.

"Hi," I told the Roitman's eleven-year-old.

I'm a little tall for a woman, certainly not basketball-star material, but it would take a major pre-pubescent growth spurt for this kid to ever look me in the eye. I widened the gap in the doorway so she could step inside.

"No school today?" I guessed. My experience with fifth-graders dated back to when I was one.

Abby assessed the living area the way dogs and cops do, checking for exits. "I missed the bus. We never bother Daddy when he's working, and Mother said she couldn't take me because the police might come back." She bit her lip and reflected. "She hates to have strangers touch her things."

She plopped herself on the blue-ticking sofa. "Did you know that bullets travel one thousand three hundred and sixty-three miles an hour?"

I knew that the velocity of a bullet was usually described in feet per second and varied with the type of ammo and even the brand, but I humored the kid and said, "Really?"

"Yep, but gravity would make it hit the ground before it got that far."

"Unless it hit something else first."

The lift of Abby's left eyebrow told me she'd made a mental adjustment in my favor.

To fill the ensuing silence, I said, "So, uh, Abby, if you're staying home, I guess you can probably wear whatever you want now." She had on the same sort of school clothes as last night, tipping me off that the no-school decision had been last minute.

"It doesn't matter what I wear," she replied with a philosophical sniff.

"I hear you." I sat on the arm of an opposing armchair. "I'm not much into clothes myself."

Abby shot me a look. "I like clothes. I meant that nobody around here cares what I do."

"Oh, I'm sure that's not true."

"Yeah, it is."

Fingers grasping the front edge of the seat cushion, she rhythmically kicked the sofa with her heels. It would become very annoying very fast. Arms folded, she asked, "How did you find out my sister's having a baby?"

I admitted that I'd guessed. "How did *you* find out?"

Abby shrugged. "I hear things." I bet she did. "Somebody shot at her last night. She's really freaked out."

I circled around to sit across from the girl. "I notice you aren't." Titillated, maybe. Freaked, no.

Abby waved her head. "My shrink said that, too. Not today, after Uncle Toby."

"And why would that be, I wonder."

Another two-shoulder shrug. "I read a lot of murder mysteries. After a while they don't seem real anymore."

"Last night was real, Abby. Chantal should have been scared."

"Nah. That doesn't make any sense. Daddy's the one people hate."

There was much I could say about that, but not to an eleven-year-old. "I don't know, Abby," I waffled. "Why do you think that?"

"Because he got mugged already. Somebody knocked him down, and he broke his wrist. He gets death threats, too. A driver and a bodyguard take him to work."

And everywhere else, I should imagine.

More double kicks to the sofa. "Chantal says the people who hate my father might kidnap one of us to get back at him."

"You don't seem very worried about that either."

"I'm not."

"Because...?"

"Because Chantal is a married grown-up and doesn't usually live here."

"That doesn't mean both of you shouldn't be extra careful."

"I told you. Nobody around here cares about me."

"That just can't be true," I disagreed.

"You don't read mysteries, do you?" she accused. "Most of the time the police screw up the drop-off and the kid they're trying to find gets killed. Or else they're already dead. Anyhow, it doesn't matter, because my father ignores me. It's like he forgot I'm his daughter."

Ah, the drama of the pre-teen. It was all coming back. "Your mother worries about you, though. If you were kidnapped…"

"Oh, she'd fuss alright, then she'd figure out how to make it all about her."

Wow. This was one cynical kid, and I can't tell you how much that depressed me. Compelled to reassure her, I launched into a pep talk that basically said I knew plenty about parents, and I was positive hers would do anything in their power to get her back home safe.

"Cops would, too," I added, just to be clear.

Abby rolled her eyes as if to say, "Oh, grow up."

Chapter 25

As my conversation with Abby wound down, I took off my still-damp sneakers and put them on a radiator under the side window.

"Feet sweat a gallon of water a week, you know," the Roitman's youngest informed me.

"Is that so?" I wasn't about to admit that I'd been tromping around in wet grass last night looking for something on the shooter.

"Yup," she said. "And twelve inches is a foot because a long time ago that's how big some king's foot was."

"Wow. Think how much smaller this room would be if you'd been king."

The kid opened her mouth, glanced to the side, and sighed. Trying to hide a smile, she popped off the sofa and marched herself over to the door.

"You should probably put your shoes back on," she recommended over her shoulder. "My dad wants to see you in his office."

"Okay. Where's his office?"

"If you find it by yourself, you'll feel smarter."

I suspected she'd been told that many times.

Personnel would probably be spread thin in a rural area on a Tuesday morning, but the absence of state police scouring the Roitman property with metal detectors still surprised me. So what if the odds for finding the bullet were daunting, I thought it was at least worth a try. Of course if the family chose not to pursue the incident for some inexplicable reason—privacy? Secrecy? Although, which Roitman would have pulled the plug, and why? Something around here just wasn't normal.

Such were my thoughts as I arrived back at the kitchen. The fragrance of freshly baked apple pie greeted me.

Rocking back and forth in the alcove by the back door, Lana remained focused on the knitting in her lap. The yarn was a thin pastel yellow, and she seemed to be working a cable up the middle of a miniature sleeve.

Early during the four years I lived in Corinne Wilder's attic apartment, my former cancer counselor and almost step-mother knitted colorful wool hats to warm my bald head. Just before her own relapse she gifted me an intricate fisherman's sweater, which I still wear whenever I miss her affectionate hugs.

Consequently, the click of Lana's needles gave me such a lump in my throat that I almost didn't ask how to find her boss.

"Upstair. Turn right," was the grudging answer.

The humongous flower arrangement at the bottom of the stairs perfumed the hall. Dust motes danced in the nearly noon sunlight angling through the narrow panes on either side of the front door, and the treads of the hundred-year-old stairs creaked beneath their carpeting as I climbed up to Frank Roitman's lair.

The door to the last room at the back of the broad hallway stood open.

Roitman rose when he saw me.

As I approached, I took in the thick drapes, the smell of old books and furniture polish. A hooded brass desk lamp illuminated the blotter area of a broad mahogany desk, and a slim computer sat open where a typewriter once rested. The setting couldn't possibly be where a modern business mogul worked very often. I suspected he had stayed home to deal with the police.

"Ah, Ms. Beck, we finally meet," he said, and my face instantly flamed.

"Please, have a seat." He motioned me onto a red leather visitor's chair opposite his own imposing black one.

"How did you...?"

"Find out?" he finished for me. "You remember George from the yacht? George is retired FBI. He ran your prints from your last beverage onboard. And Lyle Dickens—you met him last night—he's just retired police but still quite good. He researched the rest."

"So you know..."

"That you're related to the Stoddards by marriage. Yes. This would be a good time to explain why you lied about that."

Frank had remained standing even as my weakened knees lowered me onto the red chair. Now he placed his palms on the blotter the better to glare down from above.

In the pursuit of justice I lied once again. "Fantasy," I said. "Mike and I've been flirting ever since we met at my brother's wedding, and when Karen expressed misgivings about going on your trip, I jumped at the chance to take her place." I tilted my head and blinked as if the admission embarrassed me. "On the way to the airport, we were kidding around again, and I guess we got a little carried away. Mike came up with my fake name..." I threw up my hands. "I apologize for deceiving you. It seemed harmless enough at the time."

"Umph," Roitman said as if he hadn't listened. "You left the Landis, Pennsylvania, police force after only five years." Arms behind his back, he had strolled a pace or two toward the window, but suddenly he lunged around the end of the desk and stopped just short of my knees. "What do you have to say about that?"

Tell him my fiancé broke our engagement when he learned about my cancer? Tell him the emotional toll was almost greater than the physical one? Tell him that if it hadn't been for Corinne taking me in…? I don't think so.

I turned coy on him instead. "Didn't your sources tell you that?"

Frank's chin lifted. "No, but you will."

Judging by the smirk he adopted, Frank had interpreted my silence as proof of a sordid secret—the old It-takes-one-to-know-one theory in action. During my time with him and his family, I'd come to suspect that he wasn't entirely pure himself. It would be easy enough to find out.

"Why do you think I left?"

He returned to his chair as he weighed his words.

"A woman like you? I think you saw how the other side lives and decided you deserved a couple of luxuries, too."

I laughed out loud, but at my own expense. If Frank had had that opinion of me from Day One, the Lobster Thermador I allowed him to order for me must have cemented the notion.

Right now that was exactly what I needed him to think. And fortunately, it was also what he wanted to think. If need be, I would be open to a bribe.

"Okay," I pretended to concede. "You've got me. What do you want?"

He breathed in and out as if with satisfaction. Then he laced his fingers in front of him on the desk.

"I have enemies, Ms. Beck. Mortal enemies, it seems."

"Plural?"

"So it seems. Are you going to ask questions, or are you going to listen?"

I waved for him to go ahead.

"You heard us toasting the company attorney at dinner."

I nodded.

"A grieving father blamed the anti-lock brake system made by one of my companies for failing to stop his daughter's car in a rainstorm."

"Should he have won?"

My blunt interruption shocked him. "No," he blustered. "Anti-lock brakes allow you to steer during a skid, but in the heat of the moment a surprising number of people steer themselves into trouble. Also," he raised his pointer finger, "little known fact—anti-lock brakes are better at saving the people in the car you hit than they are at saving you."

My eyebrows rose and fell. "Still worthwhile," I observed.

"Yes, thank you. They are."

"You said enemies, plural." *Did one of them happen to be your CFO?* "Do you expect other lawsuits like that?"

Frank Roitman's neck reddened. "One never knows, but I think not."

"And yet...?"

"The reason we returned home early is," he seemed very loathe to say more. "Let's just call it another business emergency."

His thoughts drifted off until I asked, "What does any of this have to do with me?"

He enjoyed another breath. "Chantal seems to think she was being shot at last night. She's so worked up that my wife fears she might lose the baby. Marsha was quite upset that you knew about that first, by the way."

"Sorry. What do you want from me?" I asked again.

"My enemies are cowards and quacks—amateurs. Where I'm from? Believe me. I know." He took a moment to reflect on his distant, apparently less-privileged past before resuming. "What are the odds last night's shooter even knew Chantal was there? Eh? He probably still doesn't know. So what was the point? To rattle me? Cause me to spend more money on protection? No." He jerked his head back and forth. "No. If somebody really wanted me dead, I would be dead."

I agreed with him to a point, but he lost credibility at "cowards and quacks." Amateurs committed murder all the time. Still, it wasn't my place to argue with the man.

"I'd like you to pose as Chantal's personal bodyguard," he said, finally getting to his point. "At least until she realizes it isn't necessary."

A fake job? Interesting. "You want me to get your daughter and your wife off your back."

"If you must put it that way, yes."

"And for this you'll pay me?"

He mentioned a weekly amount. It wasn't very much.

I suggested a figure that would make a decent dent in the down-payment for an apartment.

Frank tilted his head much the same as I did when I was being coy. "You have somewhere else to be?"

"Nowhere nearly as nice as this."

He smiled, so I inquired, "Are any of Chantal's other friends licensed to carry a gun?"

A staring grimace and a final retort. "We'll meet in the middle, but two weeks max."

"That works for me."

"No. You work for me, and please don't forget it."

I mentally crossed my fingers behind my back.

"What about Abby?" I inquired.

"Abby is not your concern."

"She seems to think you wouldn't care if she got kidnapped."

Now Frank looked piqued. "My younger daughter has a flair for the dramatic. If you've spoken to her, you know."

"Doesn't mean she's wrong."

"How dare you imply…"

"I assured her you would move heaven and earth to get her back. You've hired me to mollify Chantal, shouldn't you consider Abby's feelings, too?"

Pressed lips and a sigh. "What do you have in mind?"

"Get your bodyguards to drop her at school on your way to work and pick her up after." Surely the school had safety measures in place, but riding to and from could be a vulnerable time.

"I suppose they could do that."

"What about at home?"

"We have an excellent security system on site."

Considering last night's incident, I decided to look into that myself, if only to assure Chantal that I knew my job.

"Okay," I said decisively. "Will you tell Chantal about our arrangement, or should I?"

Roitman waved me toward the door. "Be my guest, Ms. Beck. Be my guest."

Irony intended.

Chapter 26

I tried to speak to Chantal before I left the house but was forced to leave a message with Lana, the castle dragon. Whether it would get delivered was a crap shoot, but short of tossing pebbles against Chantal's second-story window I didn't know how to connect with my new assignee in her very large home. I didn't have her cell phone number or even a hall pass, two details I would have to remedy ASAP.

Back in the pool house I did text Mike. "Update. Shot fired @ hse last nite. Cover blown, but all good. Roitman hired me 2 bodyguard Chantal. Lucky, eh?"

His return message was almost instantaneous. "You're welcome," was all it said.

I couldn't dial Karen's younger brother fast enough.

"What the hell does that mean?" I barked the second he said hello.

"You got to stay on, right? So you're welcome."

My neck and cheeks felt scorched. "You fired the shot?"

Silence.

"Tell me straight out, Mike. DID YOU FIRE THAT SHOT?"

"I don't have to answer that."

"The hell you don't. You better tell me what you did right now, Mike Stoddard, or, or…"

"Or what? I'll get coal in my stocking?"

I doubled over with exasperation. Then I spun around to try to calm my breathing.

"Knowingly or Recklessly Discharging a Firearm into or Towards an Occupied Structure is a 3rd degree *felony*,

Mike. Do you hear me? And how about Placing an Individual in Fear of Serious Bodily Injury or Death? Chantal was halfway up the walk between me and the house. The shot scared her half to death. She's still terrified. If it were up to me, I'd charge you with Attempted Murder and Total Stupidity. Seriously, dude. What were you thinking?"

"You're giving me a headache."

"Good. Now answer me."

Mike exhaled heavily. "Toby was not suicidal, Lauren. He loved his life, his wife, they just bought a new house..."

"Now you tell me."

"Dammit, Lauren. I'm trying to help."

"Help," I said as if I was thinking about it. "Please explain how taking a shot toward the house of a businessman, a businessman who happens to get death threats, help anything?"

"Frank gets death threats? Seriously?"

"Yes, Mike. He has a couple of thugs who escort him to and from work and a state-of-the-art security system here at the house." Probably. Haven't checked that out yet. If I ever figured out why the family dismissed the local cops, I might share that knowledge with Mike, but right now I needed him to stay away from his brother's in-laws and my investigation into Toby's death. *My investigation* and potentially *my hide.*

"I really don't get it, Mike. Please. Tell me, what were you thinking?"

He collected himself with another deep breath before he confessed. "I figured if something scary happened before you got sent home, you would, I don't know, volunteer to look into it."

"You mean me or Lori Ruggles?"

"What's the difference? I was your cover, so I thought you needed a different excuse to stick around."

He was right, sort of.

"I SWORE AN OATH," he shouted, imitating me. "Remember that?'

"Yeah," I mumbled grudgingly.

"Admit it, Lauren. It was only a matter of time before you came clean with the Roitmans. I just gave you a good reason to own up."

Good reason? GOOD reason! Unfortunately, I'd begun to see how his cockamamie idea made sense to him.

Still, I had to say it one more time. "It was a stupid, dangerous risk you took, Mike."

"For Toby," he said quietly.

"Yes," I agreed. "And Mary," I guessed. He hadn't fulfilled her expectations, and even though he couldn't tell her what he'd done, he needed to repair his self-image. I sympathized with that.

"Honestly, Lauren," he mused. "If you don't find out what happened to Toby, I don't think anyone ever will."

After I got him to promise not to do anything that risky again ever in his life, I quizzed him on the details. No, he hadn't driven the orange Mustang, he'd put mud on the license plate of his wife's hatchback. The gun was borrowed from a friend who managed a store that had been robbed a couple of times.

"Trusting friend," I remarked, thinking of the risk *he* took.

"I told him I wanted to try it out at a shooting range. You know. To see if I wanted to buy one of my own."

"You are so lucky I'm not still a cop. Now tell me what you were aiming at."

"The ground. I was afraid to get too close to the house, but I couldn't anyway because of the electric fence. I figured the noise would be enough for you to work with anyhow. Trouble was the gun kicked like a sonovabitch, so the bullet went further than I expected, maybe all the way across the pasture."

Thank goodness the horses were inside. "Your side of the trees?"

"Yeah, I think."

Now I really had a headache.

"How's Mary?" I finally asked.

She was bored being on bed rest, but things were looking good for the baby. "I'm learning to do laundry," Mike boasted. "Can you imagine?"

"Horrifying," I said, which seemed like an appropriate answer.

I put my hair in a long braid while my sneakers thumped around in the dryer I'd found adjacent to a sauna. When the machine finally stopped, a misleading silence swallowed the pool house, not unlike sunshine the day of a funeral or a car radio continuing to blare rap music after a fatal crash. Of course when has ambience ever reflected what's actually going on?

For sure, Mike's confession had started my headache and the thumping sneakers didn't help; but I'd missed lunch, too, and was now in the clutches of an anxious appetite.

Lana was nowhere in sight, but she must have relayed that I wanted to speak to Chantal because I found a note addressed to me on the kitchen table.

"Lori—,"it began. "Will drop by the pool hse after my nap. C. PS Lunch in fridge."

Good, good, and very good. Learning whether Mike was in danger of being found out was much more urgent than confessing my sins to Frank Roitman's daughter. Plus I could look into the estate's security system at the same time. And lunch. I really really needed lunch. Bologna and cheese never tasted so good.

Revived, I plodded down the lumpy path all the way to the barn. New clouds shadowed the fresh grass on the lawn to my right, and the deciduous trees yearned for rain to open this year's leaves. Horses nickered in the pasture where Mike had discharged his borrowed handgun, and swallows shot through the sky overhead.

Lyle Dickens was saddle-soaping an actual saddle slung over a split-rail fence when I arrived at the gravel parking area beside the big red barn. In daylight he looked to be about fifty, attractive in the chiseled way of a cigar-store Indian—beautiful and immoveable.

A damp breeze whistled through the pines that bordered the pasture and blew stray hair from my braid against my cheek. After I brushed it back, I wasn't sure what to do with my hands.

"Ms. Beck," Lyle greeted me stoically, which answered the question regarding my hands.

I stuck out my right one and said, "Mr. Dickens. Did you know my name last night?"

"Yes ma'am, I did." The hand he used to shake mine was hard and dry like his face. He wore an honest-to-goodness Stetson and a red and black buffalo plaid shirt under a denim vest. Right about then I envied him the flannel.

"And did you tell the police about me?"

"No ma'am. I did not."

I folded my arms across my chest. "And why would that be, I wonder?"

"My employer prefers that the people he hires to do a job, *do* that job."

"As opposed to the police?"

"It doesn't come up often, but when it does, that would be his preference."

"So why did he call them in the first place*?" Does the family have something to hide?*

Lyle consulted the arborvitaes. "Oh, lots of reasons. You were a cop. You tell me."

I ticked off my thoughts on my fingers. "In case a neighbor heard, in case somebody got shot, in case sometime in the future the shooter returns and takes better aim..."

Lyle Dickens's smile carved creases in his cheeks and made his moonstone eyes glow.

"Come inside," he said. "You look like you're freezing."

He led me to a normal door in the side of the barn that opened into living quarters. An elderly springer spaniel resting on the blanketed sofa lifted her head with mild curiosity, and the spicy smell of chili emanated from an alcove kitchen. I detected a whiff of horse, too.

"Stay, Chloe," Dickens told the dog, and she gratefully returned to sleep.

"Sit anywhere," he told me, "except on Chloe."

"Thanks."

I chose a cushioned rocker. Lyle parked himself next to the dog. A rustic pine coffee table littered with magazines and used chili bowls spanned the space between us.

"Frank sort of hired me. Did you know that?"

Lyle leaned his elbows on his knees. "I did not know that. And what, pray tell, will you be doing for Mr.

Roitman? Something commensurate with your previous employment?"

Not quite sure how to answer, I lowered my chin and looked at him askance. "Calming down his wife and daughter by pretending to be Chantal's bodyguard."

"Ah, pretending. Makes sense," Lyle remarked as if he knew I was intentionally being tactful. "Chantal still a bit nervy, is she?"

"It would be astonishing if she wasn't, don't you think?"

Lyle sucked his teeth.

"You have anything on last night's shooter?" I asked.

"Is that a pretend question or a real one?"

"Both."

"How so?"

Unconsciously, I clasped my hands together. "Pretend because, unless you have something, I think last night's shot is a dead end," Lyle's eyebrows flicked up, "and real because of the threats Frank's been getting."

"You psychic or do you know something about last night?"

"You first. Did your cameras pick up anything?"

The security man dropped his head. "I'm deciding whether or not to trust you."

I waited, and soon he met my gaze.

"Were you a dirty cop?" he asked in a way that insisted on an answer.

"Were you?"

"I was not."

"Neither was I."

"And yet you are no longer in Landis, Pennsylvania, maintaining law and order."

"That really isn't any of your business."

"Maybe. Maybe not."

It was my turn to decide whether to trust him, but what is life if not a series of risks?

"I left when I was diagnosed with Hodgkins disease. It was a long recovery, and for a number of personal reasons I chose not to go back.

"Your turn," I said. "Why are you here? Not that it's any of my business."

He snickered. "Same as you, I guess. Different details." He flicked a piece of dry grass off his knee. "Our cameras don't reach the far edge of the pasture, and I couldn't see much of the car 'cause the shooter didn't use lights. What've you got?"

"Nothing," I lied. "Can I see your system?"

"Anything to help you pretend." His eyes shot back at me as he rose.

Through a door situated next to his bathroom was a bank of screens focused on various parts of the house and outdoor property. Lyle flicked a hand toward the monitors. "Motion-sensored. I patrol in a golf cart during the day— the horses don't take much of my time and anyway there's a stable boy who helps out on weekends. Another two guys work four to twelve and twelve to eight." He meant the shift guys were also security.

"Gotta get your beauty rest."

"Yeah, right." His lips pressed into a sardonic line. "Course I was awake when whoever the hell it was fired the shot."

"Speaking of shots, you have an opinion about Toby Stoddard's suicide?"

We had backed out of the monitor cubicle and were gravitating toward the door to the driveway. Lyle stopped in his tracks with the question. I turned to face him.

"I guess he had his reasons." His fists found his hips and a hard sort of curiosity narrowed his brow.

"You're comfortable with the circumstances then?"

"I have no reason not to be."

"Were you told specifically not to take an interest?"

Lyle inhaled deeply. Took his time exhaling. "I scarcely have enough time to do what I've been asked to do. I don't need more."

"The horses," I remarked with a nod.

"The horses," he agreed. "How about you?"

"Not in my job description either."

"But...?"

"But I do have a personal interest in how Toby died."

"Care to share?"

"Maybe when we get to know each other better."

"Sounds good. Want to start now?"

I tucked my thumbs into the waistband of Karen's slacks and gave the weathered cowboy a slow smile.

Chapter 27

"Sorry," I told Lyle with a soft smile. "Chantal is probably looking for me."

"Come back when you can. I'll saddle up a horse for you."

"What makes you think I ride?"

"A farmer's daughter? No brainer."

Did he also know that, thanks to Brent W. Cahill, TV news anchor and ex-love of my life, I didn't care for beautiful men? Unlikely. Nobody could have gotten that in the two days since Captain George lifted my prints. P.S. Who was there to ask?

I started to take my leave with a girly wave but turned back at the doorway.

"The private things I told you were private, right?" It wasn't so much that I cared who knew, although some details were more private than others. At the moment I preferred to let Frank Roitman think he was right about me. If he, or anyone else in his family, happened to be guilty of murder, a disgraced cop would be less of a threat than a retired, honest one.

Lyle Dickens zipped his lips and tilted his hat.

Trust. You've gotta trust somebody. I hoped I'd picked the right person.

Speaking of trust, Chantal was leaning against the door to the pool house when I got back.

"You wanted to see me?"

"Yes." Not that I expected the conversation to be much fun.

When I motioned her into my temporary digs, soft afternoon light made the beachy living room prettier than any other place I'd stayed, yet without question I'd rather live in a drafty attic or a borrowed bedroom with somebody I loved around.

Chantal settled across from me on the blue ticking furniture. Well rested and composed, she seemed to expect nothing less than a healthy child, nothing more than an inconsequential conversation.

Regretting that I was most likely going to ruin her mood, I told her I had a confession to make.

"Oh?" Still the benign anticipation, the pleasant smile.

I opened my hands. "My name is Lauren Beck," I told her. "Karen Stoddard Beck is my sister-in-law."

The smile lost some of its luster. "I don't understand."

"Mike and I aren't really dating. He's a very happily married man. Very."

According to the wrinkles on Chantal's forehead, my deception was beginning to take effect. It would only get worse.

"I'm afraid Karen and Mike both have misgivings about your husband's death. And so do I."

Toby's widow drew in a raspy breath. "I still don't understand. Why would you...why did you pass yourself off as someone else?"

Interesting that she focused on that, as if murder over suicide had some appeal. The human mind never ceases to amaze.

"Because I was once a cop in Landis, Pennsylvania," I explained, "and cops there don't specialize. That means I covered all sorts of crimes—including murder. I thought if your family was aware of that, I might not be able to look into Toby's death." I would also win the top slot on the killer's hit list, but Chantal didn't need to think about that.

She blinked, shook her head. "The trip was just us," she realized. "Surely you don't suspect my family."

I waved that away. "I knew nothing at that point, Chantal. I just wanted to decide for myself whether Karen and Mike's fears had any merit."

"And now?"

Stalling, I patted my leg and blew out my cheeks. "I still don't have much," I admitted, "just the basic details and a few possible motives."

I might have told her the most likely scenarios involved her father's business; but since I still had no proof that a crime had even been committed, sharing those thoughts would have been premature, maybe even slanderous.

"The shot last night. Was it meant for me?"

"Unlikely," I answered. "I think you just happened to be outdoors."

"My dad then?" Her cheeks and neck had gone red, her breathing shallow.

I gave her a moment to settle down, then I said, "There are two kinds of angry people, Chantal, the ones who raise their fists and bluster but are too cowardly to do any real harm and the serious ones who lash out however they want.

"Last night's shooter fired once—badly—then fled, which seems to suggest that he scared himself more than he scared you. I doubt that he'll come back." A real looney, who knew? But this once I could make that statement with confidence.

Chantal's eyes narrowed as if her inner thoughts were unclear. Time to drop the other shoe.

"Speaking of your dad," I began. "He asked me to stay on awhile as your bodyguard. How do you feel about that?"

Laugher burst out of her. "You're joking, right?"

Part of me wanted to assure her I was not, but a corner of my brain reminded me of Frank's cavalier attitude toward his job offer. Unless he knew something he didn't care to share, I could only attribute his refusal to acknowledge the potential danger to his daughters to egoism or pure denial. He'd hired professional body guards to accompany him when he was out and about, a reasonable response to being threatened multiple times, attacked and injured once. Yet he considered the estate security sufficient for the women. Maybe he was right, but he might also be wrong.

Chantal's reaction made an honest response my only option. With a wry smile I admitted that Frank mostly wanted her and her mother off his back.

"How about you? Do you think I'm in danger?"

Since I knew very little about Frank's adversaries, I stalled by plucking at Karen's white slacks before I replied. "Sometimes we aren't frightened when we should be, and sometimes we're scared to death over nothing." I shrugged. "Tough to tell which is which. All we can do is be reasonably careful most of the time, and, if fear is disturbing our everyday peace of mind, do whatever it takes to feel safe again."

Chantal said, "Puh."

I gave her that. Then I said, "How scared are you? Scale of one to ten."

She rolled her eyes and huffed. "What will that tell you?"

"Whether you need protection 24/7 for your peace of mind."

"I thought my father hired you for that."

I shook my head. "No one person can do that job. He hired me to hold your hand."

"So…?"

"So you have to decide whether you want 24/7 security."

"If I had it, would I be safe?"

"Safer. You could eat bad shellfish or get hit by lightning anytime. Would you be safer in general? I really don't know."

Chantal's thoughts drifted.

When she was ready, she told me, "I'm at about five, maybe four. I'm pregnant, that's one thing. Stuff I never had to think about scares the hell out of me now. But do I think I'm going to be kidnapped or killed?" She lifted a shoulder. "I didn't until last night. You say that wasn't aimed at me, and I guess I believe you. I heard the shot, but the bullet didn't exactly whiz by my ear."

She thought some more before meeting my eyes in a contrite manner. "I guess I might have laid it on a little thick this morning, but some of that was for Abby. If Sykes—or anybody—wants to punish Frank Roitman, after Frank himself, Abby would be the most likely target. My father has to acknowledge that."

"Actually, he did. His bodyguards will be driving your little sister to and from school."

"That's…that's wonderful!"

"Please," I said. "Finish what you were saying about yourself."

The young widow wove her fingers together as if making a pact then lifted her chin for punctuation. "I don't mind you staying on," she said, "but I don't think I could tolerate that 24/7 idea."

"You're sure?"

"I'm not a child, Lauren. I know rotten shellfish and lightning happen."

From the moment Frank asked, I had always intended to protect Chantal from her father's enemies to the best of my abilities. My efforts might not be enough, but vigilance and a big helping of common sense were on my side. Now it seemed I had to do whatever I could without smothering Chantal or alarming her unduly. Girlfriends, talking about nail polish and salad dressing. Yup, that's us. But as Chantal pointed out, she was an adult, and I had to respect her position. Living in constant fear wasn't much of a life.

"You'll still be looking into Toby's death, right?" Her clasped hands seemed to be raised in prayer.

"If you're comfortable with it."

She surged forward so fast it surprised me. "Absolutely."

Heads or tails. Murder over suicide. The coin was in the air.

Movement outside the window had caught my eye—Abby running and stumbling down the brick path.

Now she was hammering on the pool house door.

Chapter 28

Frank succumbed to the lure of his city office soon after he finished with the state police regarding the gunshot incident. This left Marsha free to run her errand and return before he came home for dinner.

The safe in their walk-in closet had been disguised well, sunk as it was beneath a jigsaw-puzzlelike lid of matching oak flooring. Since she used the combination almost daily, it took thirty seconds to access a selection of her favorite jewelry, the square-cut ruby earrings and large matching ring, platinum settings, or so she thought; her diamond anniversary ring, a sapphire necklace, a gold bracelet studded with pearls and amethysts; a turquoise pendant surrounded by diamonds, and a few pieces more until her purse strap protested the weight.

The tennis bracelet in its small gray cloth bag, broken pieces included, was the last item in. Deciding whether to have it repaired could wait until her jeweler rendered his opinion.

Typically, she would have informed Lyle that she was going out; but considering the gunshot last night, the security man would have insisted on accompanying her. That, of course, would not do. Determining whether her husband was a shit-heel was not something you did with a witness in tow.

The drive to the nearby small town went quickly, focused as she was on what she would say to the jeweler. Hide her anger? Amplify it? Pretend to be determining her treasure's worth for insurance purposes? An acting opportunity for sure, but was it worth the effort?

Considering how often she stopped in to browse and drop hints, she regarded Mr. Ignatious as *her* jeweler. Frank was merely the go-between, the purchaser rather than the ultimate customer.

A diagonal parking space with money in the meter two spots from her destination buoyed her. Yes! She was decided.

Seeing her face, Mr. Ignatious tore himself away from an insipid woman in a mismatched plaid jacket. A glance from him completed the hand-off to his female clerk. Clutching her purse between two gnarled hands, the would-be customer blinked and sidled farther away.

"I need to speak to you privately," Marsha announced the second Mr. Ignatious stood before her.

The proprietor's eyebrows rose and lowered smoothly. "Follow me." He indicated the rear of the store with a sweep of his hand.

From experience Marsha knew she was being guided to a room for private showings just inside the door to the workroom.

"Thank you," she replied.

The jeweler's head tilted forward permanently, it seemed. His hands were bumpy and white, fringed with unusually long, curled black hair, his nails—buffed. He wore a gray-striped cotton shirt with a gray wool vest, perhaps to hide his almost skeletal thinness. Black slacks, black shoes. A tiny diamond stud dotted his left earlobe, an oddity for his age, which was approximately seventy-five, give or take half a decade. He did not wear spectacles, another oddity of his age that probably indicated successful cataract surgery.

After they were settled in comfortable antique chairs with an intimate, well-lighted round table between them,

Mr. Ignatious leaned in the way he might with a close, but not *too* close, friend.

"Mrs. Roitman," he said, since they hadn't exactly greeted one another. "Please tell me how I can help you."

Marsha shrugged out of her red, boiled-wool Chesterfield. "I...my tennis bracelet...here." She rummaged through her purse until she found the correct bag then handed it over.

The jeweler—*her* jeweler—poured the contents onto the mauve, tightly woven tablecloth. "Hmmm," he said. "It seems that we've had a bit of an accident."

"A...yes," was all Marsha could manage at the moment.

Mr. I's gaze lifted. "Wherever Frank got this, dear, it wasn't from me."

Since that was not anything Marsha had expected to hear, she couldn't think how to respond. Her mouth opened anyway.

"You're aware these are cubic zirconia, aren't you?"

"Suspected," she said with a dry mouth. "I suspected when, when I saw that those two little ones broke."

Mr. I looked at her askance. "Must have been hit with something very hard," he remarked.

"Chair leg," Marsha admitted. She didn't care to add that she'd added considerably to the impact.

"Not as strong as diamonds, these aren't, but it still takes a lot of pressure to break one." He waited to see whether she intended to expand on her story.

She did not.

"The gold," she wiggled her fingers, "is that real?"

"I'd say so, but the gems are definitely not gems."

"You can tell that without your loupe?"

"Brighter. Surprised you didn't notice yourself."

Marsha tossed her head as if to excuse herself. "They're so small," she said. *And I only use my reading glasses when I absolutely must.*

She tried to swallow. Remembered the rest of the jewelry she'd brought along. Dug into her purse and handed each drawstring bag over as if it were the ashes of a friend.

Mr. Ignatious required no instructions. He produced a loupe and methodically examined each piece. When he finished, there were two piles, as if two pirates had divided their booty.

"These are imitation stones," the expert informed their owner, dismissing the collection on the left with a gesture. "These are not," he remarked regarding the pieces on his right.

Marsha glanced back and forth between the two displays. The ruby earrings/ring set and the anniversary ring were legitimate, a great relief. The turquoise pendant circled by diamond chips was not, nor was the gold bracelet studded with amethysts and pearls. The fakes numbered six pieces in all, and it took but a moment for Marsha to realize they were her most recent gifts.

"If these were real stones," she thought aloud, "what would they be worth?"

"The workmanship is top notch," Mr. Ignatious admitted with a contemplative wave of his narrow head. Then he calculated for a long moment before delivering a number in the high six-figure range.

Marsha had to ask. "And their actual value?"

The number aspired to tickle the top of the five figure spectrum but did not achieve its goal.

Marsha had a new appreciation for the expression "kicked by a mule."

As she began to gather her non-Mr. Ignatious jewelry into their bags, another question occurred to her.

"These settings, are they real?"

"Oh, yes."

"So somebody replaced the real stones?" Marsha sounded confused because she was.

"Doubtful," Mr. I answered, rubbing his bony fingers against his chin. "Duplicating the stones well enough that you wouldn't notice would be awfully expensive. Most likely they were never real to begin with."

"Fake stones put into real settings."

"Yes. Done at the production stage, I'd say."

Marsha slouched back in her chair and gazed vaguely into the distance. "Who the hell would do that?" she wondered aloud.

Chapter 29

The instant I opened the pool-house door, Abby lurched inside.

"Hey, baby," her older sister cooed. "What's the matter?"

When that kid dressed down, she really dressed down—jeans with bald spots and holes, sneakers with neon orange laces, and a stretched-out aqua sweater wet with tears and other related excretions on the sleeve. I reached behind me for some tissues, and before I turned back, Chantal's maternal arms were muffling her sister's sobs.

"They're fighting," Abby sniffed as soon as she was allowed to breathe.

Chantal waved her head in dismay. Then she guided the two of them onto the nearest sofa, where they landed like one connected lump.

"Who?" I asked Abby just to clarify.

"Mother and Daddy."

"Dad's already home?" That seemed to shock Chantal more than the argument, almost as if it had never happened before.

Abby nodded, a bobble-head of a preteen with uncombed hair. "He came home early." Two damp, older-than-their-years eyes magnified by stylish spectacles assessed my reaction with a glance.

Arms folded across my waist, I scowled with the appropriate concern. Never mind that I had no idea what was going on; the sisters' distress had me riveted.

"What's it about?" Chantal urged. She still looked thrown, and I thought I understood why. From my time in their presence, I'd seen petulance when Marsha felt ignored and irritation when Frank was late for lunch, but behind that sort of complaint was flattery. Marsha thrived in her husband's company, literally glowed when they were together. I'd discerned nothing but a doting dependency on her part, so a fight volatile enough to make their youngest daughter cry had to be huge.

"Jewelry," she said.

Chantal's head snapped back. "They're fighting about that?"

"Um humm." Having secured our total attention, Abby began to relish her role in the drama du jour. The gleam in her eye and curl of her lip served as a drum roll.

"A bunch of it is fake," she announced.

All at once the confusing jewelry-store transaction I'd witnessed in Punta Cana made sense. The backroom item, the cash, the *extra* cash handed over with reluctance.

Chantal's eyelids nearly stretched to her eyebrows. "I really doubt…"

"It's true," the child insisted the way children do. "Mother took it all to Mr. Ignatious. That's how she found out."

Chantal's mind was off somewhere processing, so I used the opportunity to ask where Abby was when she heard.

"Behind the living room sofa next to the vacuum pipe."

"The what? Where?"

Chantal had returned to us. "Some of these old houses had a central vacuum system," she explained, "pipes in the walls that end in the basement. The maid attached a hose to a hole in the room's baseboard and cleaned the rugs with a lightweight sweeper. We don't use that system anymore."

"It broke," Abby supplied. "When I was little I used to hide behind the sofa. One day I found out I could hear what Mother and Dad were saying in their bedroom."

"Clever," I said, and the girl beamed.

"What else did you hear?" Chantal prompted.

"Daddy said he needed some money nobody else would know about. 'Off the books' I think he called it."

"Did he say what it was for?" Chantal again.

"Nope, and that made Mother *really* mad."

I should imagine. And did. Of the panoply of possibilities—drugs, gambling, adultery, etcetera—adultery was my personal choice for Frank. I'd have forfeited half my pay to hear him spin that whopper, but he had chosen to remain silent. It was a wonder Marsha didn't shoot him on the spot.

"I heard a big crash," Abby again, attempting to reclaim the spotlight.

Her sister wisely changed the subject. "Oh! Did Daddy tell you? His bodyguards are going to drive you to and from school."

The kid's face instantly went pink, and her hands rushed to her cheeks to cool them. "For real? You're sure?" She was indeed her mother's daughter.

Chantal eyed me for confirmation. "Absolutely sure," she answered. "Now. How about you and me go back to the house and get cleaned up for dinner?"

"That's way cool," Abby was still gushing as her sister deftly guided her toward the door.

"Make mine takeout," I called after them.

I wanted to go see a horse about a man.

The chestnut gelding and I made eye contact across about twenty yards of early spring grass. He worked his nostrils to check me out, twisted his ears, swished his black tail in anticipation of a bribe.

I'd brought the apple I'd nabbed from the kitchen, scored its circumference with a thumbnail, then twisted it in two the way my father taught me. Offering one of the halves on the flat of my hand, I raised an eyebrow and whistled.

From the back corner of the pasture two plodders—probably gentler rides for newbies or guests—caught a whiff of me and my treat but chose not to investigate any further. It would be the gelding and I or nothing, just as I hoped.

I stepped onto the middle rung of the gate and whistled again.

Playing hard to get, Red stared off at the swaying pines. A huff. A headshake. With his cocky bearing and mischievous eye, I put my chances at 60/40 that he would bolt. His prerogative, so I cut his thinking time short by swinging both legs over the gate and dropping into the pasture. When he shifted his feet with indecision, I showed him the second half of the apple and made sweet talk as I inched forward. "Easy boy. Com'on. You know you want it."

"Not as much as you do," Lyle remarked, and I jumped like a cat.

The security man put two fingers against his teeth and blew a loud, high note. "Hey, Bobbyboy," he called to the horse. "Over here, fella. Lady wants to give you that apple bad." Then to me, "That all you want?"

"A spin around the pasture bareback?"

"Sure. Just let me get some reins. Bobby'd just as soon smash your leg against the fence without 'em."

"Okay then," I said, backing up against the gate to wait.

When the bit was settled in the horse's mouth, Lyle threw the reins over his head. Then he laced his hands together to hoist me up.

The horse's coarse mane bunched in my left fist, the smooth reins wound between my right fingers, I kept Bobbyboy to a walk for the length of the field before heeling him up to a butt-bouncing trot—the best our limited space would allow.

When my smile muscles began to ache, I just plain bubbled over with laughter. This was pure joy, a happiness the likes of which I hadn't experienced in months, probably not since my brief affair with Scarp Poletta.

Ah, Scarp. He'd gone back where he belonged, back to the pleasantly neurotic Rainy McQuinn. His apologetic honesty had severed my last tie with Pennsylvania and made foisting myself on my brother and Karen ever so slightly easier. I missed how he wrinkled his crooked, busted nose, his granite thighs, his wit. But I knew he wanted his own kids, and with me he wouldn't have that option.

Someone else would come along for me. Maybe even the stoic cowboy over there grinning at my expense.

I eased Bobbyboy to a halt at the gate, slid off, rounded the horse's muzzle. "Whooph, thank you," I told Lyle, handing him the reins. Then I rubbed my butt and shook my head. "Now I remember why they invented saddles."

The ex-cop chuckled. "Give me a minute to get Bobbyboy settled. Meet you in the barn. There's beer."

I gave him a look that you might describe as direct. "That's okay. I'll wait for you."

Lyle appeared to think about that. "Okay," he agreed.

And so I watched from my perch on a hay bale as he put the three horses in for the night, fed and watered them, and throughout it all watched me watching him.

We didn't talk, but we smiled. Then somehow we segued into a more serious connection, an invited exploration of the other person's thoughts, both of us imagining that what we perceived was true. As I added this elusive new knowledge to whatever had allowed me to share my personal history with him, I realized my subconscious had made a decision and was daring my conscious self to catch up.

I won't say we "made love," but we did have a lovely roll in the hay with the thoughtful benefit of a plaid horse blanket in between.

"Hello Lauren Beck," said the cowboy as he lay inches from my face.

"Hello Lyle Dickens," I said as I rubbed the stubble on his chin with a thumb.

"You missed dinner," he observed.

"Any chili left?"

"Nope."

"Peanut butter and jelly?"

"Nope.

"And Bobbyboy ate my only apple. I guess we'll starve."

"Hell no. I told you there's beer."

"Damn!" I exclaimed. "Who's been watching the house while you've been…you've been…?"

"Tom. The first night man's name is Tom. Get decent. I'll introduce you."

"Oh no. Not without a shower. We both smell like horse."

"Good point. Tiny water tank though. We'll have to double up."

I rolled my eyes.

I never did meet Tom. After we cleaned up, separately mind you—both the water tank and the shower were tiny— Lyle and I arranged ourselves about a foot apart on the sofa and settled down to a dinner of Swiss cheese on crackers topped with sweet relish. Three prominent food groups plus all the calories of beer. Apparently cowboys do not do "lite."

After my two Corona Extras, I mentioned that Frank and Marsha had had a big fight this afternoon and asked Lyle whether he happened to know anything about it.

"Yep," he said after a generous swig. The dog Chloe sat at his knee, and he scratched her ears as he answered.

"Know what it was about?"

"Jewelry."

"That's what Abby told Chantal and me. The kid was really upset. How did you find out?" *so fast?* I wondered.

Lyle hesitated, but we'd chosen the route of honesty at the outset, so I suppose it seemed foolish to balk about the Roitmans' argument. "Tom had just come on duty," he admitted. "We both heard it."

I did a double-take. "You heard it? How?"

"Flip of a switch. If we don't like whatever's going on up there, we listen—briefly—to make sure everybody's safe. Marsha stomping upstairs with Frank chasing after her seemed like something we should check out."

"How long did you listen in?"

A look. "Long enough to decide it was none of our business."

"But you heard that Frank's been giving her jewelry with real settings and fake stones."

Lyle showed me a wry smile. "Guy's entitled to save a few bucks. If my wife…"

I waved my head to interrupt. "You missed the best part. He admitted that he needed some secret cash, but he refused to tell Marsha what it was for. Do you have any ideas?"

Lyle gave off scratching Chloe to rub his chin. "*Absolutely* none my business."

"For an ex-cop you really have a limited curiosity, don't you?" Words I regretted immediately. We all are entitled to our secrets. The permanent limp, the scars on his legs. Lyle hadn't shared the details, just told me in general terms that our stories were parallel.

"We're not cats, you and me," he remarked. "We're not gonna get eight more lives."

Chapter 30

Sunrise had whipped the air into a mean wind that sent elephant-size clouds running and tackled me the second I stepped out the pool-house door. Head down, hair swirling, I questioned my sister-in-law's every last word as I plodded up to the house for breakfast.

When I phoned her last night, Karen had said all the right things; but as soon as I hung up, I shredded my brain dissecting our conversation. Had she sounded happiest when we said hello, or when I explained that I needed to pick up clothes for an extended stay? When I asked how she was, had she used the same everything's-fine, nothing-to-report "Okay" she gave when I'd inquired about the kids? Or had it been the leave-me-alone hint of a person in mourning or the none-of-your-business dismissal of a wife about to leave her husband—the guy who happened to be my brother? I would find out today, and the worrisome possibilities had me nervous as all get out.

Lyle brushed by me with a wink as he exited the kitchen, the fragrance of bacon on his breath. I heard him whistling as he shambled down the walk toward the barn.

"No, no, the other way," Marsha corrected Lana across the room. Holding a large fork in her fist, she looked like an irritable Poisedon ruling the choppy household waters. To lower my profile, I sat.

The bacon fork got traded for a plastic spoon, which Marsha applied to scrambling eggs as if she alone were qualified to perform the chore.

"Oh!" Marsha exclaimed when she turned my way. "You missed dinner last night."

"Yes, I did. Sorry, Lana. I should have let you know." I'd leaned to the side to address the cook, who was nearly obscured by the larger woman.

Lana responded with her usual indifference.

"You planning on joining us tonight, Lori?" the mistress of the house inquired. "I beg your pardon— *Lauren.*" She cast me a look hot enough to rival the spitting bacon grease. "Nice little laugh you and Mike had at our expense, *Lauren.*"

Ah, the remaining white lie, the one that continued to hide my investigation into Toby's death.

"I'm awfully sorry about that. We only meant to have a little harmless fun."

"And how did that work out for you, dear?"

I took the reprimand in silence; Chantal was wandering in wearing a pink bathrobe and feathered slippers. She'd washed her face and combed back her hair, revealing the sallowness that sometimes accompanies pregnancy.

"Morning, Mom, Lana," she greeted the other two women.

"It's okay, Chantal," I said to help her out. "They know my name now."

"Oh, of course. Good. Good morning, Lauren," she said with a bow.

As Marsha replenished the bowl on the hotplate with her guaranteed-perfect eggs, she asked her daughter, "Will you and *Lauren* be back for dinner?" as if I were out of the room.

"We're not sure," I answered before Chantal had the chance. She blinked and stared but didn't contradict me.

My interruption forced Marsha to acknowledge me again. "Be sure to tell Lana," she ordered. "It's only polite, you know."

Polite, the way that insinuating your cook can't scramble eggs is *polite*?

"We will," I reassured both Lana and her nemesis.

Chantal and I met in front of the estate's five-car garage at ten. A rain shower had emptied the last of the clouds, allowing the strengthening sunshine to tease open some purple crocuses around the courtyard fountain. A high breeze still quickened the branches of the nearby pines, so crossing the Chesapeake Bay Bridge promised to be even less fun than before.

Chantal must have been thinking that, too, because she handed me the keys to a Mercedes sedan. "Do you mind driving? I hate that bridge."

"I was going to offer anyway. Bodyguard, remember?" I'd had some training in evasive techniques, but I couldn't use them if I wasn't behind the wheel.

For instance, if anyone intended to follow us, they would most likely pick us up soon after we departed, so I frittered away fifteen minutes turning left out of the property rather than right toward DC.

"This is how it's going to go?" my assignee inquired.

"Yup."

"Well, okay then."

An inevitable silence fell, so I took the opportunity to thank Chantal for not giving me away at breakfast.

"Giving what away?"

"Mike and me," I answered. "That we're not really a couple."

She tossed a hand. "My mother wouldn't have believed me, so why disappoint her?"

I smiled with relief. The Mike fiction was still the cover that protected me and my investigation, and it would end the second the elder Roitmans realized they weren't exempt from my scrutiny.

"One more thing. Your dad thinks I was forced off the Landis police."

Chantal suddenly jerked forward. "Really?"

"I left for personal reasons," I hastened to reassure her, "but I'd rather not tell your dad he was wrong. Nothing to be gained. Okay?"

Chantal locked her arms tight across her waist and stared out the front window, so I returned my attention to the road and the rear-view mirror. The driver of the white Honda SUV that had kept pace with us for a couple of miles hadn't taken either of the opportunities I gave him to pass.

"So Dad assumed you were a dirty cop, but he hired you to protect his darling daughter anyway. What a sweetheart."

Terrific. I'd just made her feel even less loved by her father than before.

"I left because…"

"No, don't," Chantal halted me. "It's your business, and I apologize on behalf of my goddamn shit of a father for making you think you have to explain."

"I don't want you thinking you can't trust me."

A glance showed me her pale brown eyebrows had lowered like thunderclouds. "Do you know why we all came home early?" she asked.

"Something happened at work."

"You bet your ass something happened at work. Another lawsuit—retirees claiming mismanagement of their pension fund."

I took that to mean the person or persons managing the fund had used questionable judgment that caused a frightening dip in the fund's assets. Probably nothing criminal, or legal steps would already have been taken. Still, a class action suit by the people dependent on those shrunken assets could be a major disaster for Roitman Industries.

Déjà vu all over again Frank had remarked to himself after the call that sent us packing. I'd felt sorry for the man. At least I thought I did, but that was before the "money off the books" information had emerged.

Chantal and I spent several minutes with our own thoughts after that, and a good thing, too. I was negotiating the streets of our nation's capitol, using an indirect route only partly from design. Roads under repair sent us out of our way. A wrong turn did the same.

Now and then a white SUV slipped in and out of my sight, but was it the same one? Midday reflections on the windows revealed only a hint of a driver behind the wheel, sometimes ahead of us, sometimes behind, once passing by us on a one-way street. Ultimately we would join the funnel that brought us to the mouth of "the scariest bridge in the world."

After that, I would definitely use some evasive moves.

And that gave me an idea.

Chapter 31

"Isn't the hunting lodge sort of on our way?" I hinted as a blue Ford slipped in front of us.

Chantal inhaled sharply before answering. "It's southeast. Your brother's farm is northeast."

"But is it doable?" Seeing the scene of the potential crime was Number One on my sleuthing To-Do list, but I'd been expecting to go on my own. That was before the responsibility of protecting Frank Roitman's pregnant daughter practically joined us at the hip.

I assured her the detour was entirely up to her. "It's just that we're close and…"

"Sure. If you think you need to see it."

Oh, I needed to see it alright, for so many reasons. Greatly relieved, I thanked her then inquired about a key.

"We hid one in case any guests get there first."

And how many people know about that? I wondered.

Meanwhile, the dreaded bridge was upon us. Chantal clutched the passenger door as if she thought it might fly off in the wind, while I settled the Mercedes in behind a smoke-choked pickup whose driver didn't have a snowball's chance of earning a checkered flag.

To distract us I asked what I expected to be a harmless question. "What's up with your mother and Svetlana?"

Chantal's head snapped my way. "What do you mean?"

Looming beside us were the wire fans of the eastbound span. Seagulls soared in the wind gusts swirling to our right. The pickup slowed even more, so I did, too.

"The dynamic," I answered. "I can't figure out if they like each other or not."

"Good question."

Really? As a conversational dead end, I thought it was right up there with nail polish, but Chantal stared at the passing scenery as if getting it right actually mattered.

"A little of both," she decided. "Lana came over from Belarus with one suitcase and a university degree, which, unfortunately, she can't use here. My mother..." Chantal paused to consider her words. "...She grew up on a rented farm that 'couldn't support a flock of crows.' Her words. Once she got so hungry she ate some of the neighbor's carrots right out of the ground."

I could see where Chantal's love/hate assessment was probably right. Her mother's jewelry obsession, her attitude toward me, the symbiotic relationship with Lana all added up. If Marsha was terrified of becoming poor again, Lana's presence would keep that fear sharply in focus.

As for Lana, being grateful for food on her plate and a roof over her head seemed perfectly compatible with hating the snide, controlling dictator her boss seemed to be ninety percent of the time.

A fist of wind punched the side of the Mercedes and jostled us toward the left lane. As a result, the pickup truck over-steered toward the rail. Only slightly, but the sudden movement made my stomach lurch.

The smoky pickup slowed even more, so much more that the vehicle behind me actually honked. Jeez. Nothing I could do. The lane to my left was clogged with Richard Pettys.

Way below us the seagulls had become white dots that resembled ripples on the blue-gray bay. I gave Chantal's silence a glance. She was biting her thumb, thinking her thoughts.

"Dad got another death threat at the office," she informed me, and I thought I detected a smug pleasure in the statement, as if others inflicting pain on her father relieved her of the need to do it herself.

Just what I needed—something else to think about.

The left lane finally presented an opening, so I used it to pass the stinky pickup.

A white SUV eased in behind me.

Great! Just *great.*

To deal with the overload bombarding my brain, I resorted to an old Silva mind-control trick. I pinched my middle finger and thumb together and counted down 333-222-111 in my head. The calm clarity I needed was far from guaranteed, but I liked the idea of doing something positive for a couple of seconds.

Chantal simply gazed out the window toward the sky.

We completed the bridge ordeal in silence.

At the second turnoff after the bridge I pulled a quick right, but so did the white SUV.

"This isn't..." Chantal protested. "Oh, another...did you see something?"

I didn't reply, just steered into an office parking lot, continued around to the back of a huge brick building, and stopped in the middle of the driveway.

Three-three-three, two-two-two...

The white SUV continued out of sight.

I put the Mercedes in Park before revisiting a serious question. "Tell me again where you are with this bodyguard idea. Are you really on board?"

"No, not really," Chantal finally admitted. Our eyes met and locked. "I guess I should be, right?"

"Eyup," I told her.

"Because...because my dad..."

"Is pissing off lots of people. And because..."

"…because my husband is dead."

Having promised myself not to state the obvious, I held my tongue. So proud.

"What were the last things Toby said about his work?" I prompted. "Anything about a disagreement? About the lawsuit? About…I don't know…"

Chantal burst into tears.

Waiting out her emotions, I scanned our surroundings. Raised stainless steel lettering labeled the place as a medical building. Bushes in a decorative clump on either side of a wide rear entrance rustled in the chilly air. While Chantal sniffled and sobbed, an elderly woman holding the arm of an even more elderly man exited, an ordinary occurrence but nothing Chantal would ever get to do with her husband. The crying lasted a while.

When at last it subsided, I assured the young widow she could get back to me about Toby and the business. Then I handed her my smartphone. "How about putting the cabin into the GPS for us? I think I've screwed up your directions."

Four miles later we stopped for lunch, choosing a family diner over a hamburger chain because the parking lot was fuller. Chantal ordered waffles and sausage; I ordered the chicken pot pie special and regretted every bite.

"Who was there?" I inquired after requesting the key lime pie, another risk this far north but fortunately one that paid off.

Chantal met my eyes over her thick white mug of herbal tea. She knew perfectly well I referred to the night Toby died. Nothing else was on either of our minds this close to the cabin.

"You really believe he was murdered, don't you?" she said with grim resignation.

I lifted a shoulder, glanced at the ceiling. Waited.

"Everybody was there," she answered as she set down her drink. "Gavin, me, Toby, Mom, Dad, Abby. Dad's birthday comes during light-goose season, so we always have his party at the lodge. It's a family tradition."

"You said everybody. Was Gavin's girlfriend there too?"

"Oh, no. God forbid."

Right. God forbid.

"You mentioned the key to the place is available for other guests. Was anyone else expected?"

"Not this year. Dad's people had just celebrated the lawsuit win, an impromptu thing that got out of hand and lasted well into the night. Mother suspected everybody probably had enough of each other for a while."

"By 'Dad's people' you mean the Roitman Industries management team?"

"Yes. My guess is most of them were delighted to skip the hunting party. Not too many business types are into shooting geese, and anyhow who wants to be on their best behavior on their time off?"

"Not the bonding experience the weekend was supposed to be?"

"Exactly."

Of course, if light-goose season stuck in your memory, as it would now stick in mine, and if you happened to remember directions to the Roitmans' hunting lodge and had a pressing reason to kill the CFO...

"There." Chantal alerted me to an arrow-shaped board pointing to the right. It's fading white letters said "Chinook Acres."

"Why Chinook?" I asked.

She shrugged. "I think maybe the previous owner had one of those Chinook dogs."

The crushed stone lane, rutted and pocked by former puddles and littered with detritus, meandered into a woods ready and eager for spring. Squirrels foraged for acorns they'd planted last fall beneath underbrush blooming with fresh, almond-shaped leaves. Above, the oak trees were tipped with swollen red buds ready to burst.

I took it all in with an eye toward sneaking up on the Roitman's lodge. Way back at the road I'd noticed a half-moon clearing large enough for one vehicle, but considering the woodsy surroundings a parked car or truck probably would be remembered.

Walking in from the road was also rife with hazards. Toby's death had occurred well after dinner, so an intruder who didn't want to risk a branch in the eye or tripping and breaking a limb would have needed a flashlight. Between what seemed like thousands of tree trunks were rocks laced with moss. Pine straw and leaves obscured runoff ditches you could spot in the daylight but probably not at night. Tramping through sticks and leaves and underbrush wouldn't exactly be quiet either. Even the lane had drawbacks—potholes, open exposure, and distance, for we'd driven easily half a mile already and I still hadn't spotted a building.

"Turn left," Chantal ordered suddenly.

"Where?"

"Between those two trees. See it now?"

Barely visible was another small board shaped like a shotgun nailed to a tree. Since Chantal chose to mention the trees rather than the firearm, I worried once again how returning to this place would affect her.

A quarter mile later we finally arrived, and I have to say I was underwhelmed. Built of logs, the one-story structure spread across a clearing of about half an acre. The lichen-laced cedar shake roof had grayed and curled with age. All the windows were simple squares edged in "hunter" green. Cordwood stacked between two pines had been winnowed down to a low pile shaped like a camel's back, a clue that a fireplace was a primary heat source. The absence of electric lines suggested that one of the small out-buildings housed a generator, and three large propane tanks seemed to confirm my guess. Ankle-deep leaves blown against the door told me no one had been here in a while, perhaps not since light-goose season.

Chantal climbed out, slammed the car door, and hugged herself. Trying not to interrupt the internal adjustment she appeared to be making, I closed my own door with extra care.

As soon as I could, I asked the whereabouts of the key. The ground was musky-damp and the air crisp. We could think our thoughts just as well indoors.

As expected, the key hung on a nail on the cabin side of the nearest tree, a convenient five feet from the doorknob.

Chantal led me into a kitchen Daniel Boone's mother might have admired, but probably not Lana and certainly not Marsha. Linoleum countertops in beat-up yellow, the interior wall papered with yellow wallpaper resembling tiles sporting red roosters and whitish chickens, a dulled stainless steel sink, a white oven topped with thick black burners, a once-white refrigerator with rounded corners, an ancient Starbucks coffee can sprouting spatulas and spoons on the four-foot long prep counter—it was old to the point of being unsanitary. I could envision cans of Dinty Moore stew being opened and heated but very little real cooking.

I felt Chantal watching me. "You look shocked," she remarked.

"Sorry. I guess I am."

She nodded as if she once felt the same. "Poor Lana. This is the only place my mother leaves her alone." Hearing that Chantal didn't care for Marsha's interference any more than I did made me warm to her even more.

We proceeded into a long room almost blocked off by a lengthy mahogany dining table. Although it once may have been somebody's prized antique, now it was quite beat up and surrounded by a dozen neglected chairs sporting a fan design on the backrest.

The farther part of the room was defined by a narrow storage cabinet supporting a lamp featuring a ceramic duck. Next, a U of three brown leather sofas faced a stone fireplace large enough to roast a beast on a spit. A couple of trite hunting prints moldered on walls covered in water-stained wallpaper.

Inside the lodge felt only marginally warmer than outside, and a whistling draft seeping in from a screened porch (presently storing lawn furniture) wasn't helping. As soon as Chantal seemed ready to talk about the here and now, I would ask her permission to light a fire. In the meantime I made do by tucking my fingers deeper into my pockets.

Beyond the porch lay a patio (I think) and some open space sloping down to a lake about three times the size of the lodge's footprint. A crow squawked from the top of a naked oak, and others answered back from the woods. I couldn't tell from their voices if they were warning each other or inviting their friends to a late lunch.

Chantal crooked a finger to suggest I follow her down a back hall to the right of the fireplace.

Several bedrooms on either side contained twin beds except for a slightly larger room to the right. Two bathrooms faced each other across the center of the hall. At the end we turned right, passed a linen closet and another bedroom and four strides later faced the infamous gun room.

Chantal waved a hand at it like a reluctant tour guide. "I think this is what you want to see," she said, "but there really isn't anything left."

Except for the sensation that something repellant had happened here, the eight-by-eight room was practically empty. A barred and padlocked display case of shotguns hung on the left-hand wall, and a formidable black safe sat back in a corner. No curtains covered the barred window that faced the direction of the road. The knotty-pine paneling had been cleaned within an inch of its life, and the floor lacked anything but the lightest coating of dust.

Chantal had slouched against the doorjamb, and I joined her respectfully on the other side. If we'd been sisters, we might have held hands. I monitored her face for a second, discreetly I hoped, and saw a sorrow that seemed to come from her very bones. But no tears. Thankfully, no tears.

"Can you talk about it?" I asked.

She blinked before meeting my eyes. "Isn't that why we're here?"

That was when I got it. She had only come to assuage my suspicions. Had I not offered an alternative to Toby deliberately leaving life—and her—she would never have stepped foot in here again.

"Yes," I answered, and so we began.

Chapter 32

"What's the combination for the cabinet?" I asked as Chantal and I stood fixed in the doorway of the gun room. We'd started the information ball rolling, and I wanted to get as many answers as I could before Niagara Falls resumed again.

"Dad's birthday," she admitted with a wince, because now the day would always remind her of her husband's death. The date would also be easy for the hunting guests to remember and scarcely a chore for anybody else to guess.

"Who cleaned out the room?" Whoever it was not only eliminated any trace of Toby's demise, they also removed every bit of furniture.

"A company that specializes in…in jobs like this. The sheriff recommended them."

"There must have been furniture, right?" At least a chair.

"Sure. A table in front of the window, an old wooden chair, a lamp, a rug."

More detail would have been helpful, such as which way Toby had been facing, the position of the body after death; but I might be able to get that information another way.

With little else to do I went over and jiggled the window. Nailed shut, and all the glass panes were evenly etched a dirty white/gray by years of rain. Nobody had broken directly into this room.

"Tell me more about the evening. Anything strike you as odd?"

Chantal shrugged. "Dad got drunk."

"He doesn't usually?"

"It's rare."

"Why that night? Any guesses?"

Here Frank's oldest daughter balked.

"What?" I prompted.

"Toby and Dad exchanged a couple of looks I didn't understand."

"Ah. And Toby didn't say anything to you that might explain the…what was it? Tension?"

"Not tension exactly. Discomfort? My father's a brilliant businessman, but he's also a hardheaded SOB, and it wasn't Toby's job to always tell him what he wanted to hear."

"For example?"

"Oh, maybe Dad was all hot to buy some company Toby thought was a dog, or sometimes he had to tell Dad one of the subsidiaries wasn't performing up to expectations. Stuff like that. That's really all I thought was going on."

So maybe being Frank's son-in-law and closest advisor wasn't such a lucky coup after all. Maybe Toby was performing for an audience of critics eager for a trapdoor to open under his feet. *And maybe he got tired of it.*

"Know of anybody who was rooting for Toby to fail?" *Your brother, for instance?*

A wry laugh. "Sure," she said. "Absolutely. But if they did anything to undermine Toby, they were really undermining Roitman Industries; and if Dad caught wind of that, they would have been fired."

Right. Disgruntled ex-employees equaled suspects. When the time came, I would request a list.

"Your brother?" He was already on my list.

"No. Oh, no. He and Gavin got along. They even invested together now and then."

"Any idea how that worked out?"

Chantal shut her eyes and shook her head. "Up and down, I guess. I don't really know."

I pointed my chin toward the nearest bedroom, the last one before a tiny bathroom and only half a dozen feet from where Chantal stood. "Who slept over there?" I wondered.

"Abby usually. It's got that little bathroom, but mostly it's away from the adult's late-night shenanigans."

My heart clenched hearing how close the eleven-year-old had been to the shotgun blast.

Although now that I thought of it, the child exhibited surprisingly few outward symptoms of trauma. The resilience of youth? Exposure to TV violence? Those books she reads? A top-notch therapist? Whatever it was, I was glad for the girl.

If only I'd recovered from *Brent W. Cahill's* reaction to my cancer diagnosis so well. I can still see his perfectly photogenic face turn away, watch the roll of his clenched jaw in the candlelight, follow the movement of his closed eyes as he previewed the rest of his life with—or without—me.

"I can't," he announced, standing so suddenly the chair from the bistro set in my attic apartment crashed to the floor. Breath coming in short, greedy gulps, he looked like a captured animal frantic for escape. I loved the man, but suddenly he frightened me.

"Please," he said extending his hand.

Please what? What did he want?

When I failed to respond, he curved his fingers in a come-on gesture.

Finally, I got it. His right hand had been signaling to my left, obscenely demanding that I return his ring.

In time I understood that breaking our engagement was the best thing he could have done for me. Yet in the four years since that awful night I've only had half a dozen second dates.

I eased past Cantal to check the adjacent bathroom's window, another possible entry. It had a lever type of lock that moved as if it had been opened many times. Of course, with no exhaust fan in the room that made sense.

Chantal shuddered from the cold, reminding me of my vow to light a fire ASAP. She readily agreed, which bode well for satisfying my curiosity. We would need to stay long enough for the fire to burn itself out.

"I'm sorry, but I don't know how to get one started," Chantal admitted. "Do you?"

"Farm girl," I said. "Piece of cake."

I moved the empty grate aside and used the poker to check for a cinder depository. And there it was, a metal plate in the back of the hearth that pivoted open.

As I began to sweep ashes into the hole, something clinked. I swept it toward me on the gray slate hearth, brushed away the ashes, and picked it up. It was a J-shaped piece of lightweight wire about two inches long. Rubbing it revealed a hint of pink and dirtied my fingers with sticky goo.

Was it important? Hard to say, but I was curious why someone had thrown it into the fire.

Behind me Chantal stretched and yawned. "Lana," she suddenly exclaimed. "I remember now. Lana stayed in the back room that night. Dad snores when he's drunk, so Abby and my mother slept in that green side room together."

Mention of the Roitmans' cook made me realize what I'd found was a knitting tool. I'd seen Lana using one to make a cable up the sleeve of the yellow baby sweater.

Since the hook was sticky—maybe with birthday cake or toasted marshmallow—Lana must have set it aside and reached for another or, depending on her mood, tossed it into the fire herself. Either that or somebody who didn't know what it was couldn't find a wastebasket.

The only way to satisfy my overactive curiosity was to return it to its owner. However, putting the sooty, sticky item in my pocket would cause me—or Karen—a laundry problem, so I stuck it in a sandwich bag I found in the kitchen and stashed it in my purse.

Naturally, thinking of my sister-in-law and laundry summoned up my anxiety about how Karen and Ron were getting along and how soon I needed to move out. I admit I was grateful to delay those answers a few hours longer.

By the time I'd brought in kindling and extra logs, built the fire, opened the flue, lit the kindling, waved a lighted twist of newspaper up the chimney to start a draft, and replaced the fire screen, Chantal was half asleep under a fleece comforter.

I disturbed her only long enough to tell her I was going outside for a while.

The solid log exterior revealed no signs of forced entry into the "lodge," a description that flattered what was essentially a clubhouse for overgrown boys. I could not for the life of me imagine Marsha here. Deciding which jewelry went with a sweatshirt and jeans must have been agony.

Two outbuildings had been plunked down at the edge of the clearing, strategically away from the sightline to the lake. Both of plywood siding, they seemed to be recent additions, perhaps only twenty years old or so. One had a window I couldn't see through; but with two vents under the eaves and propane tanks flanking the far side, I assumed it housed the generator and possibly some tools.

The other was about six feet by eight. Its double doors were trimmed with white Xs like a barn. I fiddled with the padlock for a few minutes, but I didn't know Frank's birthday so I had no luck getting inside. Maybe when Chantal woke up.

For a few minutes I stood listening to the woodsy noises—the breeze through the high branches, the squirrels crunching across last year's leaves, the squawk of ducks as they landed on the little lake. Silver ripples formed Vs behind the water fowl, a fleeting, beautiful sight. I was pleased nobody was around to shoot at them.

Back inside Chantal's sleeping face remained a smooth canvas of contentment, her eyelashes twitching with what I hoped was a pleasant dream.

I added a few logs to the fire. Then I took my phone into the kitchen where I'd noticed a ragged phone book in a drawer. The book had expired years ago, but the non-emergency number I needed probably hadn't changed.

"Sheriff's office," answered the dispatcher. "How may I direct your call?"

I explained that I was "former police" and that I was "only in the area for the afternoon." Then I asked if it would be possible for me to meet with the sheriff.

As if he'd been right there listening, the gentleman himself came on the line.

"Seth Troxell here. Former police? What's that mean? Retired?"

The melodic, virile voice came across as curious rather than hostile, so I allowed myself to laugh.

"Not even close," I replied. "I left for health reasons. If you want a reference, I can give you a number." Since Troxell had signed off on Toby's suicide, revealing that

Scarp Poletta worked Homicide might have tilted the scale toward hostile, so I skipped that part. That I'd had a brief affair with the guy was also irrelevant.

"First things first. Why do you wish to speak with me?"

I filled him in on my connection to Toby Stoddard and explained how I'd been hired to protect his widow.

"From?"

"Unclear. That's why I need to talk to you."

While Troxell connected the dots, I imagined a rugged but kindly man chewing his lip and furrowing his brow. I convinced myself that he carried himself like a portly rooster and all his employees but one, who clearly had ego issues, loved him. Especially endearing were his glasses, which he knew perfectly well were way, way out of style but couldn't care less. I fervently hoped I wasn't going to ruin his day.

"You have anything that's going to cause me more paperwork?"

"Not yet." Not for sure.

"Do I hear a 'but' at the end of that statement?"

"Yessir, you do."

"Damn. Gimme that reference you talked about, will you? I gotta pick up my granddaughter pretty soon, and I promised her ice cream. You know where Hubbard's is?"

I recited Scarp Poletta's cell phone number from memory. Then I admitted the only place I knew in this area was the Mom and Pop diner where Chantal and I had eaten lunch. Troxell gave me easy directions from there, and we agreed to meet in twenty minutes.

The note I left for Chantal promised take-out ice cream upon my return.

Chapter 33

"So, Ms. Lauren Beck, why are the Roitmans suddenly dissatisfied with their son-in-law's suicide?"

The county sheriff's large hands surrounded his untouched cup of chocolate ice cream, while his eyes discreetly monitored his granddaughter. Holding her cone like a bouquet, the four-year-old tiptoed pretend "moose tracks" in and out through the dozen pink, mostly occupied, honest-to-goodness ice cream parlor tables and chairs. Lively and blonde, she looked like a Disney child, round-faced and wide-eyed and perfect, and I suspected that picking her up early from daycare was a favor to Troxell's quite likely cash-strapped, single-parent daughter. That he did it personally suggested he was divorced or widowed himself and that his daughter and grandchild might even live with him. All speculation, of course, but connecting such dots was a habit I've never been able to kick.

"Not the Roitmans," I admitted. "The death threats against Toby's father-in-law make my nose itch."

Troxell sighed and poked his melting ice cream with a pink plastic spoon. I'd gotten the paunch part of his appearance right and the glasses, but his real face was all bulldog folds and caterpillar eyebrows. He hadn't removed his tan uniform hat, but with little Devon's random wandering and me pretty much accusing his office of muffing a murder he might have forgotten the thing was still on his head.

"What else you got?" The intensity in his eyes warned me my answer had better be good.

"Stoddard's wife is pregnant and, even though it was early-on when her husband died, Chantal insists they both knew."

Troxell's stare said *So what?*

"Plus they bought a larger house." Even to me my argument sounded flimsy.

The sheriff poked his ice cream so hard I almost said ouch. "The threats. What are they about?"

I filled him in on the failed lawsuit regarding the young woman who died in the car crash. "Plus there's a brand new lawsuit claiming mismanagement of a Roitman subsidiary's pension fund. Plenty of people are angry about that."

"So you're being paid to protect his oldest daughter, whatsername." He waved his spoon. "Chantal. Aren't you stretching your job description a little thin?"

"It pays to be careful, don't you think? If killing Roitman's CFO was a message directed toward Frank, what's to stop the sender from hitting him even closer to home?"

"Grandpa!" Having completed her circuit, Devon slipped a hip onto Troxell's leg.

He pulled her onto his lap without a thought for her dripping cone—or the nature of our conversation.

"Or, what if Toby Stoddard knew something he shouldn't, and the *disgruntled person* is afraid his wife knows it, too?"

Troxell bounced his granddaughter to a better balance on his thigh. "How about this? What if the suicide ruling is correct and nobody wants to touch a hair on Chantal's head?"

"I would go home happy."

Troxell sent a glance to the ceiling and slid me an oblique smile. "All I want in the world is to make you go home happy." Then he concentrated on spooning chocolate soup into his mouth.

"You going to humor me, or not?" I asked.

Devon had begun to poke the curly hairs sticking out of her grandfather's ears.

"Stop that, Sweetie," the sheriff said then wiped his lip with the back of his free hand.

"I'm here, aren't I?" he told me.

"Yessir, you are. Anything interesting in the trace evidence you gathered at the scene? Hair, fibers, fingerprints?"

Troxell's visage hardened, and an awkward silence stretched. Bored, Devon wriggled free, only to descend upon an even smaller boy, who drew back in terror.

"Well?" I pressed now that we were without an audience.

The sheriff made a sucking noise. "Remind me why I'm telling you anything."

"Because getting at the truth usually involves some give and take."

Troxell rolled his eyes in a way he probably thought wasn't obvious. "The trace evidence mostly belonged to family members."

"Mostly."

"The Roitmans often entertain guests there. We believe the non-relative prints and material belonged to them."

"Fair enough," I agreed just to be nice. "It was a, um, sudden death, so I assume you took pictures."

"Yes," Troxell replied, and I thought I detected a slight blush brightening his deeply creased cheeks. "Actually, the cleanup company I recommended to the Roitmans did the photos."

"Because it was an obvious suicide."

"Yes. I mean, no. We've used Warren and Son for years. Pete Junior is quite good with a camera. Knows exactly what we need."

"And it was an obvious suicide anyway." My smile aspired to be generous, but it felt a little tight.

"Right," Troxell replied without looking my way.

"So may I see them?"

Another stalling cluck before he said, "Sure."

While he recited Warren and Son's number and I put it in my phone, I tried not to grind my teeth.

"One more question." Troxell had stood and begun to head for his granddaughter. He wasn't pleased about turning back. "Were there any sedatives in Toby Stoddard's bloodstream?"

The sheriff stuffed his hands into his pants pockets and eyed me like a bug that was about to meet his shoe.

"Yes, Ms. Lauren Beck, ex-officer from Landis, P A, there was one, which I assume an ex-officer from Landis P A would know is not uncommon for a suicide."

"Thank you," I said with sincerity because he'd just saved me a whole bunch of trouble finding that out. Also because we both knew if my investigation—unofficial or not—turned up any damning evidence, I would be causing him a whole bunch of trouble, not to mention embarrassment.

He and little Devon departed hand-in-hand, and I threw his scarcely touched ice cream in the trash on my way to the counter.

My intuition and I were feeling pretty good about ourselves right about then—not smug, we were a long way from knowing what happened to Toby Stoddard, but I was encouraged enough to reward my inner self with a double scoop of Rum Raisin.

Chantal fell on her container of Fudge Ripple like a teenage boy who'd missed his last meal. I'd chosen the safer flavor because I didn't know her ice cream preferences and, in my experience, Rum Raisin melts too fast for take-out.

While I was gone she must have shifted into yet another phase of grief because she seemed more subdued, distracted, and bone-crushingly morose than I had previously witnessed. I'd expected being where Toby's soul had departed to have an effect, but I hoped it would be a salutary and necessary one. For sure, whatever she was experiencing was private. When I excused myself to call Warren and Son, she didn't even spare me a glance.

Still, I stepped out into the driveway to use my phone, partly because the signal was better, and partly to protect Chantal from the content of my call.

"Warren and Son," a warm, male voice said with the appropriate mix of friendliness and concern. "Pete Senior at your service."

I introduced myself, mentioning that Sheriff Troxell had given me their number. Then I briefly explained my Stoddard/Roitman connections, adding that I got my current bodyguarding job "because of my police training."

"Okay," Warren said tentatively.

"I'm familiar with the sort of work you do…"

The business's founder laughed. "That helps. Not many people are."

I smiled to myself. "Not until they have your sort of problem."

"Very true. What do you need?"

"I know when the Roitmans hired you to clean the gun room, they asked you to dispose of the furnishings. Where did they end up, if I may ask?"

"We send anything the family doesn't want to an auctioneer. Wasn't much in this case—a table, a couple of chairs, a lamp. Oh, and an oriental..." Pete Senior held the receiver away and shouted, "Andy, what did you do with the Roitman's rug?"

"Forgot about it, to tell you the truth," came the near-distant reply.

The boss grunted. Then he mentioned that they used a high-end carpet specialist to clean expensive orientals. Again to the employee, "Where is it now?"

Andy must have moved closer, because I heard his answer clearly on speaker-phone. "Still in the shed, I guess. The weather was below freezing back then, so...."

"Was it dry or wet when you rolled it up?" I inquired.

"Already dry," Andy admitted. "Pete Junior met the sheriff there to take photos, but we couldn't do anything else until the undertaker came. The Roitmans left right after that, but in the meantime we got an emergency puff-back call, furnace soot everywhere and a family of seven waiting to get back in..."

"We figured the Roitman job could wait another day," Warren Senior abbreviated for me.

"Makes sense."

"Yeah, and then my van broke down before I could pick up the rug," Andy added. "Didn't get it back for two weeks. Probably why the rug just plain slipped my mind. Sorry," Andy threw in for Warren Senior's benefit.

Another grunt. "Don't you worry," the boss told me. "We'll pick it up today, right Andy?"

"Right on it."

"No! I mean no rush now." How could I examine what was probably the only remaining piece of hard evidence regarding Toby Stoddard's death if they rushed over and took it away?

"It's okay. We'll be right there."

"No, please. Chantal's having a tough day. Let's not make it any harder. Anyhow, it's not that important."

Not much it isn't.

Chapter 34

As soon as I disconnected with Warren and Son, I ran—
ran—back into the house.

I was about to shout for Chantal to tell me how to open
the shed's padlock, but I stopped just in time. The last thing
she needed was to see that rug again, and the last thing I
wanted was her watching me examine it.

"Chantal," *honey, baby*, I wanted to say like a lover
with an agenda, "do you happen to know the combination
to the lock on the shed?"

The young widow's head rested on the arm of a sofa
facing the fire. Her legs stretched out under a blue fleece
throw, and her hands rested gently on her abdomen.
Nothing else going on but whatever was on her mind. "Did
you try Dad's birthday?"

"Didn't know it." My face would have given away my
eagerness, so I kept myself safely out of sight in the
kitchen.

She gave me the numbers, then added, "If that doesn't
work, try my mother's, April twentieth," and then a year
Marsha Roitman probably wouldn't care to have anyone
remember.

I was back in the kitchen five minutes later. "How
about your parents' wedding anniversary?" Other than his
wife's birthday what date was a man never supposed to
forget?

"August seventh." The time elapsed coincided closely
with Chantal's present age, but who cared about that
anymore? I thanked Chantal and exited quickly, but quietly.

The anniversary date worked.

A funky, earthy smell wafted over me as soon as I tugged the right half of the door open. The left was fixed in place by a sliding bolt that poked into a small hole in the floor. I blamed mice for some of the fustiness, the rolled up carpet for much of the rest. Old blood, after all, might as well be spoiled meat.

Leaned upright against some shelves, the rug was between seven and eight feet tall and, rolled up, about a foot in diameter. The underside showed that wool yarn had been looped cheek to jowl about as closely as humanly possible, which was surely why Warren's people assumed the "oriental" was valuable.

I wanted to haul the thing out like a wrestler tackling his opponent, but I forced myself to think first. If this really was the best and last physical evidence of a crime, the legal folks would string me up by my thumbs if I didn't protect the chain of custody.

I took a couple pictures with my phone. Then I looked around to see what might help me move the rug without straining any important body parts.

The shed contained the usual suspects—snow shovel, rake, weed-whacker, gas can, bucket, axe, a pruning saw hung on a nail—all dusty and old. No wheelbarrow, unfortunately, but I found an old denim drapery panel spotted with dried paint on a kitchen chair in need of glue. When I spread the drape on the ground, it measured four feet by eight feet; and since it had been folded, it wasn't as dusty as everything else. In other words, it wouldn't add or take away anything that wasn't already on my precious "evidence."

Carefully, I wrapped my arms around the rolled up rug and began to back up, which tipped the tall tube onto the drape and almost took me with it. Another picture just in case. Then, bunching the corners of the drape in my fists, I dragged the rug on my makeshift sled twenty feet across mud and dried grass to the somewhat cleaner gravel driveway. Taking it inside would have been better and opening it in the gun room ideal, but Chantal was in there grieving or coping or whatever was going on with her, and anyway my arms and shoulders couldn't have pulled the thing much farther.

Another picture, and then the moment of truth. I unrolled the rug, took photos, then put my phone away. "Talk to me," I urged the inanimate evidence before me. *Please,* I added with gusto.

The rug's design was mostly ornate curlicues with bands of solid colors forming a border. The reds had faded to shades of brick, the blues to gray. There were probably yellows and maybe white and teal, but I was partly guessing because of the age and wear, and to be honest the dried blood and bone chips and brain material commanded most of my attention.

Initially, there was always an emotional jolt, the shock of seeing the result of violent death. I'd responded to gunshot deaths on the job, of course, not as often in my small city as you might expect; but the results were nothing you'd be likely to forget. Yet you can't do police work without learning to distance yourself from life's more unpleasant realities. Also, I'd nearly died enough times during my cancer treatments to have made peace with my own mortality. In a few moments I settled down and allowed the mental process to begin.

The forensics expert Landis employed for questionable situations loved to lecture us cops on blood spatters and such. When she spoke, I listened. Now as I studied the gory patterns spread in front of me, I hoped common sense would make up for whatever I might have forgotten.

It took fifteen minutes or more for the rug to reveal its secret. I walked around the perimeter at least three times, pausing for long intervals to imagine where Toby Stoddard's chair stood before it fell. The position of the table was easy; the legs had left clear impressions over time. I knew where the body landed because of fainter smears where liquid had been absorbed by Toby's clothing. The largest pool of blackened blood was where it should have been. Even the mark to the right where the shotgun fell wasn't too difficult to discern.

It was when I stood at the fringe end of the rug opposite the indentations for the table, which I assumed had been closer to the window than the door, that I noticed an unexpected pattern. The majority of the spatters spread toward me and what I'd determined was the doorway. The body marks occurred just my side of the table marks, the shotgun strip to my right. Next, the chair, then a relatively untouched span of dried matter fanned my way again.

What seemed odd was a strip of dried blood that came toward me from the shotgun to my feet, almost as if a line had been drawn in the blood…*by a string!*

Toby Stoddard had been murdered.

Chapter 35

My reactions included much more than fury. Astonishment at the murderer's gall accompanied my amazement that the chancy trick worked. Low on the list, but there nonetheless, was a hint of vindication. Just as Karen, Mike and my gut suspected, Toby Stoddard had not killed himself.

Afraid the angle of daylight that exposed the murder method might shift, I snapped several more pictures. Then I called Sheriff Troxell's office and stated my case for speaking with him again as soon as possible.

"He's not here," the dispatcher responded in that lifeless voice they use.

"I know. I met with him an hour ago." Tell her where? Sure. "At Hubbard's. It was business," I added, and now it's urgent business."

The dispatcher promised to do her best.

What had been a halfhearted breeze was now kicking up leaves and mussing my hair. To prevent further contamination of the rug, I set about rolling it up.

"Lauren!" Chantal's shout from the kitchen doorway made me jump. "What are you doing?"

"Just a sec," I told her as I hurried to cover the evidence in the folds of the old drape.

My phone rang.

"Oops, excuse me," I said, then added, "Sorry. It's, uh, personal." Eavesdropping was no way to hear that your husband had been murdered.

"Oh, okay," she said and, much to my relief, withdrew back into the kitchen.

"What's so urgent?" Sheriff Troxell inquired evenly. From the background came the sound of cartoon laughter.

I explained about the rug and what I believed it proved.

Troxell's pause lasted so long that I had to ask whether he was still there.

"Gimme a minute," he snapped.

I gave him two.

"You're positive about this?" Meaning, *You're sure you're not seeing things just to prove your theory?*

"You saw it yourself. It was an extremely messy death." Understatement. A hundred fifty BBs to the head probably inspired the description 'bloodbath.'

"Maybe the line I'm seeing now became more obvious when the blood dried. Hell, I don't know. All I can say is *it's obvious now*, and it's the best evidence you're going to get. If it was my career on the line, I'd store the thing in a guarded vault." Refrigerated, I might have added, but I didn't want to push.

Troxell grunted, not with delight. "Don't go anywhere," he ordered.

It couldn't be helped. I reminded him he'd agreed to show me the crime-scene photos.

"Get 'em from Pete Junior," he said, and yes. Now he sounded peeved.

I placed that call before I went inside.

Chantal had returned to the sofa by the fire. I sat on the edge of the one opposite her and folded my hands on my lap.

"I have new information," I began carefully. "Evidence that your husband was murdered."

Chantal eyed me like a stunned bird too frightened to fly away.

Giving her time to process, I continued slowly. "The cleaners stored the rug from the gun room in the shed," I said. "That's what I was looking at outside. I could see that a string or cord had been pulled across it toward the doorway."

"You're sure?"

"Yes. Toby's death was rigged to look like suicide."

Chantal swung her legs to the floor and stared at her knees. "But...but that's crazy," said with a bitter laugh, "like something out of a book."

"You believe it though, don't you?"

She ignored me. Focused on the space beyond my shoulder. Finally met my eyes. Her breath hitched as she tried to speak. "I thought he had to be suffering, you know? Wrestling with something he couldn't tell me."

"He probably was," I agreed, "just not in the way you thought."

"What do you mean?"

"If it had to do with your father, he might have thought it was something you didn't need to hear."

"You mean the pension mess?" She waved her head. "All Dad did was approve a bad investment. Name one executive who hasn't made that sort of mistake."

"Not that. More likely it was something damning the public still doesn't know about. Wouldn't Toby try to protect you from something like that?"

"Yeah, possibly."

"How about probably?"

Our eyes met again, and I watched her make the mental connection. "The fight with Mother, the money off the books."

Smart guess, but not a healthy one for her to entertain.

I tossed a hand. "Maybe your dad was trying to replenish what the pension fund lost." A lame suggestion, but it was all I could come up with.

Chantal wasn't having it. "Roitman Industries has thousands of employees," she rightfully pointed out. "The jewelry money wouldn't begin to fix that problem. You didn't really think that did you?"

I shrugged. "What do you think?"

She was done thinking for now, because she answered, "No clue," and I must admit I was relieved.

The jewelry money had been spaced out over time, so whatever Frank needed it for had also been spaced out over time. To me, that suggested blackmail; and unfortunately, Toby might very well have been the blackmailer. Who would have known his father-in-law's secrets any better?

Unfortunately, that made Frank the most likely murder suspect, although far from the only one. I could think of half a dozen leads to follow, none of them local to the Roitmans' hunting lodge. Would Seth Troxell travel outside his domain to pursue those possibilities, or would he confine his investigation to the wild geese closer to home? I would soon find out.

Chantal's face had gone pink, and her eyes were pooled with tears. When she stood before me, her left hand trembled even in the grip of her right. "I...I have to...This is..." She wheeled around and fled out of sight.

I poked the fire but added no more logs. Then I systematically examined each room of the sprawling cabin, beginning with the kitchen and pantry, proceeding to the dining area and living areas, then the chilly screened-porch crowded with outdoor furniture. Having been unoccupied for about a month, they were cubicles of cold, damp air smelling of musty fabric and plaster and dust.

Since Chantal had sequestered herself in the first bedroom, the green one where Abby and Marsha slept the night of the birthday party, I continued onto the turn in the hall to finish my search. Procrastinating the inevitable gun room, I detoured into the tiny bathroom. Shower curtain concealing a dusty, gritty tub—moldy and gross. Check. Toilet tank, no surprises. Medicine cabinet: the usual aspirin, band-aids, Colgate toothpaste squeezed almost down to nothing.

"Quit stalling," I scolded myself, then made sure the window was locked before moving on.

The afternoon light confirmed that the gun-room ceiling had been scrubbed; years of dirt still showed in shadowy swirls. The safe remained inaccessible, but no big deal. I doubted that the murderer had been in it anyway. Eight twelve-gauge Remington 870 shotguns hung in the wall cabinet behind glass and metal grids. No slots were vacant, so I assumed the murder weapon had been cleaned and returned to its rack among the others. Anyone hunting geese in the future would have no way of identifying which was which. Nor would I.

Once again leaning against the door jamb, I tried to envision the mechanics of the murder. Toby would have been seated facing the table, which, judging by the depressions in the rug, had been situated slightly forward from the window. He'd had a sedative in his system; Troxell admitted that. One of his feet would have been bare to pretend he pulled the trigger with his toe.

The stock of the loaded shotgun would have rested on the floor, the barrel positioned in the traditional spot. A string would have been temporarily looped around the trigger, which was spaced approximately a quarter inch from the back of its guard. The string would have run down from the trigger, under the rung between the chair's front legs, then run at a right angle along the floor and under the closed door into the hall. Afterward the murderer would have reeled in the loosened string, temporarily hid it for later retrieval, or took it with him through the opened bathroom window.

Much commotion would ensue, and so on.

A horn honked. Sheriff Troxell had arrived.

I hustled out to the driveway to meet him.

Not Troxell after all. It had to be Pete Junior and Andy driving his repaired van.

Junior wore his light brown hair military-short and pointed his nose at me from a height of six-foot-five. Even in the cool spring weather a faded, olive-green t-shirt seemed to be enough warmth for him. His pale, ropy arms stuck out like handles ending in fists at his hips.

"Troxell's pissed," he said instead of hello.

"I don't care," I replied, and the cleanup company designee/part time photographer had the grace to laugh.

"Know what you mean."

Andy had walked over to the covered rug and appeared unsure of how to lift it.

I asked Pete if he'd noticed any unusual pattern in the spatters when he took the photos.

"Call me PJ. And no I did not."

"Why do you suppose that was?"

"Because I'm not police and I was trying to hold onto my dinner."

"You're an honest man, PJ," I observed.

"I try."

"You know how to preserve the chain of evidence?" I wondered.

"Yes, ma'm. That I do."

"Good, then you'll want a copy of the pictures I took when I removed the rug from the shed. Got any pictures for me?"

"Yes, ma'm, I do." He had an adorable crooked smile and the pent up energy of a young stallion. Not my type, but surely someone's. A wedding band sparkled from his left fist.

He reached into the cab of the truck and handed over a nine by twelve brown envelope containing my requested photographs. Then he gave me his cell number and Troxell's so I could forward the pictures I took that eventually the county prosecutor might need.

Whether my precautions would hold up in court I really couldn't say. Somebody was probably going to have to build a convincing circumstantial case as well, and since Troxell had delegated the pickup of what I'd described as the best evidence he was going to get, I suspected that person might have to be me. After all, the sheriff had signed off on the suicide, and he had implied that I'd imagined the string marks to justify my murder theory.

"Nuts," I thought. "PJ, you got any paper to wrap the rug in?"

"Sheriff didn't say nothing about paper."

"Plastic speeds decomposition. Better if organic matter can breathe."

PJ made a scoffing little huff. "If you say so."

Honest, *but not police*, I reminded myself. Give the guy a break. "Then just take it the way it is. Yeah, in the drape, but wrap it in paper when you get...wherever you're going, okay? Will wherever that is have air-conditioning?"

"I'll ask."

"Fine." Only so much a volunteer can do.

Of course if the rug got thrown out as evidence, all the circumstantial support in the world might not assure a conviction.

In that case, somebody just might have to confess.

Chapter 36

PJ did give me a receipt for the rug, written on a Warren and Son tablet with an old-fashioned carbon copy underneath. He and Andy loaded the rug in its paint-spattered drape into the back of his Chevy van, and they lumbered back to the road on the bumpy lane. I did not have high hopes for the rug's use as evidence, and that gave me a rattled, panicky feeling. Still I saw what I saw and had a load of previously gleaned raw material to process.

And maybe Sheriff Troxell would surprise me and arrest somebody all by himself.

In the meantime I still had at least one leg to stand on, my ersatz assignment to protect Chantal, which, unfortunately, had gained legitimacy in the last couple of hours.

I sidled up to her in the doorway to the gun room, where she stood sniffling and hugging herself.

I rubbed her shoulder in sympathy. "After the shot," I began, "who was the first to arrive here?"

"What difference…who cares…?"

"We both should," I replied honestly. "Finding out who killed Toby—and why—will tell us whether you and the baby are safe."

She made a dismissive sound. "You really think…?"

"Yes," I insisted. "So please tell me. Who got here first?"

"Dad did."

"Was he staggering drunk at that point?"

Chantal riveted me with a look. "No," She seemed surprised to be saying that. "No. He was fine. Took charge the way he always does."

"Okay. Who was next?"

"Me. I was right behind him."

"Was the door open or closed when you got here?"

"Closed. I remember seeing Dad hesitate before he turned the knob."

PJ's pictures had confirmed that the body fell to the left, the shotgun to the right, and, as was obvious from the rug, the room was a helluva mess.

I steered Chantal back to toward the couches, questioning her along the way.

"Again. Did Toby say anything to you about what was going on at work around that time? Anything at all?"

"Just that the lawsuit was a huge worry, and he would be glad when it was over."

"The antilock-brake one, right?"

"Yes."

The fire would be out in a few minutes, which was good. I didn't want to risk cracking the hearth by dousing it. "Anything else?" I asked.

Chantal rubbed her hands together and reached for the fleece comforter. "The week before the birthday party Toby came home in a mood. I asked him what was wrong, and he admitted he'd had a tough talk with Dad. '*Another* tough talk,' I said, but he didn't laugh, just left the room for a while." She shook her head. "Funny, I'd forgotten about that until now."

"Toby didn't mention anything about the company's stability." *Or lack thereof.*

"No, not really."

The fluffy ashes were finally ready to spread thin with the poker. After I closed the flue and secured the screen, Chantal locked up and we sauntered out to the car.

Rush hour on the back roads of Maryland would still be rush hour. I phoned Karen to let her know we would be late for dinner.

We arrived at the farm an hour and a quarter later. Twilight had pillowed our surroundings by then—the long stretch of plowed and planted fields, the distant tree lines of neighbors, the utility poles, the powder blue sky fading to pink. Nightfall on a farm always comforted me, the restful sight of work done and the promise of what it would yield.

Karen met us at the end of the walk. Wrapping her arm around Chantal's neck, she told her other sister-in-law, "I'm so glad you're here! We'll put you in Lauren's room." A sideways glance at me. "You can do the sofa for a night, right Lauren?" Then the usual more welcoming chatter. "Hope you like chicken pot pie...I'll put towels on your bed..."

I tried not to mind their instant bond. Mine was a familiar face, and Karen and Chantal were joined by a mutual grief.

Still, I allowed myself to lag behind. Light from Ron's barn office was spilling onto the driveway.

"Be right in," I called across the growing distance.

Karen glanced back from the porch and waved her assent. My dinner had been held this long. What were a few more minutes?

I caught Ron dozing on the unforgiving chair, his booted feet crossed at the ankles on his desk, an International Harvester ball cap shadowing his eyes.

"Hey, bro," I greeted him from the doorway.

He grabbed the cap and thumped his feet to the floor. "Jesus, LB. You about knocked me over."

Naturally, I flashed back on the day I'd done that literally, floored him the way I'd dumped Gavin Roitman on the sand. Ron had remarked that the police academy seemed to be overtraining me for "walking the streets." Exhausted by the rigorous obstacle course I'd completed that day, his attempt at a joke did not go over well.

"Patrolling," I corrected with venom.

To me, his offhanded, "Whatever," was the last straw. I flexed my knees and circled. "Try me," I dared. "Make my day."

Ron laughed, so I grasped his arm and flipped him onto the front lawn. His expression as I helped him up haunts me to this day.

"How's it going?" I inquired mildly. The barn office possessed only one chair, so I leaned against the shelves of dusty cow catalogs left behind by the farm's previous owner.

Elbows resting on his thighs, Ron considered how much or how little to disclose, which was revealing all by itself. Whatever ground I'd gained living here had receded back to the line he'd drawn between us so many years ago.

Disappointment made my chest ache. I wanted to be reassured that everything was okay between him and Karen. I wanted to know that whatever had prompted him to drink was resolved. I wanted to know if he loved me as much as I loved him.

I wanted to know whether he loved me at all.

"Miss me?" I opened when he still hadn't answered, and because we were so very far apart.

"Like jock itch." He laughed. "How's it going with you?"

"It's…it's going," I said.

Ron bobbed his head as if my non-answer satisfied him. "Good. Good," he parroted. "You want a drink?"

My mouth opened, and my face reddened to the roots of my hair.

His hands shot out in a 'whoa-there' gesture. "Joke!" he said. "That was a joke."

I pretended to wipe sweat from my brow. "So you and Karen have figured things out?"

Ron feigned a reflective pose. "Seems that way. For now."

I said "Hmmm," as if I'd received real information, too. "Happy for you."

"Thanks, Sis."

"Well, um. Dinner's waiting."

"Yup. Yup. Can't let dinner wait. Not in this house."

I wanted to cry. Instead I walked over and lightly tapped the shoulder seam of my brother's brown plaid shirt, impersonally, the way you touch an ATM machine or dial an iphone.

"Love you," I said. Then I turned tail and got out of there.

Let him handle his astonishment and horror in his own way. If it involved opening the bottom desk drawer with the key in his muck boot, so be it. He was an adult.

And so was I.

The fragrance of chicken pot pie filled the kitchen. Karen was about to pour Chantal some coffee, but Chantal hastily turned over her mug. "Can't touch the stuff," she remarked. "Not since…"

Karen gasped. "Oh, sweetie. Really? A baby? I'm going to be an aunt?"

Chantal's eyes misted over in spite of her smile. "Early October."

"Wow." Karen spun on her heel with glee before landing on the chair next to the mother-to-be. "That's absolutely fabulous." Her fingers twined in her fine platinum hair as if to hold her head erect. "Wow," she repeated.

Here we go again, I thought, feeling a pang for myself unlike the others that had come before. I recognized it as jealousy, of course, Karen connecting to Chantal in a way she would never connect with me. A percentage of my envy was probably wishing for the impossible, but I refused to acknowledge that. My lifestyle was fine the way it was. My *life* was fine the way it was. I had purpose, accomplishments, happy moments and sad. Let other women ooh and ahh and squeal with maternal delight. I was content with my role as their guardian.

More than content.

Proud.

I heated myself a bowl of chicken pot pie in Karen's microwave and sat at the end of the table eating it with a spoon. Two chairs away the other women chatted about maternity clothes and morning sickness. I washed down my dinner with coffee.

Reporting that Karen's brother had been murdered could wait.

Chapter 37

Perverse as fate, the rising sun painted the following morning in technicolor. The men were already gone, the girls probably watching the countryside slip by through the window of their school bus.

Chantal pushed a stray caper into the cream cheese of her bagel and lox. Then she lifted an eyebrow at me as if to say, "Isn't it time?"

Leaning toward Karen, I dabbed my lips with a paper napkin then cleared my throat to secure my sister-in-law's attention.

"I've got something to tell you," I said carefully. "You were right to think Toby wouldn't commit suicide. He didn't."

Karen took it like a slap—swaying, blinking, palms pressing the kitchen table as if she were about to rise and flee. "Do you believe it?" her shock silently asked Chantal. Their hands reached out to each other and held.

I laid out all the facts I knew by rote, then excused myself to go pack. Chantal and I were supposed to return to the Roitman estate today.

I felt Karen's gaze follow me down the hall toward the room Chantal had used overnight. My clothes were there and my duffel bag. My cosmetics. My pillow. For days I'd yearned for the soft snug feel of my favorite jeans, the ease of my long-sleeved t-shirts, my real running shoes, not the clean, for-show sneakers I'd taken on the trip. I wore the comfy stuff now, but bodyguarding Chantal meant adapting to her lifestyle, a far more public and put-together one than mine. I extracted a black pencil skirt and my best black slacks from the closet and brushed the dust off the folds. I grabbed a striped pull-over sweater from my dresser drawer, then turned back to the closet for whatever else I could find.

Warmer days were on the way. The leaves had popped while I was eating Lobster Thermador and spying on my host, prying personal tidbits from Chantal's background, learning Marsha's mercurial ways and Lana's fears. I'd concluded that Frank's upbringing had prepared him perfectly for success without perfecting him, and his son's childhood environment had accomplished much the same.

Were any of them capable of murder? I'm afraid so.

Were any of them likely to confess? Not without the right provocation, and that was something I hadn't worked out quite yet.

Was there still a chance Frank's business troubles provoked Toby Stoddard's death? Absolutely. But did I think someone outside the family, someone I hadn't yet met, was responsible? Extremely improbable. Troxell admitted that the deceased had a sedative in his system, and those medications don't act instantly. An intruder would have had to gain access to the lodge, force the sedative on Toby, then keep him out of sight and quiet long enough for it to work. And, since Toby had every reason to live—Chantal, the baby, the new house, the lifestyle—I couldn't imagine him risking the dangerous combination of a sedative and alcohol on his own.

Tragically, the faked suicide better suited a killer unable to extricate themselves from the aftermath, someone who needed Seth Troxell to believe what he saw and close the case without a second thought.

I was mulling all this over as I folded a loose jacket that, if needed, could conceal my Glock. To my favorite saddlebag purse I added some mini binoculars wrapped in a silk scarf. My indispensable phone would be kept either in a pocket or a belt clip. The turquoise necklace from Corinne, my so recently departed mother-figure, stayed where it was. Some things are just too precious to risk damage or loss.

Zipping my stuffed duffel and hoisting it to my shoulder, I released a deep sigh. I wasn't just feeling lonely. I was anxious. Prickling-skin, heart-racing anxious, and with good reason. Since Chantal was present when Troxell's minions picked up the rug, telling her what was going on, and why, had been unavoidable. I didn't dare tip my hand by suggesting she keep the news from her family, so if the murderer hadn't already learned I was onto his or her secret, he or she would surely hear by the end of the day.

Congratulations, Lauren, I told the worried face in the bedroom mirror. You've not only warned a killer you're on his trail, you've put anyone who knows even part of what you know at risk. *You need to end this fast.*

I closed my eyes and visualized success, breathed in deeply, breathed out slowly. Only when my impatience was under control and my face showed nothing of the churning inside did I dare venture back into the hall.

Still at the kitchen table, Karen and Chantal looked up when I returned. *Make it believable* I reminded myself, but *make it work.*

"Hey, Karen," I began with my fists clasped together. "I just got a call."

"Oh?" She released Chantal's hand. Spared me a glance.

"A dear friend is undergoing chemo," I fibbed, "and she's sick as a dog. She'll be okay, but her husband has business out of town and he needs somebody to help out for a couple days." Except for what I was saying, I might have been a teenager begging for car keys. "Could Chantal please stay here awhile longer? Dave really doesn't have anybody else to ask."

"No, no," Chantal protested. "Why don't I just go home?"

"Because I'm supposed to be protecting you," I reminded her. "You'll be safe here," I argued. "Nobody knows where you are." None of the people angry with her father, anyway, which was another matter altogether.

"But…"

Karen raised her palms like a teacher ordering her class quiet down. "Done deal," she insisted. "We'll kick back, get to know each other better. Plus I've got a maternity shop I think you'll love. Would that be okay?" she asked, finally consulting me.

"Sunglasses and a baseball cap should do it." I joked, but the mother and the mother-to-be took me seriously. "I think you'll be fine," I assured them.

Still jazzed by the urgency of my mission but also pumped with anticipation, I crunched across the gravel drive and threw my stuff in the trunk of the Miata. Unless Chantal told her relatives I was driving a rusting red convertible, and why would she? I was free to roam with impunity.

Gavin's widget factory, and presumably his condo, were located in Frederick, Virginia, geographically between the farm and my second destination.

Standing in the crotch of the open car door, I ran my eyes over Ron's fields, the barn and its outbuildings, the flawless sky and the distant hazy horizon. I listened to the breeze and the squawk of a crow, the drone of a tractor, and the rush of a truck on the road. I breathed in the smells of fresh earth and grass and the first dandelions of the year.

Then I bid them all good-bye.

Chapter 38

I fueled up at a nearby crossroad and checked the Miata's oil, Dad's wise recommendation for a nearly vintage vehicle. Its radio was in a staticky mood, so I created a Lyle Lovett station on my phone in honor of my security cowboy back at the Roitman estate. The Texan's voice proved to be nice company, interrupted only by my GPS "recalculating" my occasional premature turn.

Gavin Roitman's turf, Fredricksburg, Virginia, is very historic, very Americana, and proud of it. The buildings tended to be traditional brick or painted clapboard. Contrasting shutters were the norm, columns an infrequent upgrade to a facade. The city struck me as too quiet for an attractive, well-off, single guy. I pictured Gavin as a Georgetown man, or maybe Richmond if it was more convenient to his work.

During one of my unscheduled neighborhood tours, I pulled over next to a historic building with a broad front porch, "originally built in the 1760s for George Washington's younger brother Charles" and christened as a tavern in 1792. Somebody came across a sign and thought the tavern's name was Rising Sun, but that turned out to be wrong. Oh, well. A bar by any name was still a bar, which prompted me to wonder if my extended absence from the Pelican's Perch was costing me my job.

Another worry for another day.

Right now I mostly cared about the bars on my cell phone. If I wanted to grill Gavin Roitman, I needed to know where he was. As it was only 11:15 AM on a weekday, I tried the widget factory first.

Mr. President was out of the office.

"All day?" I quizzed the woman who had answered the phone.

"Yes."

"Fishing in Alaska?" I felt compelled to ask. "Big car-matt convention in Tampa?"

"I really can't say," the humorless voice replied. She sounded approachable though, so she was probably good at her job.

Next I phoned Gavin's home number, and to my surprise a female answered.

"Oh!" I said brilliantly. "Is Gavin home?"

"No he isn't. May I tell him who called?" Not *May I take a message?* Not even *Who the hell are you?* Nice polite response, but less welcoming than the widget-factory receptionist. Perhaps I had best explain myself.

"Lauren Beck, I work for Gavin's father."

"Doing what, if I may ask?"

That was when I crossed off cleaning-person and underscored girlfriend. "Bodyguarding his sister Chantal at the moment, which is why I'd like to speak with Gavin. And you are…?"

"Julianna."

"Would that be Julianna Sykes by any chance?"

Silence.

"…because if you are, I think you can help me."

Silence.

"Please," I said. "I won't take up much of your time. It's about his sister. I'm already in Fredericksburg. May I stop over? Please? This isn't something that should be discussed on the phone."

In the end I thought I was going to get brushed off, but Julianna finally relented. "Apartment 4C," she confided.

"I'll put you on the list at the gate, but I'm going to want to see some ID."

"Perfectly fair," I agreed.

The apartment complex was a sprawling, upscale assortment of units, each divided twice by a stack of square white, wooden outcrops that served as decks. The faces of the buildings sported the Fredericksburg assortment—brick, clapboard, and once in a while stone. My progress between buildings one, two, and three also took me past a clubhouse, a fitness facility, a pool, and two tennis courts. The surrounding landscape had just been planted with annuals and mulched with dark brown stuff that smelled like chocolate. The grass awaited mowing for the first time this spring, and pink petals from a Japanese cherry tree next to my parking spot spun through the air like confetti. A beautiful day in the neighborhood, which was too bad because everybody seemed to be at work except me and Julianna; and in a way I was working, too.

My first sighting was Julianna's shadow eclipsing the peephole of 4C. I held up my driver's license and a photocopy of my expired Landis, PA, police badge.

The door opened and the fragrance of beef and vegetables seasoned with bay leaf greeted me before Julianna did. Had to be a crockpot recipe judging by how completely it permeated the apartment.

"Come in," she said, stepping aside.

The living room and kitchen were open concept, with granite countertops and stainless steel appliances to the right opposite white leather sectional furniture grouped around a rustic coffee table. The rug appeared to be Native American, but the lamps and knickknacks were an eclectic assortment probably gleaned from around the world.

"Please sit down," Julianna said as she tossed a dish towel onto the kitchen counter. "Can I get you something?"

"I guess whatever you're cooking isn't ready yet."

She smiled and folded her hands in her lap.

"No, nothing," I answered. "I promised to make this quick."

"What's this about Gavin's sister?"

"I've been hired to act as Chantal's bodyguard, and I'm trying to gauge how much danger she's in."

"I don't see how I can help. I can't even imagine what you're protecting her from."

Julianna wore her blonde hair up in a clip. Her shirtsleeves were rolled to the elbow, the waist area wet as if she'd been cleaning up dishes and got splashed. Like a person whose only criteria was to be comfortable, she, too, wore jeans and casual shoes.

"We're worried that whoever killed Toby might have the same reason to silence Chantal."

Gavin's live-in girlfriend closed her eyes and winced. Then something astonishing happened. Julianna Sykes, who surely never met Toby Stoddard in her life, began to tremble and cry.

"What?" I asked, as in *What am I missing?*

"I heard the shot," she answered, which absolutely flummoxed me.

"I don't understand," I said truthfully. "How…? I didn't think you were there."

She lifted her chin and wiped away tears. "I wasn't," she said. "Gavin and I were talking on the phone when…when the shot was fired. I can still hear it now. It reminded me of…"

"…losing your sister." The gunshot, the crash, equally awful sounds. Who wouldn't make that unfortunate connection, even nearly a year apart? "I'm so sorry."

Julianna sniffled and blinked. "You know about Luanne? Oh. Of course. You're working for the Roitmans." She looked alarmed. "You won't tell them I'm here, will you? Gavin wants to…"

"None of my business," I interrupted. "None of theirs either."

"No. No, you're right. Thanks. Thanks for that." She hugged herself and stared out through the slider to the deck. "Rotten luck," she mused. "I'm always first in line." She flopped back in her armchair and dug a tissue out of her pocket.

"You've got questions?" she asked.

I did, but not the ones I'd planned. Now I wanted details about the traumatic event she had just described, the event that unintentionally gave one of my prime suspects an awfully good alibi.

"What did Gavin think happened?" I wondered.

"Think? The same thing I did, I guess—What the heck *was* that? Is everybody okay?"

"I guess I meant what did he do?"

"He said he would call me back and hung up."

"Did he?"

"Did he what?" She was getting exasperated, and so was I.

"Did he call you back?"

"Oh, sure. Two hours later." She waved her head and stared into the distance again. "I've never heard him like that. I hope I never do again."

"Like what?"

That earned me a disparaging stare. "What do you think? He was horrified. His whole family was. The police came, the medical examiner or whoever the heck it is who pronounces you dead. I don't know about things like that."

"I'm sorry to stir up such bad memories."

"You've got your reasons, I guess. Do you have any more questions, because…?"

"The rest probably don't matter."

She seemed to reconsider. "Ask me anyhow. I'm curious."

"Alright. How did Gavin and Toby get along? Were they friends, rivals? Do you know?"

"Friendly rivals, I guess. Toby gave Gavin investment tips now and then."

"Did Gavin act on them?"

"I think so. Sure. That was Toby's field of expertise, after all. Analyzing that sort of thing."

"Any idea whether the investments worked out?"

She gestured vaguely at our surroundings. "Mostly, I guess. Toby put his own money into them, too." She gave a short laugh. "He said if they didn't pay off, they could cry in their beers together. They also co-owned a couple of industrial properties. Gavin seems to think they're pretty solid."

"So he must have thought Toby was a pretty upstanding guy?"

"Oh, yes," she agreed with a heartier laugh. "Gavin called him Mr. Clean." Her brow furrowed slightly, "…but not always in a nice way."

I stood up to leave but abruptly turned back. "He should marry you, you know," I remarked.

Julianna's pretty lips spread into a sly smile.

"He already did."

Chapter 39

"Congratulations!" I exclaimed regarding the Sykes/Roitman nuptials. "When was the lucky day?"

Julianna eyed me askance. "February," she replied. "Why do you ask?"

"Just happy for you, that's all," I told her, hoping she hadn't already intuited the worst, that her new husband had made moves on me shortly after we met.

She folded her arms and scowled. "Did Gav make a pass at you?"

My shock probably deserved Julianna's snicker.

"The Roitmans were around, right?" she stated, further surprising me by her confidence.

"Not *around*," I hedged.

"It was on the trip, though? While you were staying on that obscenely huge boat."

"Yesss…"

"Did you mention it to Chantal? Marsha? Anybody?"

"No."

"But they could have pieced it together on their own?"

Thinking back, I realized they certainly could have. Gavin and I went off to the disco together and came back separately. He happened to be sandy from head to foot; but when I returned, my clothes were still pristine. If the yacht was equipped with a security camera, such details might have been noticed. Also Chantal had exclaimed over lunch, "You're not interested in him, are you?" If she hadn't believed my answer…

"You think I was a shill?"

Checkmate!

"Have a nice life, Ms. Lauren Beck," Julianna told me as she began to close the door.

No sooner had Julianna Roitman nee Skyes shut the door in my face than I knocked on it again.

She opened it with a Now-what? expression and the body language of a bouncer.

I elbowed past, marched back to the seating area, and placed my butt on the still-warm white leather armchair I'd vacated only a moment before.

The mistress of the house gave me a wide berth. Passing passed through the kitchen, she retrieved her wedding band from a cut-glass dish by the sink. Most likely she had removed it to conceal her marital status from me, a person who admitted direct access to her secret husband's parents. Putting it back on conveyed, perhaps deliberately, that this was her home I'd invaded, and she knew where the knives were kept.

Julianna returned to her previous spot on the sectional, clasped her hands together, and lifted her chin.

I had no trouble appearing contrite. "I'm sorry, but I need to ask you something about your sister. I should have asked before, but I...but I didn't."

In my defense, I'd been blindsided by Julianna's unwitting, and therefore convincing, alibi for Gavin at the time of the murder. An alibi with her here and her husband at the hunting lodge? I never would have imagined it, so I never could have formed the question. Even if I had, she probably would have guessed what I was after and lied.

"That's over," she told me now. "All of it. What can Luanne's death have to do with anything?"

"Maybe nothing," I had to admit, "but yesterday I came across proof that Toby Stoddard was murdered. I don't know who killed him or why, but the most likely motive would involve business." I shrugged. "Until recently your father's lawsuit against Roitman Industries was their most pressing problem." I glanced down at the floor before looking straight at my listener. "Frank really did hire me to protect Chantal—mostly to humor her—but he did hire me. And, as it turns out, my private agenda may ultimately insure her safety."

"I don't understand."

"Do you know who Karen Beck is? Toby's sister?"

Negative head shake.

"Mike Stoddard?"

Another shake.

"Okay. Karen is married to my brother, Ron—I'm temporarily living with them—and Mike is Karen's younger brother. I used to be a cop, so I got myself invited on the burial-at-sea trip to learn whatever I could about how Toby died."

By now I had a lump in my throat, so I swallowed hard before I asked, "Do you believe your sister's death was due to a mechanical failure?"

Julianna's chest heaved, and she looked away. "The future always hinges on the past, doesn't it?" Her hands bracketed her face, and her eyes briefly closed. "No," she replied. "No, not really. Do you?"

"I don't know enough about it."

She straightened up. Lifted her chin in a different way. "Luanne couldn't wait to tell our parents she got engaged. It was already dark, raining hard, but she set out for Illinois right after work anyway. She didn't see the broken-down truck in her lane in time to pass safely..." Tears slid down Julianna's cheeks. "The ruling was accidental death, and I accept it. I have no other choice."

"How about your father?"

Gavin's wife wiped her face with the back of her hand. "He was desperate to unload his pain onto somebody else. He couldn't find out who actually made the part he thinks failed, so he sued the whole food chain—up to and including Frank Roitman. 'Let the legal system figure it out,' his words." She waved her head. Swiped her cheek again. "Turned out it was Luanne who made the mistake."

I thought of her brother, the one who'd attacked Frank Roitman and caused him to fall and break his wrist.

"What do you think your family would do if someone somehow discovered the part in question was defective?"

Julianna's forehead creased. "Nothing," she said. "They've already done it and lost."

I rose from my seat. "Thank you," I said, sticking out my hand from habit.

Gavin's wife just stared at it.

"Right," I said and let myself out.

Chapter 40

The good news: Julianna's magnanimous version of her sister's death further helped me believe she actually did hear the fatal gunshot while she was on the phone with Gavin. The bad news? The bell had been rung for me on the faulty-part idea, and it wasn't going to un-ring just by covering my ears.

I set my phone's GPS for the antilock-brake arm of Roitman Industries called Nolan Company.

Two hours later I stopped for a late lunch at the Potomac St. Grill in Brunswick, Maryland. So hungry and anxious that my stomach hurt, I dithered over the battling American, Mexican, and Middle Eastern choices and finally opted for the Cuban Ham and Cheese Panini—comfort food that would have to last me longer than I knew.

The restaurant's logo featured an old-time locomotive, so while I waited for my order I asked my dining neighbor, a slope-shouldered fellow in short sleeves and a clip-on tie, what was up with the trains. The gentleman raised his white eyebrows, dabbed his lips, and smiled as if pleased to be asked. Turned out the Baltimore and Ohio railroad figured prominently in Brunswick's past. When diesel engines rendered the huge local rail yard obsolete, their "Big town/Small city" became home to "more than a few" Washington, DC commuters.

"You?" I inquired.

"Not anymore," he replied with a mischievous wink.

Nolan Company lay slightly northwest of Brunswick, another fifteen minutes from downtown. The two-story building was brick fronted, sided with functional white stucco and approximately a city block in size, if the city happened to be Brunswick. Since antilock brakes were bound to be smaller than a breadbox, I concluded that they could make quite a lot of them inside those walls.

The office faced west, opposite the shipping docks located to the far right. I parked in one of the few visitors' spaces. On a subconscious level I suppose my animal brain expected to encounter mostly men, so on a whim I swapped my sneakers for the heels I'd packed in Chantal's honor. One walks differently in heels. One thrusts out one's chest and extends one's neck in a self-aware, but more or less natural, womanly way. Oh, hell. It seemed a good idea at the time.

And it was.

The person manning the opening in the low glass partition turned from his computer, looked me up and down, pursed his lips and said, "I suppose you can't help it," with a smile that dimpled his cheek.

"Help what?" I asked.

"Looking like that. I have friends who would kill to look half that good. On weekends, of course."

"Of course."

Fielding a similar compliment from a straight male would be like stepping barefoot into a briar patch. Conversely, faux jealousy from a gay flirt felt like simple, harmless fun.

I introduced myself.

"Timothy," he said as well-kept fingers adorned with a gold signet ring, initials entwined, grasped my hand with a pleasant squeeze. Amusement over my amusement shone from behind stylish, black-rimmed spectacles.

"What can I do for you?" he inquired. No trace of innuendo of any sort, just a pretty, boyish smile.

"Would it be possible to have a few words with the president?"

"The White House is that way," Timothy gestured toward our nation's capitol, "but if you mean our leader, that would be John Schug, the Plant Manager. We call him John to his face."

"Is he in?"

Those perfect hands clasped under his chin, Timothy's elbows now rested on the three-foot shelf of smudged green Formica, the opening from his work station to the lobby. Behind him a pale gray cement-block wall said "Nolan Company" in raised, polished-aluminum letters. Tiny, stylized stop signs served as the Os. "Yes," he answered, "but you'll need an appointment, and to get one you have to tell me why you want it."

I said I worked for Frank Roitman, "and I think I'd better keep my reason confidential."

Timothy made a chucking sound with his dimpled cheek. Smile unwavering, he said, "Sorry. You're going to need an appointment even if you do work for the Grand Poobah."

"Okay. When is Mr. Schug's next available?"

The phone rang, and I waited while Timothy forwarded the call. He sounded efficient, friendly, and straight. When he finished, he consulted his watch.

"It's 3:27 now. Mr. Schug's next opening is 3:30."

"I'll take it."

"Thought you might." He lifted the receiver again, poked the first extension button and spoke when someone answered. "John's three-thirty is here." He covered the instrument and mouthed, "Name?" which I provided again. "She works for Frank Roitman." An eyebrow raise with an eye-roll. "Not my fault, Lydia. You must not have typed it in." He hung up, waved toward the hallway on the left, and told me, "First door you come to."

The narrow hall was paved with brown linoleum tiles, and each hit from my high heels reverberated like blows on an anvil. My hips swayed nicely though.

Lydia, a frumpy woman, whose work space should have been a walk-in closet, stood at John Schug's open doorway and verbally backpedaled. "I don't know," she said, "but she's here." She turned to look at me, made a brusque gesture with her arm that said, "Get in there right now or else," and dropped herself back onto her ergonomic chair. Her computer instantly devoured her attention.

I approached the open doorway like a supplicant Dorothy approaching the Wizard of Oz.

"Mr. Schug?"

"Who are you?" he asked from behind an oak desk littered with spreadsheets and post-its. His white shirtsleeves were rolled up, his soft face an unhealthy, sweaty glow. Everything about him commanded rather than requested, which automatically straightened my spine.

"Lauren Beck," I announced. "I work for Frank Roitman."

"So you say, but Lydia doesn't make mistakes. So tell me why you're here before I call security."

"Do you mind if I close the door?"

"Yes, I mind."

I reminded myself that I was rattling the tiger's cage on purpose and my adrenaline glands needn't bother to speed up my heart. Too late. My pulse pounded in my ears. Nothing to do but push on. I was too close to the end and needed information too badly to back out now.

"You're aware of how Frank's son-in-law died?"

"Suicide. Yes. What's that got to do with me?" He hadn't risen from his chair and had no interest in offering me one.

An inward sigh. "No sir, it was murder, and Frank hired me to protect his daughter Chantal."

Humph. "From what?"

"I'm getting to that. I'm wondering if Toby Stoddard might have had knowledge of your company using faulty parts, and..."

"What the hell...?" If he were a bomb, he was about to explode.

"...and if his wife knew it, too, she might be in similar danger." I'd been making it up as I went, but at least I was learning something. John Schug adhered to the court's verdict. Vociferously, you might say.

"Lydia," Schug shouted over my shoulder. "Get Frank Roitman on the line."

"Yessir."

"On second thought, call Security."

Schug once again addressed me. "I don't know who you are or why you're really here, but for the record that's the damnest, most lowlife attempt to incriminate an innocent company I ever heard. You must be mental to come in here with that cockamamie story. Now get the hell out of my office. Lydia," he shouted, "where's Danny?"

I assumed Danny was Security.

I turned on my high heels and pock, pock, pocked my way back to the lobby, crossing my fingers in the hope that Schug's calls for Security were so rare as to be non-existent, or that Danny was eighty and slower than a snail.

Behind his partition Timothy was hunkered down laboring at his computer, nobody else in sight.

"Who should I ask about parts?" I whispered.

My flirt-buddy appeared to be stunned by the question. "Purchasing Agent."

Fine. I could manage without a name. "In a hurry. Where's Purchasing?"

He pointed to the hallway on my right. "There's a sign."

Footsteps resounded from the hall back to the left, Lydia's hurry-up gait most likely; John's brogans probably would have shattered the tiles.

"I've got this," Timothy whispered as he shooed me along.

The Purchasing Department was indeed labeled with a rectangular brown sign I almost missed because the door was open. A guy visibly more slender than his clothes stood at the desk facing the hall.

"I'm Lauren Beck and I work for Frank Roitman," I spieled off hastily. "Would you be the person who bought the part that was in dispute in the Sykes trial?"

Behind him a female worker glanced at me with something more than surprise. For the rest of the conversation she wouldn't even pretend to work.

"You're the purchasing agent, right?" I addressed the man. He was maybe forty, losing his blond hair, married because I noticed his spread fingers tented on the desk. Probably a nice guy since he hadn't shouted for Danny yet.

"Yes, what is this about again?"

"The Sykes trial. I need some information about the part in question."

"Why? The trial is over."

"It's a long story, and I don't have much time."

"Why not?"

"Sorry," I said, forcing myself to slow down. "Dentist appointment. She's a bear when you're late."

"No," said the PA.

"No what?" This was how people developed migraines.

"No, I did not purchase the part that was mentioned in the Sykes trial." He spoke with extra patience, as if English were my second language or perhaps I'd recently emigrated from the moon.

"May I ask who did?"

A glance back at the woman, who quickly looked away. "My predecessor, of course. Shouldn't you know that already?"

"I'm new, too," I ad libbed. "Just trying to save time."

"Oh, right. The dentist." Sarcastic, but deservedly so.

A rustling out in the hallway turned all three of our heads.

False alarm.

Different alarm, I should say. Timothy walking back and forth past the open door like somebody who had no idea where he was going or why.

The PA stared at me with an impatient twist to his lips.

Meanwhile, the woman, a nice-looking brunette wearing bright pink lipstick was poking her cell phone. Odd because an ordinary phone was within reach right there on her desk.

No time to speculate. The ball was in my court. "Do you know how I might reach your predecessor?" I pressed.

"No idea." The PA's peeved expression warned me he was running low on patience.

"Can you at least tell me his name?"

"Jerry Emper? Was that it, Lucy?"

Lucy confirmed the name.

"Thanks," I told them both. "And he left because…?"

"None of my business, and probably not yours either."

"Ah but it is," I said. "Frank Roitman, remember?"

"Your dentist?" The PA folded his arms across his chest while I pondered how to respond.

Meanwhile, the woman, Lucy, was waving her lighted cell phone screen at me like a concert groupie. "Health reasons," she mouthed behind her boss's back. With her free hand she pointed to the ground three times then held her phone to her ear. The message couldn't have been clearer if it had been written on a billboard: Jerry Emper was listed in the local white pages. I smiled my thanks, told the PA "Never mind," then made a hasty exit.

A man, Danny from Security, I assumed, leaned on Timothy's shelf with his right leg crossed over his left, just kibitzing since the nervy woman he was supposed to chase was nowhere around.

I'd removed my shoes for stealth, but paused to put them back on at the edge of the lobby. Unfortunately, this gave Danny time to realize he wasn't doing his job.

"Hey!" he accosted me.

I trotted toward the reinforced steel door. "Sorry," I said. "Wrong turn."

With the Miata loaded with my stuff, I'd been sure to lock it; but I'd left the driver's window open a crack for ventilation. A chartreuse post-it lay on my seat.

In tidy printed letters it warned, "JS called FR. T."

Chapter 41

When he was young and naïve, Frank thought having money would protect him, a cruel deception he had learned to despise. In exchange for not starving to death in a freezing gutter, the size of his problems had multiplied exponentially with his responsibilities. At times he felt like a fireman pissing on an inferno.

After he hung up with John Schug, he helped himself to an outside line and dialed his most trusted bodyguard. Three rings later, he remembered the ex-linebacker moonlighted as a bouncer and slept into the afternoon.

Four rings became six. Frank's watch read three thirty-nine.

"Yuh," eventually came the sleep-laden answer.

"Oak Leaf Mall," Frank stated, confident that his voice would be recognized. "When can you be there?"

"Twenty minutes?"

The arrangement was infrequent but established. Frank and the young thug he thought of as "Goliath" switched cars in a prearranged strip mall, a different one each time. Goliath left in Frank's current Lexus sedan, and Frank went about whatever the day's clandestine business happened to be in the young man's anonymous black SUV.

Frank watched for its arrival with his engine running and the air conditioning on. Every other minute he closed his eyes and sighed. In between he slapped the soft leather seats and cursed Lauren Beck for insinuating herself into his life.

"I shouldn't have to do this," he muttered. "Damn you, woman. Damn you," and other angry mutterings that boiled down to feeling enormously sorry for himself. He had regained visible control by the time the SUV roared into the lot, but it was close.

The Oak Leaf Mall lay parallel to a four-lane highway. Six enterprises lined up like inches on a ruler. Two were vacant. Two others sold pizza and Chinese food respectively, which nobody wanted at this hour. A harried mother of two exited the Dry Cleaner with shirts on a hanger and her eyes on her kids. Frank and his employee would be the briefest of dots on her radar screen, there for a second and gone.

A conspiratorial smile tilted the bodyguard's lips as he leaned down to open Frank's door. The assumption was that he was enabling Frank to meet a woman, and Frank preferred to leave it at that.

"See you in the morning," he said as they exchanged keys.

"In the morning? Yes *sir!*" Since the young man hadn't lasted a year at West Point, the military affectation came off as an arrogant conceit. Perhaps Frank had placed too much trust in the fellow after all. The last thing he needed was another mouth to shut.

"Uh, where?" he was asked, much to his surprise. The usual arrangement was to switch back before Frank went home. Nothing for Marsha to suspect that way.

Frank sighed from his toes up. The problem was much worse than an angry wife. As bad as Toby Stoddard. In the long run about as bad as it can get.

He replied, "The usual. Pick up the driver and meet me at the estate."

Goliath's eyebrows shot up nearly to his crewcut. "Yes *sir.*" He spun on his heel, smoothly lowered himself into the Lexus, then entered the quickening traffic like a stunt driver in pursuit of a cinema felon.

Another check of his watch told Frank that Lauren had probably arrived at Jerry Emper's house by now, a monumental complication and extreme regret, but there was nothing to be done.

In the end, Frank supposed he was better off biding his time. Let Lauren grill the down-and-out purchasing agent; Jerry wouldn't give her anything. Then after she was long gone, Frank would solve that problem for now and forever.

The turn of the SUV's key blasted his ears with shouting so loud and raucous it couldn't possibly pass for music. He poked the double arrow on the dashboard until he came to a familiar station out of Washington, DC.

Next he searched for the source of a strange stink. A pair of "graphic novels" lay on the passenger seat. He'd smelled their sweat-dampened ink from the back seat of the Lexus before, but these lurid rags were curled and dry.

Taco wrappers crumbled and thrown on the floor proved to be the culprits. Once Frank recognized the spicy smell, he realized his mouth was watering. A "stress eater," his doctor described him, alluding to an unsatisfactory weight gain. "You're of an age, Frank," he said. "Slow down, buddy. You're not sixteen anymore."

"Neither are you," Frank reminded the doctor, another overachiever from the neighborhood. Frank's accomplishments had outdistanced the internist's by miles, nothing either one would ever mention, but as he turned north on the four-lane highway, Frank pondered how many of the doctor's admonitions might be sour grapes.

Two miles later the acid in his stomach actually hurt. Did he dare stop? Yes, he dared. He was hungry, dammit. Oh hell yes, stressed, too. But he would prevail. He always did.

At the first opportunity, a McDonald's, naturally, he bought a double cheeseburger and fries. If it still agreed with him, he'd have ordered chocolate milk, too, which was when he admitted the doctor was probably right. He was as stressed as a man faced with life or death.

The afternoon was one of the warmer ones so far, so despite the highway exhaust tainting the cooling breeze, Frank took his meal to a picnic table next to the deserted children's play equipment. The breeze might be better described as a light wind, but he'd eaten cold hamburgers before. Eaten them and been grateful to be eating anything at all.

Before the first bite his cell phone startled him with its distinctive irritating noise, and he squeezed the sandwich so hard ketchup squirted back onto the wrapper.

"Frank!" Marsha shouted in her stage voice. "Where are you?"

"Please," he beseeched her, "my eardrum."

"Where are you, Frank?" she asked at a lower volume.

"On the road. Something urgent came up."

"Lana said you won't be home for dinner." The way she said it, it sounded like a serious matter. So serious in her view that he finally comprehended the smallness of her world. How had F. Scott Fitzgerald put it? Life balancing on a fairy's wing? Something like that, except Marsha's world balanced on him. The realization produced such a burden of responsibility that he put down the sandwich and doubted that he would pick it up again.

"No, darling. I will not. What are you having?" Hearing the empathy in his own words, he realized how much he loved the woman but also how sorry he felt for her. The sorrow was new.

"Beef burgundy," she lamented.

"Sounds delicious," he lied. Nothing appealed to him now.

"Will you be late?"

"Yes, I expect so. May I wake you? I think we should talk."

If it were possible to sense terror vibrate through miles and miles of moving air, then Frank felt Marsha freeze with fear.

"Yes, alright," she said at last.

Frank returned his food to its oily bag then dropped the bag in the nearby trash can. A wash-up in the men's room and he was back on the road, his clean hands gripping the wheel as if it were a rope dangling over a ravine.

Chapter 42

Swiftly putting Nolan Company in my rear-view mirror, I drove until I found a quiet side street and pulled over as if to make a phone call. The spring leaves all around the cottagey neighborhood had nearly achieved their heavy summer hues. Dried daffodils stood among healthy green stalks, indicators of what had just been and what would return next year.

My plan was far less certain. With a post-it slipped through my car window, Timothy, the rebel receptionist, had warned me that his boss phoned Frank Roitman, most likely to complain about me. Which meant Frank already knew I'd alluded to the use of faulty parts—parts that had been legitimately ruled out as the cause of Luanne Sykes's death. Whether or not Frank was guilty of anything worse than bad luck, he would not thank me for reopening that wound. I didn't especially care about that, but I cared very much that my privileged insider status was probably toast. Such was the risk of rattling a tiger's cage, but it really couldn't be helped. When an investigation gets as stuck as this one, you have to do whatever you can to shake it loose. If that means showing up at a potential witness's home without warning, well, Ms. Manners would just have to forgive me.

Sitting there in my relaxing surroundings, I Googled how long it would take to drive from the Middleburg, Virginia, area to Brunswick, Maryland. On average the 31.4 miles up Route 287 took 46 minutes, or 49 minutes in current traffic. Should Frank Roitman decide to join me at Jerry Emper's house, I had less than an hour to find the place and pry whatever information I could out of the Nolan Company's former purchasing agent.

With sweaty fingers I poked my phone back to the GPS then shifted the Miata into motion.

Jerry Emper's abode stood out, but not in a good way. His front porch leaned to the right, and its rain gutter lacked a downspout. The clapboard siding wasn't gray any longer, but the cream-colored trim was. Also, the six-foot long cement walk that both guests and residents had to negotiate, sober or otherwise, rocked and rolled like an oldies band.

I knocked on the dust-caked screen door. From inside came the sound of an aluminum can crinkling, then the thump of feet dropping to the floor. My spiel was simple, but I rehearsed it in my head while I waited.

Thirty seconds later Jerry peered out through the ten-inch opening he risked on a stranger. He appeared to be a tall, gaunt guy with four-day stubble disguising a psoriasis rash and dirty black hair that sprouted unevenly from his head and ears. He blinked at the daylight and emitted a tiny burp.

"Not buying any," he said as he attempted to shut me out.

I pushed back his ten inches and added few more, permitting him to focus on me for real.

"I work for Frank Roitman," I said. "He asked me to check in."

"Why?" When he tried, Jerry Emper looked reasonably intelligent. He also had beautiful, if weepy, eyes. He might even look decent again if he rethought his grooming routine. Something serious must have happened to him, but I couldn't guess what.

In lieu of answering his question, I asked if I might come in.

Jerry's hungry eyes peeled me like an orange while he moistened his lips with beer-scented saliva. For at least the thousandth time I thanked the police academy for teaching me self-defense and the trainer whose fitness regime I adopted soon after I finished chemo. The Glock in my purse didn't hurt my confidence any either.

"Certainly," said the spider to the fly.

The inside of Jerry Emper's house, surely a rental, rivaled the set of a horror movie. It smelled like skin and tobacco ash and beer. The ottoman where his booted feet had rested was an old typewriter crate most likely left behind by the first railway worker who lived here. There were no drapes on the casement windows, just milky-blue smoke residue.

"Have a seat," my host offered, watching me askance as he wet his lips once again.

The available chair was a well-shaped wooden specimen, also of an expired century. Painted black, it sported a faded pattern of fruit across the top done in gold-leaf. I found it surprisingly comfortable. Dusty, but comfortable.

Jerry returned to a soiled green overstuffed armchair facing the twenty-nine inch television on the dresser to my left. Beyond Jerry was a dining room with no table, and past that a kitchen I couldn't really see. Against the wall to my right was a stairway to the second floor.

Jerry caught me looking up the stairs as he lit a cigarette, and the left corner of his mouth lifted.

"Frank sent you," he stated.

"Yes."

"I don't believe you." The former PA's shining eyes narrowed as he drew in a lungful of smoke.

"I can give you Frank's private cell phone number if you like."

Jerry's emaciated shoulders rolled forward as he leaned on his knees. "Shit. What the hell do I care?"

Another awkward thirty seconds ticked away.

"So. How are you?" I asked without demonstrable concern. I didn't yet know whether I was speaking to a blackmailer, a victim, or a co-conspirator. It was like walking across the peak of a roof.

"Not well, thank you." As if I hadn't noticed. "Just got out of the hospital, if you must know. But you would be aware of that if you know Frank."

"He didn't mention it."

"Umm," Jerry hummed skeptically.

"He just wants to know how you feel about things," I said, making *things* sound as ambiguous as possible.

"You mean am I going to keep quiet?"

"Exactly." What am I talking about, Jerry? Toss me a crumb.

"Put another way, do you need anything?" More jewelry money, for instance?

The man flopped back and breathed in some regular air. Looked out the window then back at me.

"Hell, yes," he said. "I beg your pardon. *Yes.* I need a new hot water heater and probably a new set of lungs. I'm told I need a colonoscopy and a new carburetor for my car. I need meds for depression, and I need a goddamn good night's sleep. I could also use a winner on a long shot at Santa Anita. You wanna help me with any of that?"

"Gotta pass, Jerry, but I advise you to get the colonoscopy. I've had cancer and it's no fun."

"You had cancer?"

"Hodgkins disease."

"You don't look like you've been sick a day in your life."

"Trust me."

He looked me over again. "Sure. Why not? What do you want to know again?"

"What part was it they thought was defective in Luanne Sykes's car?"

Emper looked at me differently yet again. "I guess you do know Frank."

"That I do, but he wouldn't answer me when I asked that." Should have said *if* I asked, but whatever.

"I don't suppose he would. So why are you asking me?"

"I'm trying to understand why the case went to court. You put your foot on the brake and the car stops, right?"

"I may be screwed up, and I may be sick, but I got eyes, and I can see you're not that dumb. Not even close. So tell me right now why you asked me that, or you're outta here, whoever the hell you are."

I crossed my legs. Took a deep breath and confessed. "Because I think Frank may be on his way here to kill you."

Jerry's arm jerked out in such a sudden spasm that he knocked his ashtray to the floor. He glanced down at the mess as if he couldn't fathom what it was.

I walked over and rubbed out any embers with the toe of my shoe. I was sitting down again before Jerry recovered enough to talk. "You sure about that?"

"No. That's why I'm hitting you up for information."

"Who the hell are you?"

"I'm an ex-cop. That's the short version. We don't have time for the long one."

"Shit."

"You got that right. Now tell me about the defective part, Jerry. I think it's the key to everything."

It turned out to be a sensor, and its job was to tell the antilock brake whether to engage or not. The Nolan Company usually bought theirs from an American supplier, but as with every other manufacturer, they couldn't help but notice that overseas parts cost less. Jerry tried a shipment of sensors from a Chinese company, but his quality control guy discovered that a certain critical portion of it was thinner than the American counterpart. "He recommended dumping the new supplier and scrapping the imported shipment.

"I figured it wasn't exactly defective, just inferior," Jerry explained, "so I just had the warehouse guys set them aside."

"Then what happened?"

Jerry waved his head and snorted with disgust. "Our regular supplier got backed up at the worst possible time. We had an order from our biggest auto manufacturer coming up fast, and missing their deadline would have cost us the contract."

"Not good," I sympathized.

Jerry's moist eyes widened with disbelief. "Not good? Try catastrophic. The end of the company if you want to know the truth."

"So you dusted off the Chinese parts and filled the order?"

"You make it sound easy. No, I called Frank and we decided together."

"You know him that well?" I had trouble believing a purchasing agent from one of many companies owned by Roitman Industries would have direct access to the CEO.

"Frank and me grew up in the same New York neighborhood. Looked out for each other since we were kids."

I read that as Frank took care of Jerry ever since they were kids, but I kept my impression to myself. "That how you got the PA job?" I wondered.

Jerry had been consumed by his story, and the interruption brought him up short. "Yeah. Sure. What of it?"

"Nothing," I apologized. "Go on."

He eagerly returned to his tale. "Like I said, it wasn't that easy. I had to change the shipping containers and all." He'd been talking with the cigarette stuck in the corner of his lip, and now he sucked in smoke while his eyes solicited my empathy.

"Got it," I said, worrying more and more about the expenditure of time.

Jerry's right knee bounced and his left eye had developed a tic. He smoked faster and ignored me more. If he wasn't processing what I said about Frank being on his way here to kill him, he was even crazier than he claimed.

"And then Luanne Sykes happened," I said.

"And then Luanne Sykes happened," he agreed. Then he began to cry.

Chapter 43

Touching Jerry Emper would be neither sanitary nor wise, so I resisted the urge to comfort him. As he dried his face with his sleeve, I tried to focus him on what was already an urgent problem.

"Actually, I misspoke," I remarked as if I were a rational person about to correct a trivial error. "Frank probably wants to kill *both* of us."

Momentary confusion. Then Jerry dove right back into his own dark hole as if the idea of his long-time protector wanting him dead had depleted an already meager reservoir of joy.

"Did you hear me?"

"No. Not Frank." The former PA waved his head and sniffled. Apparently Frank's potential treachery had also short-circuited Jerry's ability to process information, including the fact that I was now on his side. Why? Because blackmailers were not the sort to cry if their mark turned on them; the sickos simply carried out their threats. On the other hand, weak people who had been bribed to go away quietly, who literally depended on their benefactors to keep them alive, might fall apart at the thought of betrayal.

"Hey!" I said to get the guy's attention. "I have a gun." I dug it out. "See?"

Jerry flinched and huddled deeper into his chair. Whatever his problems were, I seemed to be making them worse.

"What've you got for dinner?" I asked.

"Whaa?"

"Dinner. What've you got planned?"

"Uh, tomato soup."

"Okay, Jerry. Why don't you go into the kitchen and make your tomato soup. I'll wait here for Frank."

The man had the survival instincts of a feral animal; I didn't hear so much as a clinking dish for thirty-five minutes, which was when Frank tapped on the screen door and I released the safety on the Glock.

"Come in," I said, hiding the gun under the purse on my lap.

The screen door squeaked, the regular door eased open, and I received a view of Frank's derriere as he entered backwards to pull the door shut. Very civilized. Marsha would be proud.

"Don't even think about it," I told him before he uttered a word.

"About what?" Frank inquired mildly. He was dressed in business clothes, okay for an air conditioned office, not okay for this dusty, stuffy shoebox. Already he had begun to sweat. Or perhaps the cool, collected Frank Roitman, CEO and multi-millionnaire, was a bit nervous, too. I could only hope.

"Don't think about doing what you came to do," I clarified as much as I intended to.

"And what is that?" he asked, rhetorically, I assumed.

Jerry had appeared in the doorway of his kitchen. When he sensed the motion, Frank turned and said, "Hi, Jer."

Jerry chose not to reply. He had something in his hand. A kitchen knife would be my guess.

During a brief silence we took turns looking at each other, which was when I realized something was off. My flight-or-fight system hadn't flipped on. I decided maybe I should lighten up a little, at least until I figured out why.

"So Frank," I began as if I were opening an ordinary conversation. "I guess you must be aware of my visit to your antilock brake company, and I can think of only one reason why you'd ditch your bodyguard and rush up here to see Jerry. Why don't you tell me why I'm wrong."

"Are you sure I 'ditched my bodyguard?'"

Involuntarily, my eyes jerked toward the front door, making Frank chuckle.

"May I?" He gestured toward Jerry's chair too suddenly for me. As he sat down, I dropped my purse on the floor and showed him the Glock.

He stared. "What would you have done if the pilot found that before the flight?" he wondered.

I guess I shouldn't have been surprised that Frank knew the gun was with me on the trip. Lyle would have told him about giving it the sniff test the night Mike pulled his stupid stunt.

"Stayed home," I admitted, which made Frank shut his eyes and wave his head with regret.

Jerry had eased himself into the living room. Now he stood toward the window, making a triangle of the three of us. At his side a hunting knife of frightening proportions glittered in the flickering daylight, adding yet another worry to my lengthening list.

"How are you?" Frank inquired of his old friend.

"She already asked that."

Frank switched back to watching me. "What was the answer?" Unconsciously, he rubbed his hands along his thighs, a good place for them in my opinion.

"Lousy," Jerry said. "Worse now that you're here."

"Oh? Why is that?"

"She thinks you want to kill us."

"Is that true, Lauren? You really think that?"

I wiggled the Glock in lieu of an answer.

Frank suddenly rose again and stuffed his hands into his pants pockets. *Not* a good place for them, in my opinion. I adjusted my aim accordingly.

Turning his head toward Jerry just as nonchalant as can be, Frank remarked, "We go way back, right Jer?"

No answer. Just a quick glare—at me.

"And we've always looked out for each other, right?"

A quick nod.

Frank rocked back and forth on his heels. "After the sensor business, when you got…sick…I funded your early retirement, didn't I?" The way Frank italicized the word *sick* led me to believe he referred to a nervous breakdown.

Hey! HEY! Now who's the bigger threat? my psyche yelled into my ear so insistently that I almost switched my target.

Jerry shot me a glare newly laced with distrust.

"…so why would you think I'd harm a hair on your head?" Frank finished.

"You…you wouldn't," Jerry stammered.

His point made, Frank raised his hands in surrender. "Lauren, please," he said, "put down the gun. I'm afraid it might go off."

"Not just yet."

"Really? Aren't your arms getting tired?"

"I'm fine, thanks."

Frank sucked his cheek. "Just before I left to come up here," he began, "I did something that will interest you, Jerry. You, too, Lauren, since you seem to be so worried about the so-called faulty part from the Sykes lawsuit."

Jerry and I were back together again, if only because both of us were thinking, *What the hell…?*

Frank folded his arms smugly and squared his feet. "I phoned Nolan's biggest customer, the one we were so desperate to keep, and told them a bad batch of sensors got used by mistake and they should enact a recall."

"But...but that's..." I thought Jerry was going to say 'wonderful,' or 'fabulous' or even 'about time!' After all, anxiety over the potential fallout from his and Frank's mutual decision had literally made him ill. Instead he said, "...*financial suicide!*"

Potato/potato.

"Maybe not," Frank allowed. "Nevertheless, it's done. Now will you please put that gun down, Ms. Beck?"

I did as he asked.

Chapter 44

Twilight in Brunswick, Maryland, and the air had turned cool and damp. Frank and I strolled out to our cars over Jerry's bumpy sidewalk, both of us acting as if we hadn't been frightened half to death by our just-ended, unbelievably delicate rollercoaster of a conversation. Since Frank was exceptionally good at being in charge, it's possible he wasn't acting. Me, I was quaking inside from adrenaline withdrawal.

In parting, the two men had hugged, and I sensed a bond so deeply established that no newcomer could completely appreciate it. My closest comparison was me and Corinne, my cancer counselor and recently deceased landlady. We had recognized each other's voice with one word. We finished each other's sentences. We knew what the other needed on levels nobody else could, and we'd only known each other for six and a half years. What must it be like to have a lifetime connection? I doubted I would ever experience a friendship that close and wondered if it would be worth changing who I was to try.

"Where's Chantal?" Frank inquired, perhaps to rebuke me for abandoning his pregnant daughter. *...you work for me, and please don't forget it.*

I said she was with my family.

"Where?"

"If I told you, I'd have to kill you."

Frank's expression said, "Ha," in the sarcastic way.

"Speaking of killing people, why did you have to ditch your bodyguard to come up here and tell Jerry the good news?" In other words, why the secrecy if you didn't plan to kill anyone?

An ominous silence fell, and the cogs in my brain began to mesh. Maybe the Glock had been more persuasive than I thought.

The turning gears gained traction. "You didn't call your customer about the recall yet."

Frank shot me a glance, and I realized there hadn't been time. I had just visited Nolan Company spouting nonsense that happened to be true. If I also found my way to Jerry, the possibility that I might learn the rest of the story must have motivated Frank to get himself up here to make sure Jerry and I were contained.

The question was had he done what he originally planned, or had my preemptive approach been a game changer? Alone out here on a darkening street I realized I was no longer sure.

"You will make the call, right?" I asked with more hope than certainty.

Frank's lips compressed into a sour moue. "My arrangement with Jerry must remain private," he warned. "Understood?"

I breathed again.

"Meaning you'll tell the customer he was merely following orders."

"That's right, and you won't tell anyone otherwise." I thought of U.S. presidents taking the blame for things they didn't directly do. It was the-buck-stops-here scenario, the way things worked.

"Jerry's that fragile?"

Without a sidewalk we'd been walking down middle of the street, and the halogen lamp overhead suddenly revealed the lifetime of struggle on Frank's face.

"Jerry's father was a mean sonovabitch," he seemed to think aloud. "Mine was gone, which was for the best." He kicked at a piece of cardboard lying in the way. "My mother had a steel backbone. Jerry's was a born victim."

"Jerry took after her?"

"No," Frank decided. "No. Instead he developed an overly acute sense of right and wrong."

"Was it the Luanne Sykes case what broke him?"

Frank's eyes narrowed as he paused to think. "No," he decided. "The ruling was driver error, and all that happened later anyway. Jerry 'broke,' as you call it, because he was torn between loyalty to me and fear of potential disasters—Luanne Sykes, but with only us to blame."

"Was he worried about what would happen to your company?"

The beleaguered CEO waved his head. "To my family and by extension to him."

"No more jewelry money?"

"Something like that."

"Will the company be okay?"

"I haven't the faintest idea."

We'd arrived at the Miata. In the lamplight it looked even worse than Frank. "This is my car," I admitted.

He gave it the once over and smiled.

"See you back at the estate?" he inquired mildly.

Stunned as I was that he expected me to return, I still managed to reply. "Not if I see you first."

Frank huffed out a little laugh, stuffed his hands back into his pants pockets and sauntered along down the street.

As I steered the Miata out of its slot and turned back in the right direction, I thought about Frank's mother and her steel backbone. Maybe Frank was doing the same. When I drove past, he was staring out the front window of a monstrous black SUV.

Chapter 45

"You got any chili?" I quizzed Lyle as soon as he opened his door. Chantal had texted me that she'd returned to the estate late this afternoon, and I had assured myself that the Mercedes was tucked safely in the garage before I wandered down to the barn.

"Nope," Lyle lamented, "but I bought peanut butter. Lucille likes peanut butter."

"Who's Lucille?"

"The dappled mare."

"I'll buy her more. Where is it?" I sidled past the Roitman's head of security and over to the kitchen nook. The drive back from Brunswick had been easy except for the demons in my head and my hunger. The empty beer bottle in Lyle's tiny sink reminded me I was thirsty, too.

"How was your day?" I asked as I bit into calorie-laden bread.

Lyle kissed me with my mouth full. Then he said, "Fine. And yours?"

I swallowed and sipped the beer he handed me. "It was two days, actually. Miss me?"

"Sure. What have you been up to?"

"Toby Stoddard was murdered. What do you think of that?"

"Not much. You got proof?"

"Yes I do." I explained about the rug and Sheriff Troxell's disinterested approach to it all.

"You messed up his suicide," Lyle observed.

"I'm afraid so."

We smiled at each other.

"I don't have a motive though. Not for sure anyway. So I don't have the killer either."

"You will."

"You think?"

"I'm beginning to suspect you get whatever you want."

I grinned a little wider, perhaps because of what he was doing with his hands.

"Hurry up and finish that, will you?"

"Itz peanub budder," I said. "I cand eab any fastr."

I'd parked in the estate's front circle and had no interest in hauling any of my stuff back to the pool house. I would probably have to haul it all back to my car tomorrow anyway. With no food in the bungalow and no idea what my reception would be at the main house, I'd gravitated down to the barn where a warm welcome was more assured.

"Tom's here?" I presumed as Lyle tugged my shirt over my head.

"Obviously." If the night man hadn't been on duty yet, Lyle wouldn't have been free to lead me up to the loft. We made ourselves comfortable on the bed.

"Ouch! What is that?"

"A band-aid, you big baby. I cut my finger."

"Who's calling who a big baby? Wait a minute." I sat straight up. "You got another one of those?"

"Fingers?"

"Band-aids. I've been trying to figure something out since yesterday."

Lyle looked crestfallen, grumpy even, but he climbed down the ladder and headed toward the tiny bathroom.

"Hold it," I called after him. "I'm coming down, too." I pulled on my jersey and followed him barefoot.

He handed me a band-aid from a box in a drawer and folded his arms to watch me unwrap it.

"Got a match?" I inquired.

"Seriously?"

"Yes."

He didn't bother to ask why, just limped four steps around the corner to the kitchen nook, opened another drawer, and extracted a small green box from a restaurant called Antlers. Inside were mini wooden matches that lit on the first strike.

I held the band-aid over the little stainless steel kitchen sink and carefully waved the flame under the latex. When stinky melted rubber dripped into the sink, I blew out the match and the smoking band-aid and proudly announced, "Mystery solved."

"Swell. Can we go back to bed now?"

"Don't you want to know why I gunked up your sink?" I held up my trophy.

"No."

"It tells me who murdered Toby Stoddard." Then I thought twice and added, "Probably. I found something in the fireplace of the hunting lodge." I hustled over to my purse for the plastic bag containing the burned stitch holder. Then I held the opened bag under Lyle's nose.

"Smell familiar?"

His eyes widened, and I was pleased to see he was finally taking me seriously. "Okay, explain. What's this have to do with Toby Stoddard?"

I said it bothered me that the string the killer tied to the trigger of the shotgun released so easily. "If the knot had been tight enough to fire the shotgun from outside the gun room, how could the string have come free for the killer to reel it in? He'd have had to open the door, walk in and untie it himself."

"Or herself." Lyle ran the back of his hand down my cheek. "Women can be lethal, you know."

"Right. But there weren't any footprints in the blood spatters and really no time to go in and get out before people in the house came running."

"So you think it was this thing." He pointed at the sandwich bag containing the J-shaped stitch holder.

"Yup."

"And the band-aid?"

"Knitting needles are smooth, otherwise you couldn't knit with them. This hook thing is slippery, too, so the string wouldn't stay on it with just a knot. He or *she* needed to attach it with tape, and when I searched the hunting lodge there wasn't any, just band-aids in the bathroom next to where Toby died."

Lyle rubbed the stubble on his chin. "So how'd the killer get rid of the string?"

"When Frank and Chantal ran back to the gun room, nobody else was there. I figure the killer took the string out the bathroom window, hurried around to the kitchen—which would have put him or *her* behind everybody else—then tossed the string in the fire while the others were freaking out in the back hall."

"Before the sheriff arrived."

"I guess. Although I'm not sure Troxell's team did much of a search."

This displeased Lyle, and I couldn't blame him. "Okay," he said finally. "Who did it?"

"Let me get back to you after I return this." I held up the baggie.

"And when, may I ask, do you plan to do that?" His hands were rocking my hips, and I could think of no reason to disappoint him.

"In the morning," I said. For my plan to work I needed to behave normally, and waking up my suspect wouldn't exactly seem normal.

There was also the matter of motive. Until tonight I'd bet heavily on Frank for business reasons. Toby's family had described him as a goodie-goodie, a guy with a conscience, as it turned out probably a fatal flaw. If he'd learned about the use of the faulty part, he would have insisted on telling Nolan's customer immediately. Every day of delay would strengthen any suspicion that the substitution was deliberate and make the legal and financial exposures for Roitman Industries much much worse. Since Frank seemed resigned to do the right thing now, I regarded him more as a gambler owning up to a loss than a murderer protecting his assets at any cost.

Gavin and his investments, his jealousy? Never a strong enough story to persuade me, and his wife's volunteered alibi upheld my earlier inclination.

I did have a first choice, but without convincing physical proof, and the entire witness pool potentially hostile, securing a confession would still be best.

A good night's sleep was in order, but it wasn't about to happen.

Two hours later Tom shouted from the bottom of the loft's ladder. "Hey, up there. Wake up."

"What you got?" Lyle called back as he switched on a light and tugged on some jeans.

"Intruder. Just entered the pool house."

That got me moving, too. To my own jeans I added the closest decent thing I could reach, one of Lyle's sweatshirts, then clambered down the ladder after him.

Tom had returned to the monitors. On the main screen, one of six, he pointed at the door to the sauna, an indirect and quieter way to enter the cottage. "Entry," he confirmed.

A moment later a figure in loose clothing emerged from the lighted front door. The person wore a floppy hat that hid her face, but the shoes and overall shape suggested a woman. The monitor's clock read 2:10 AM and counting.

"You recording?" I asked Tom. He wore an Atlanta Braves warmup jacket in the chilly security cubbyhole.

"You betcha," he replied. "Whatdaya think, Lyle?"

Lyle glanced at me. "I think we got ourselves a murderer."

Tom's unshaven face recoiled in shock. "Somebody else was in there?"

"Nope. Long story," Lyle clapped his associate on the shoulder.

"I got all night to listen," Tom reminded us as the shadowy silhouette hustled up the brick walk toward the main house.

"Can you replay it for me?" I requested.

Tom did. Then he did twice again.

I thanked him after I'd gotten what I needed. Then I took Lyle's hand and tugged him back to the ladder.

We'd just gotten back to sleep when Tom woke us again. "Car's leaving."

"One of ours?" Lyle called down.

"The Volvo."

In the glow emanating from downstairs I watched Lyle reach for his jeans.

I halted him with my urgent, "Wait!" before he could grab his shirt. "You have any tracking on it?" I asked.

"Yeah, sure. An anti-theft tracer."

"So Tom can see where it is at all times?"

"Yes, but..."

"Then let him tell us where it went when we get up in the morning." Three reasons: I thought I already knew where it was going, we had no authority to stop it, and *I really needed some sleep.*

Conflicting thoughts crossed Lyle's face like cloud shadows across a field.

"Your murder. Not mine," he concluded. Then he climbed down the ladder to explain it all to Tom.

Chapter 46

"Good morning," I told Marsha as I entered the kitchen.

Standing by the center island, her hands embraced a coffee mug as if it were a wishing well or perhaps the Fountain of Youth. Without makeup her complexion was even and bland as pizza dough, and her white chenille bathrobe added twenty pounds to her waistline. I'd forgotten about her age, but I remembered now.

"Umph," she answered, clearly no good until the caffeine kicked in.

I took my turn with the coffee pot while she slipped a couple slices of whole wheat into the toaster.

Lyle had not been pleased that I elected to do this by myself, but he had to admit I was right. Descending on the Roitman household together might do more than raise eyebrows; it could put a nervous murderer on Red Alert.

I also won our disagreement over the Glock, which was safely locked away in the Miata's glove compartment. Having been picked up by his bodyguard and driver, Frank wasn't around, but Abby was.

Elbows splayed on the kitchen table, the child shoveled Cheerios into her mouth with a concentration suitable for the SATs. Her orange juice remained untouched, but the amount of sugar on her cereal probably made the juice taste like vinegar.

"...so then the troll got so angry he..." she continued another of the verbal book reports she couldn't seem to resist.

"Abby, please," said her mother with a hand to her forehead. "Enough."

Abby looked to me for a diversion. Any diversion.

I considered complimenting her pajamas, but their sky-blue background dotted with rubber duckies struck me as so age-inappropriate I simply couldn't.

"No school?" I remarked absently.

"Orthodontist," the kid mumbled with an eye-roll. Abruptly popping up from her seat, she gathered her bowl, set it in the sink, and pushed through the swinging door.

Marsha and I were alone at the table.

"Oh!" I exclaimed, dipping into my pocket for the baggie containing the stitch holder. When I slapped it on the table, the clank sounded so loud I almost jumped.

I did jump when the pantry door swung open again.

Abby pushed through and made a bee-line for her juice. While she drank, she monitored the silence between her mother and me over the lip of the glass.

"Go get dressed, Sweetie." Marsha spoke in a tone as cloying and outdated as the pajamas. Meanwhile, she seemed mesmerized by the sandwich bag.

A final slurp and Abby was gone. I listened but didn't hear the expected footsteps hammering up the stairs. Slippers, I guessed. Or socks.

"What's that?" Marsha asked when enough time had elapsed for her daughter to be out of earshot.

"Lana's stitch holder. Thought I'd return it before I forget." I rose and made like I was headed past the stove toward the cook's bedroom door.

Marsha's chair scraped on the floor as she rushed to stop me. "She's not there."

I feigned mild surprise, because I knew Lana was already gone. "Dulles," read the penciled note Tom left for Lyle and me at the end of his shift, confirmation that the

Roitman's Volvo had traveled to Washington Dulles International Airport and back.

"Family emergency," Marsha informed me.

"Oh my," I sympathized. "When do you think she'll be back?"

Marsha shrugged with ambiguous despair.

"Oh, that sort of family emergency," I observed. "Lucky you're such a good cook."

A sharp glance told me an employment agency would be getting a call this morning.

"You know Toby was murdered, right?" Another answer I knew in advance. Chantal had called her mother regarding dinner right after she'd seen the rug, and there was no way my conclusion about Toby's death wouldn't have been the first thing out of Chantal's mouth. Just as there was no way the rest of the family wouldn't hear it within moments. These days, for better or worse, everybody might as well be standing right next to each other.

Toby's mother-in-law blinked and breathed and lifted a finger as if she might reach out and touch the baggie, perhaps to steal it and bury it and thus erase the final evidence that Lana had ever been part of her household.

She refrained. Instead turned her head to look out past the pool and the barn, maybe as far as Belarus.

"I have to get dressed," she said to the window. The chair scraped on the tile. I was on her heels, but the pantry door swung hard into the cabinet and bounced back at me.

Marsha turned right into the hall and put on speed as she ran up the stairs.

I followed close, even when she cut diagonally across the upper hall into the master bedroom. It was lovely if you like French provincial, but it was also a mess. The lavender sheets lay tangled in the middle of the bed. Frank's aftershave spiced air still damp from his shower. Yesterday's clothes were strewn on a window bench, and two window shades were crooked while the third remained down. Adjacent to the opened closet to my right sat a mirrored vanity, its satin-cushioned chair the very one that crushed the faux gem and sparked the argument that upset Abby so badly. "They're fighting," she'd sobbed as if it were the end of her world.

Marsha wheeled on me, "Get out," she ordered.

"Not until we've talked."

Her jaw suddenly set in concrete. Just like that. As if she'd been practicing all her life to play Scarlet O'Hara.

I made my next line sound like an accusation. "You realize what Lana's stitch holder means, don't you?"

Her helpless hand grasped the air. "Since Chantal's call, I've thought of nothing else."

"Say it."

Marsha shut her eyes and bowed her head. "Lana murdered Toby."

"Why do you suppose she did that?"

"She must have heard Frank telling me Toby was going public with damning information, information that could mean financial ruin. She was probably terrified of going back to Belarus."

"But isn't that exactly where you sent her?"

Marsha looked shocked that I should mention this. "Lana was...is...very dear to me. Did you expect me to let her go to jail?"

A regular thumping noise came from the hall. Footfalls on the steps. Abby hadn't come upstairs to change after all. Noting the strain between her mother and me, she must have slipped into her safe haven behind the living room sofa, the spot where she used to suck her thumb when she was frightened, where she discovered that the old vacuum ducts built into the walls were ideal for eavesdropping.

"I'm curious," I told Marsha. "How did you plan to kill me? Smother me with a pillow? Stab me in my sleep?"

"What? I didn't…"

"You did. There's a security recording of you exiting the pool house. Your diamond ring flashed in the light by the front door. Here. I've got a copy on my phone. You want to see…?"

Abby burst into the room running, threw herself at her mother, and nearly toppled them both.

"Mother, tell her. I helped you, not Lana. Lana didn't do a thing."

"No no, Abby. Hush."

Tears smeared the child's face. "Don't you remember? You asked me to tell you about that book again. You said I was brilliant, and you were proud of me. You even hugged me until I fell asleep."

"Please Abby, no."

Abby was sobbing now, huffing out big gasps of air between her damning words. "You said I was 'The smartest girl in the whole world,' because I knew things you didn't. Tell her, Mother. You said I saved Daddy's company."

"Abby, please. No more, baby. Please be quiet."

The girl grabbed at her mother's chenille sleeves. "You said I was the smartest girl in the whole world." Her sobs deflated to a heart-breaking whimper.

"Yes, Sweetie. You arc," Marsha finally agreed. "Now please be quiet."

Marsha was no longer acting. She was glassy-eyed but eerily calm. She clutched Abby's head to her breast and petted her daughter's hair so hard it was a wonder the girl could breathe.

Other feet trotted up the stairs. Uncertain whether they belonged to friend or foe, I glanced around for a weapon. Nothing in sight but a hand mirror or maybe the vanity chair.

Abby mustered all the strength in her neck to look Marsha in the eye. "You thanked me, don't you remember? Tell her, Mother."

"What's going on here?" Chantal stood in the doorway, one hand steadying herself, the other lightly touching her abdomen.

"Get Abby out of here," I urged, but Chantal needed time to catch on and process. "Your mother killed Toby," I explained, figuring that pretty much summed it up.

I might as well have kicked Chantal in the head. She gasped and staggered and skewered me with her disbelief.

While her older daughter reeled, Marsha broke loose from Abby's fists, intent on attacking me. Abby ran screaming from the room.

No choice. I giant-stepped to the vanity and grabbed the hand mirror, a thick silver thing resembling a ping-pong paddle.

"Go!" I instructed Chantal as Marsha dove toward me. As she tackled my hips, I whacked the back of her head, a satisfying sound, but she simply stumbled past into the shower of glass. I swatted at her again, but the dented silver paddle had no effect. Marsha latched onto my calf, drew it to her mouth and bit.

Time for stronger measures. I reached for a certain pressure point in her neck that had proven useful in the past, and within a minute her eyes fluttered and she dropped the rest of the way to the floor.

I had just finished tying Marsha's wrists behind her back with the bathrobe sash when Lyle came puffing in.

"Jesus," he said. "You're bleeding."

"Yup," I agreed. "I hope she's had all her shots."

Chapter 47

Chantal gave the hysterical Abby half of one of her mother's tranquillizers, which caused the child to sleep for hours, plenty of time for the local sheriff to respond to Lyle's 9-1-1 call then to debrief Lyle and begin on me. Sheriff Troxell would coordinate with the local man on Monday, and they would swap custody of the prisoner. Marsha's bone-deep fear of losing her comfortable lifestyle had become reality. Bail was out of the question. Frank's wealth made her a flight risk.

Before the local law arrived, however, Marsha succumbed to reason and cut a deal with Lyle and me. We agreed to withhold Abby's blubbering condemnation (recorded remotely on the estate's security equipment) and promised never to involve Abby in any way, *if* Marsha volunteered to sign a confession in front of official witnesses. Chantal agreed to explain Marsha's too-little-too-late (in my opinion) maternal gesture toward Abby to ensure the girl's everlasting cooperation.

Three Tuesdays later I was polishing glasses at The Pelican's Perch when Anthony slapped a palm on the mahogany bar.

"Lady ask for you," he stage whispered, his lips wagging back and forth in concert with his pelican earring. I took that to mean the woman looked out of place among his summertime lunch customers. The rakish lift of his eyebrow expressed the hope that she came with a big appetite.

I'd been hired back because, "dose college kids jus' pay attention udder college kids.'" Also, because Anthony was a soft touch. Frank had reneged on paying me to bodyguard Chantal, a not unexpected move considering that I got his wife arrested for murder. However, that left me without a down payment on an apartment. Karen and Ron accepted my status report graciously, perhaps even with sympathy, but a whiff of disappointment hung in the air like the stink of sweaty sneakers. Nobody said a word, but it was there just the same.

"Go, go," Anthony ordered. "I do dat." He grabbed the towel from my hand.

Chantal Stoddard waited on the bench by the restaurant's opened front door. Midday sun spilled across the worn wooden floor like paint and filled the rectangular opening with white glare.

We embraced in the melancholy way that seemed appropriate. Chantal's belly-bump was now a solid presence impossible to ignore, a not-so-subtle reminder that he or she would be a presence in her life for all the years she had left. I envied her that, but it didn't hurt like it once had. For me, children were a regret to be stored in my attic of regrets, the place I occasionally deposited something new but one day hoped to lock and leave for good.

"Let's…" I gestured toward the privacy of outdoors. Alongside the restaurant a green employee's picnic table waited in the shade of a tall red oak. We held hands like grammar school girlfriends until we'd settled down face to face.

"How are you?" I asked.

Chantal tilted her head and slanted her eyes toward the river just below. Hundreds of diamond flashes, not unlike the one that revealed Marsha as a murderer, bounced off the water onto the leaves of the trees.

"Coping, but just," Chantal replied as her eyes returned to me.

Surely, mourning her husband would continue to progress at its own unalterable pace, but Marsha's pathological behavior was so harsh, so unprecedented, I thought it might be nearly impossible for Chantal to process. I felt I owed her an apology.

"I'm sorry about your mother," I said.

Tears sprang to her eyes, but she swiped them away. "My mother has always been a controlling, narcissistic bitch," she remarked bitterly. "Now I can hate her without feeling guilty."

We listened to the river splash for a while. Then Chantal wiped her nose with a tissue, gave the view a glance, and remarked, "Abby's back at your brother's farm. She's going to babysit while Karen and I do some more shopping." A short laugh. "Karen thinks two hours should be enough all around."

I blew out a breath to unlock my shoulders. "Think you can get everything you need in two hours?"

Chantal suddenly looked terminally sad, making me regret my unfortunate phrasing. I reached across and took her hand again. "You'll be happy again," I assured her.

"When?"

"Oh, in about four months would be my guess."

She laughed at that, thank goodness, and I realized it was probably true.

"So what else is going on?"

"Gavin and Julianna are married. Did you know that?"

"Wonderful," I hedged. "About time he grew up."

That rated a smile. "And of course Dad is up to his ears in lawyers."

"For your mom?"

"And for the company."

The recall mess, of course.

"What about you?"

"The house Toby and I picked out for the baby is still up for sale. I'm almost tempted to buy it again. What do you think?"

"Sounds perfect."

There was a glitch. It was written all over her face.

"I just don't know. Dad spends very little time with Abby, as you can imagine." I could. He never did, and now would be even worse. "And he's pretty much of a wreck himself. He works," *works*, as if he shoveled coal all day, "but it's more of a Herculean effort than ever. Abby's already in counseling…"

Déjà vu all over again, I thought, and the lock's tumblers clicked, the door of my mental vault swung wide, and there it was: Frank's own "Déjà vu all over again" remark as he turned off the Metro-wreck news back on the yacht.

"By any chance does Roitman Industries own a company connected to trains?" I wondered aloud.

The seemingly random question pinched creases between Chantal's eyebrows. "Used to," she said. "Not anymore. Why?"

I stood and crossed my arms to hold myself together. "Remember the name?"

It took Chantal a minute, but she came up with it.

Jacked up like a racehorse crammed into the starting gate, I waved my hand beside my head to release some tension. "Remember what they made?"

Chantal's pregnancy pallor had drained to a dangerous gray. Her fingers touched her temple as if anticipating pain. "Um, uh, brake parts, but Dad sold…"

"Buy the house," I told her with grim conviction. "Everybody needs a place of their own." And after I phoned the National Transportation Safety Board to suggest that another Roitman subsidiary may have used sub-standard parts, she may not have a choice. The NTSB's head Metro-crash investigator would attack the new lead like a Doberman on steroids, and the Roitman's grand estate just might become cannon fodder in the fight to secure its remaining owner's freedom.

"Take Abby with you," I suggested. "Short term? Long term? Up to you."

"Yes," Chantal agreed obediently as if she saw it all spread out before her. Her own attic of regrets. Her very own fresh start.

"I'm sorry," I said again.

Understatement of the century.

#

Dear Reader—

I hope you enjoyed investigating this modern-day "locked-room" mystery along with Lauren. For me it was fun imagining how she would behave outside her comfort zone pitted against a family of intelligent misfits. Pretty much like a camel inside a tent, wouldn't you say?

If you did happen to enjoy Lauren's "guilt trip," I would be very pleased if you would do me the great favor of contributing a review to one or more of your favorite book sites, such as Amazon, Goodreads, Barnes & Noble, etc. More and more readers—and authors—rely on the guidance offered by fans such as yourself, and I can personally assure you that the couple of minutes it takes to share your thoughts are very greatly appreciated.

Also, if you'd like to be the first to know about any **contests** I've got going, **free offers, new books, new blogs, or special appearances,** please visit my website (http://www.donnahustonmurray.com) and sign the Guest Book.

While you're there, why not introduce yourself? There's an easy link for that, too.

Cordially,
Donna

Acknowledgements

As always, this creative journey could never have been completed without the help of some very talented and generous people: Robynne Graffam, my extraordinary daughter *and* editor, and Hench Murray my wonderful husband *and* copyeditor. You wouldn't think relatives could be so good at this, but they are! And then there's Daniel Middleton, my excellent cover artist. I'm grateful to all of you more than you can know.

Huge thanks also to beta readers Nancy Labs and Sonja Haggert for their extremely valuable feedback. Thanks, too, to Donald Shrawder for sharing his expertise and to Gretchen Hall, for guiding me to Pamelia S. Stratton and Jerri Williams, retired FBI agent and Media Director for SEPTA. Your help was exactly what the book needed.

Donna

In real life Donna assumes she can fix anything until proven wrong, calls trash-picking recycling, and, although she probably should know better, adores Irish setters.

Donna and husband, Hench, live in the greater Philadelphia, PA, area. They have two adult children.

More at http://www.donnahustonmurray.com

CPSIA information can be obtained at www.ICGtesting.com
Printed in the USA
LVOW07s0523070616

491424LV00001B/38/P

9 780985 688097